THE FINAL TRUTH

MORAG PRINGLE

Storm

PUBLISHING

Copyright © Morag Pringle, 2025

The moral right of the author has been asserted.

To request permissions, contact the publisher at rights@stormpublishing.co

Ebook ISBN: 978-1-80508-390-0
Paperback ISBN: 978-1-80508-392-4

Cover design: Sara Simpson
Cover images: Shutterstock

Published by Storm Publishing.
For further information, visit:
www.stormpublishing.co

ALSO BY MORAG PRINGLE

A Rachel McKenzie Mystery

The Liar's Bones

The Highland Dead

For Flora

PROLOGUE

Eric Hunter paced the ridge.

His contact had changed the venue at the last minute and Eric hadn't been happy.

But when he got here, he'd understood. The peninsula was the bump on God's nose. As far away from anywhere as it was possible to be on the island. At least on the ground.

Not wanting to attract attention, he'd left his van at the end of a dead-end road and walked the rest of the way, a matter of a couple of miles by the most direct route. He'd not come across another soul – an increasingly rare event in this part of Scotland – only a vast expanse of moor, a herd of cattle and a farmhouse, a thin trail of smoke spiralling up from its chimney. A barely worn track led up to its front door, a beat-up Land Rover parked outside, the croft fenced off with a sign on the gate forbidding entry to vehicles and warning walkers to keep dogs on the leash.

Nevertheless, despite his precautions, his finely tuned sixth sense for danger, developed over years of putting himself in perilous situations, jabbed at him, in the same way his mother had poked her finger into his chest when he was a teenager and already gaining a reputation as Scotland's best under-eighteen climber. 'You'll overreach yourself one day, my lad, and where will that leave me?'

Likely the same place as she was now. Six feet under. He never thought he'd miss that poking finger but, Christ, he did. Every single day. Now that he had children of his own he recognised the love behind the stiffened finger, the fear in the angry, trembling voice.

He'd also learned there were worse things than finding yourself upside down, 400 metres above the ground at the end of a rope.

That's why he was here. Despite his underlying unease, this meeting was too important to miss. Gee had names. Even better, proof. The last pieces in the jigsaw he needed before he submitted his article exposing the evil fuckers threatening the country he loved and, indirectly, the people he cared for most: his wife and children. Failure didn't bear thinking about.

When he'd arrived at the meeting point a few minutes before six, it was already light and had been for a couple of hours. A haar had drifted in from the sea, making it difficult for him to see more than a metre in any direction.

Gee – as she wished to be known, as if he hadn't made it his business to discover her real name – was late. Possibly waiting for the mist to clear. When the sun broke through the cloud he'd been hopeful. Gee would appear, apologise for keeping him waiting, they'd conclude their business and he'd get the hell back to his family. Leave it to the police to arrest the bastards.

A further advantage of meeting out here was that, now the mist had cleared, if anyone approached he'd see them easily.

Like the four-by-four hurtling over the tracks left by a tractor.

Gee was too cautious to draw attention like this, so it couldn't be her.

The Range Rover pulled to a halt outside the farmhouse. Probably the crofter who owned the farmhouse returning from checking on their cattle, many of which had calves. Only vehicles belonging to the crofter were allowed access beyond the gate.

Eric carried on strolling along the edge of the cliff towards the lighthouse, pausing every now and again to look out to sea, smiling as a pod of dolphins cavorted past. He glanced around. Two figures were striding towards him. What the fuck? Although the hood of her jacket obscured most of her features, he recognised Gee. She was supposed to come alone. It was part of their deal. No one else to be involved until they were done. She could do what she liked once his article was published. The man with her was big with blond hair pulled away from his face. He was wearing jeans, a leather jacket and a shirt open at the neck – no tie. Was he a plain clothes police officer? In which case, why had Gee brought him to the meeting?

The man reached into his jacket pocket. Pulled out a gun. Fuck. Fear fired like electric shocks throughout Eric's body. Not police then. Gee must have tipped off the fuckers he'd been investigating.

Tantalisingly close to breaking the story wide open, he'd made a major error. He'd ignored his instincts. The draw of the story had been too strong to resist.

Worse, he'd not told anyone where he was and who he was meeting, not even Ella. He'd been determined to protect her and their children at all costs.

Should've, would've, could've.

Too late now. All he could do was try to get away.

He scanned the peninsula. He'd studied the map before he'd set off and knew there was nowhere to hide. The lighthouse and the keepers' cottages were too obvious. They'd find him there easily. He could run along the cliffside. He'd negotiate the narrow, crumbling path better than they would but, standing where he was, there was a chance they'd intercept him before he could reach it. He had to try. Decision made, he started running, pumping his arms, speeding across the uneven ground. With a yell, the man started to follow.

Eric continued at full pelt, scrambling over the moor, looking over his shoulder, his boots skidding on the slippery rocks under his feet. He hadn't been totally reckless. Aware that he was poking the nest of some extremely dangerous people, and knowing this could all go pear-shaped, he'd taken precautions, made a backup plan. He was putting his faith in Rachel McKenzie. She was like a dog with a bone. If anything happened to him, he trusted her to finish what he'd started, although he knew he was putting her in danger, maybe the worst danger of her life.

He considered his options. A sheer drop down a cliff to the sea many metres below or—

There was no damn 'or'. He was trapped. He turned to face his pursuers.

The sea breeze cooled the sweat on his oxters.

They'd split up, the man heading right, Gee left, looking to cut him off with a pincer movement. It wasn't over yet. No way was he going to lay down, give up without a fight. Hold up his hands and say, *Sorry. Shouldn't have done what I did. Is it OK if I go home now?* There was still a chance he could outrun them. He must be twice as fit as either of them. Then again, perhaps not. The man had a chest like an Olympic swimmer, biceps like he lived in the gym and only went home to sleep. But bulk didn't make a man fast. Climbing mountains, a Munro, sometimes two, in a morning, did.

What would Ella do if he didn't come home? What about the kids? Would these people come after them next?

Fear put wings on his feet. If he didn't get out alive, he

prayed Rachel would solve the puzzle he'd set, find his notes, ensure his wife and children were given protection.

The big guy was closing the gap. Eric gathered himself for a final sprint. Before he could move, something punched his leg. His legs buckled and he fell to the ground. His last sight as his vision began to blur was of a cloudless sky.

ONE

THREE DAYS EARLIER

Rachel McKenzie leaned back in her chair and suppressed a sigh. Another day, another death. Jenny Hammersmith, the mother of the dead nineteen-year-old, was in her mid-forties. Her hair was twisted into a hasty bun, a smear of lipstick her sole attempt to present a brave face, although no amount of make-up could disguise the bags under her eyes or the clammy pallor of her skin. Although it would be summer soon, it had poured throughout the night and not ceased, a cold wind coming from the north, driving rain into faces and down collars. Despite the weather outside it was sweltering in the open-plan office. The central heating was pumping out heat and facilities had so far been unable to turn it off. Jenny was shivering despite wearing a thick sweater, and a scarf up to her chin. She sat, hands dotted with eczema in her lap, raw from continual washing, or wringing. Like she was doing now – twisting her fingers as if she could peel off her mental anguish along with her skin.

Brian, the father, was equally nervous although he was trying not to show it. Grief was etched into gaunt features made more haggard by his receding hairline. He was wearing black corduroys and a T-shirt.

Jenny and Brian's daughter, Poppy, had been found dead in her student flat, a needle still embedded in her elbow.

'Someone must have given it to her,' Jennifer insisted again. 'She never would have taken drugs. Our Poppy wasn't like that.'

That's what Jenny wanted to believe. But it wasn't true. The police had interviewed Poppy's university friends, who'd reluctantly revealed her slide into addiction, starting with the occasional tab of ecstasy and wrap of coke, then steadily progressing to heroin and crack cocaine. Her friends had begged her to get help, but Poppy had been adamant she could kick the habit by herself – and in time to pull her abysmal exam results around and graduate.

She'd failed. In every respect. Now a life with so much promise was over. And it was Rachel's job to impart the findings on behalf of the Crown Office and Procurator Fiscal Service: death from accidental overdose.

It was another three-quarters of an hour before Rachel escorted the parents to the door, promising to keep in touch should anything change, while encouraging them to go ahead and make arrangements for Poppy's funeral.

Rachel stretched the kinks from her back and headed towards the small office kitchen, and coffee.

Her boss, Douglas Mainwaring, the fiscal depute in charge of Inverness's Death Unit – or, more formally, the Scottish Fatalities Investigation Unit – was to be on sick leave for longer than they thought, according to Linda, the office manager, who knew those things. Linda had kept the office up to date since Mainwaring's heart attack a few weeks earlier. He'd had a couple of stents put in his coronary arteries, but was expected, 'if he followed the lifestyle advice given to him by professionals' as Linda put it with a sceptical purse to her lips, 'to make a full recovery'. Rachel had been relieved. Despite his crabby, irascible temper, she had a soft spot for her boss. At least as soft a spot as she allowed herself to have for anyone.

She winced, recalling the last time she'd spoken to him. He'd phoned her from his home, where he was supposed to be resting and recovering, to give her a bollocking. Among other things, he'd berated her for crossing the line AGAIN, putting her life and her career in danger, bringing the office into DISREPUTE. Hadn't they HAD the same conversation on more than one occasion? HOW was he supposed to get better when she caused him so much stress? He'd been shouting so loudly she was worried he'd have another heart attack. But when he'd finished his tone had softened and he'd asked how she was. The concern in his voice had brought a lump to her throat, even while her feathers ruffled at the idea she needed protecting. She'd managed to look after herself just fine for years. But that wasn't totally true. She wasn't doing OK. Physically she was fine, mentally she was bruised, struggling at times to hold it together. Her insomnia was getting worse, the nightmares more frequent. One in particular kept recurring. In it, the murderer she'd helped catch had anesthetised her – just as he'd done to his victims – leaving her paralysed, but able to hear and feel everything he was doing to her.

Rachel glanced around the open plan office. Suruthi's dark head was bent over her keyboard, Alastair was perched on the corner of his desk swinging a fashionably clod foot as he perused a report while Linda was taking calls.

Until Mainwaring's return from sick leave, the team had been temporarily placed under the wing of Virginia Plover.

Ginny – as she liked to be called – was as thin as Mainwaring was fat. She had a short blond bob, tonged into razor-sharp edges, fashionably cut so that one side was shorter than the other, sharp features with thin lips and huge baby blue eyes made her look almost doll like. Since she'd tripped into the office in four-inch heels, she'd taken roost in Mainwaring's eyrie in the corner.

Alastair Turnbull, the fiscal put in charge when Mainwaring had gone off sick, and royal pain in the butt, had been transferred to Homicide, heading up the division and reporting directly to the procurator fiscal, lording it over his own domain although he remained based in the ministry of justice with the rest of them.

Also gone was Clive, who'd been the junior member of the unit's office staff under Linda. He'd finished his forensic science degree and would be graduating in a couple of weeks. In the meantime, he'd applied and been accepted as a crime scene investigator. He'd already taken up his new role.

Rachel would miss his mischievous sense of humour, his quick wit, his inability to take himself seriously and, in particular, his lack of curiosity about her personal life. However, given that he'd joined the local SOCO team, she was bound to come across him in the course of her job.

That left Suruthi, Rachel's fellow fiscal and a ruthlessly efficient prosecutor, to handle the sudden and unexpected deaths and serious crime between them. They'd divided the work roughly in two: Rachel investigating sudden deaths, deciding if anyone should be prosecuted, and Suruthi taking responsibility for rape, assault and other serious crime.

His former colleagues had theorised that Alastair would have been put out to be relieved of his temporary elevation to power but, to their surprise, he had taken his temporary demotion – if that's what it was – without a whimper.

While Mainwaring had treated them like a litter of badly behaved puppies, Plover appeared embarrassingly eager to be liked and approved of. So much so that Suruthi, always quick to come up with nicknames, had started referring to her as Ginny Pushover. Despite his uneven temper, Rachel would rather have Mainwaring any day.

On her first day, Ginny had come into the office with cardboard trays of take-out coffee for the team and spent far too much time perched on the edge of their desks, trading make-up tips with the 'girls'. Before he left, she'd told Clive that many of her friends were Black, and Suruthi that Indian food was her 'fave'.

Meanwhile she tiptoed around Rachel as if she were feral and couldn't be trusted not to bite off her hand if she got too close.

Alastair was the only one of the team she seemed truly at ease with. He was a frequent visitor to her office – in reality, a small section separated with a plywood partition constructed by Mainwaring when they'd first relocated to their new space. Their laughter – hers shrill, his a low rumble – was often heard.

Linda, who was never anything but civil to everyone, could be heard muttering under her breath about it being time to retire.

Rachel turned her attention back to the notes she was entering onto her computer. She was due to prosecute a case in the sheriff court in a couple of days and wanted to make sure she was well prepared.

Her phone vibrated. Practically did a foxtrot over her desk.

It was Selena, the detective constable she had recently become friends with.

'Hey,' Rachel said, tucking her mobile under her chin while continuing to type.

'Hey,' Selena replied. 'I've a body, a real doozy for you. I thought you'd prefer to know about it sooner rather than wait for us to send a report. Given that it looks like this one might turn out to be of particular interest.'

'Go for it,' Rachel said, pulling her notepad towards her.

Selena paused. Rachel could hear traffic in the background. 'Look, I think it's easiest if you come to the scene. You'll find us and the body in Tomnahurich Cemetery. And before you ask – no, he did not emerge from a grave in the middle of the night.'

'On my way.' Rachel picked up her cycle helmet, slung her backpack over her shoulder and headed out the door.

TWO

The dead man lay in a fetal position, legs drawn up to his chest, face pressed into the earth, hands trapped between his knees like a child seeking comfort.

Rachel shivered as she stood over the body. For a sickening moment she'd thought it was Louis. He had the same fine features, the same dark, silky hair flopping over a pale forehead. But Louis had died over a decade ago. Rachel knew, because she'd been with him.

Rachel took a steadying breath, hoping the shock hadn't shown on her face. Keeping her distance, she hunkered down and studied the body.

It looked like he had been in a sitting position, possibly using the gravestone for support, but had toppled over after death. Lividity would confirm if that was the case.

His face had the pallor of death, his full lips were blue, his eyes half open and unfocused, already misting over with a milky film. Even so, she could tell he had been a beautiful man. He had thin, sharp features, a couple of days stubble on his chin. He was wearing light-coloured chinos, muddy on the back, a thick cotton white shirt, and blue socks. One of his shoes – the ones that had intrigued the uniformed PC who had first attended the scene – had come off, the sock on that foot was half on, exposing a pale clean sole. At first glance, no blood or wounds were visible. His mouth was open, with flecks of froth in the corners.

All this Rachel took in with a sweeping glance. Like the first responding police officers and DC Selena MacDonald, Rachel's gut was telling her that something wasn't right here. This was no ordinary drug death.

She stood to scan her surroundings, trying to visualise how the man had come to be here. Tomnahurich Cemetery had been built around, and partly into, a hill. It was circular, the perimeter enclosed by a stone wall. Entry was by two gates, the main gate wide enough for a hearse, usually securely padlocked, with the smaller pedestrian entrance permanently left open. Rachel knew this as she often ran along the canal, cutting through the houses in Ballifeary to get to the cemetery, running up the hill of yews in its centre which gave the cemetery its name, and doing a loop before rejoining the canal. Sometimes she'd pause to examine the headstones, read the inscriptions. People appeared to look after the graves of their dead much the same way as they cared for their living. Some were lovingly tended and weeded, with fresh flowers or plants, others, the older ones, maybe because there was no one left to care, lay with their headstones face down in the dirt like passed-out drunks. Almost all of the still standing stones were engraved with lines identifying the deceased and how long they'd been on earth. Some epitaphs were personal, little nuggets of history, pain and loss; others more to the point, with only dates and names. But all of them claimed and mourned.

She made a silent promise to the man at her feet that she would give him a name and history and return him to those who loved him.

Over the years, dozens of houses and flats had been built

outside the cemetery perimeter. Most of them would have views over the cemetery from their upper floors, so it was possible someone had seen him arrive, and if he'd been with anyone. Perhaps they'd get lucky and someone would have heard a disturbance. Rachel knew the police would be on it. They'd likely already started going door to door to ask the same questions. But Tomnahurich was huge, more like a large park, and partly wooded, so there were plenty of places that would be concealed from anyone happening to look out their bedroom window – especially if their John Doe had come after darkness had fallen.

Rachel ducked back under the crime tape and approached her detective colleagues. Audrey Liversage, the detective sergeant, was in her forties, with a world-weary expression and a no-nonsense attitude. She was just the kind of police officer Rachel would choose to have with her in fraught situations. Selena, the detective constable, was both a friend and a colleague. Her recently cropped hair framed a heart-shaped face. Full cheeks and bright blue eyes were finished off with a wide smile. Her consistent good humour had never failed to impress Rachel. Today, however, there was something different about her demeanour. Rachel thought she detected anxiety in her expression, hesitancy in her smile. Understandable. Selena hadn't been a detective for long.

Although fiscals were notionally in charge of any investigation into sudden, unexpected deaths, murder included, they weren't required to attend the scene, but Rachel liked to be involved as early as possible. Photos were fine, when there was nothing else available, but there was nothing like actually being there, seeing it firsthand.

'Who found him?' Rachel asked.

'Take a guess,' Audrey replied.

'A dog walker?'

'Got it in one,' Selena said, nodding to a bench where an

elderly woman wearing walking boots and a Barbour jacket sat
next to a police officer who was listening attentively to what she
had to say and writing it down in her digital notepad. 'Mrs
Hillington always walks through the cemetery when she takes
Crispin for his walks. It's the first time she's come across a body
though.' Selena hunched her shoulders as a blast of wind tore
through the cemetery, rustling the leaves like sighing ghosts.
'Less distressed than I might have expected. She was a nurse in
A&E before she retired, so is used to dead bodies and' – Selena
gave Rachel a wry smile – 'knows when they're beyond resus-
citation.'

Crispin, a short-haired fox terrier, sat at Mrs Hillington's
feet, taking in the activity around him with interest, wagging his
tail when anyone looked his way.

'Did the pathologist attend?' Rachel asked.

'Yes. He came for a quick look on his way in to work.'

'What does he think?'

'No obvious cause of death that he can see. Says they'll
know more after they've done the PM but can't promise it will
be any time soon. He's about to go on leave.'

'Drug overdose?' Rachel asked.

'That's what PCs who attended the call thought at first: a
straightforward drug death. You know – man seeks privacy of
graveyard to inject himself, overdoes it and dies. But something
about the man's appearance didn't fit with that scenario. "He
just didn't look like a junkie" – their words, not mine. As soon as
I saw him, I got what they meant. He's well-dressed, in clean
clothes and wearing expensive shoes. One of the PCs is a bit of
a fashionista and recognised the brand: Prada. Apparently, they
sell for hundreds of pounds. So why come here to take drugs?
Why not take them in the comfort of his own home or that of
a pal?

'He clearly hasn't shaved for a while but it looks like his hair
has been recently cut and expensively dyed. I know none of

that means he couldn't have died from a drug overdose – plenty rich folk take drugs – but when they couldn't find any ID on the man, not even a phone, they called us and we got the crime scene examiners in.'

The wind whipped Rachel's hair into her eyes and she pulled her beanie lower down on her face. It was nearly summer, for fuck's sake!

'Who leaves home without their phone?' Selena continued. 'Maybe old people, but he's in his twenties – early thirties max. Everyone I know practically has them surgically attached. In fact there is no ID on him at all – no wallet with a driving licence or even credit cards. No work ID either. If it wasn't for the missing ID, I'd think he'd been heading to or from the office. And before you ask, the cemetery has been thoroughly searched.' She gave Rachel a wry smile. 'I won't make the same mistake as in Uist.'

Selena was referring to the first case they'd worked together, where Rachel had found a phone which had been overlooked by the police and turned out to be critical in solving the murder.

Phones weren't always found with bodies. Drownings, for example. But when one was found with a body, police could access emails, texts, last movements, social media accounts all which made identification more straightforward.

Looking at the body, Rachel could see Selena's point; for someone like their John Doe not to be carrying one *was* strange.

'Maybe he was mugged and robbed?' Rachel suggested.

'Possibly. But there are no marks on him – at least, none that are visible – to suggest he was a victim of physical violence.'

In cases like this, without a phone or anything else to identify the victim, the pathologist would take DNA and search for a match on the police database. In the meantime they'd wait for someone to come forward, desperate to trace a missing loved one. Sadly, some were never identified. Rachel hoped this John Doe – the name all male bodies were given until they were identified – wouldn't stay one of those for long.

'None of the local coppers recognise him,' Audrey continued. 'Although that doesn't mean he doesn't live in the area.'

At one time Inverness had been a relatively small town and most of the locals had known each other. But over the last couple of decades the population had grown significantly as tourism and an expanding business sector brought more people to the area.

'Initial thoughts?' Rachel asked Audrey.

The DS shrugged. 'Looks like he found his way here and collapsed. It wasn't cold enough overnight for him to have died from hypothermia.'

'Maybe he took poorly, sat down, died or passed out and someone found him, thought he was drunk or on drugs, and took his phone and wallet,' Selena continued.

Audrey flashed Selena a disapproving look. 'All this is speculation until we find out cause of death.'

Audrey was correct. At this point they hadn't a clue how he'd come to be there or what had happened to him. Rachel would need to wait for the preliminary reports from Detective Inspector Kirk Du Toit and his team.

Rachel's thoughts turned to the people left behind. This man was someone's son, or husband, or brother. Some poor soul was going to get the worst possible news.

But in order to deliver the news, they needed to find out who their John Doe was.

'If he's not local, he could be a tourist,' Rachel speculated. At this time of year, visitors from across the globe flooded into the Highlands and Islands, swelling the local population many times over.

'We plan to check that out. If he came by car, he must have left it somewhere. Although finding it will be near impossible without a number plate. If we're lucky, we might find him on

CCTV. We'll check the cameras at the bus and train stations too. Whoever he is, he must have been staying somewhere. If we can find out where, we might learn more.'

'Fingers crossed someone will miss him and come forward before then.'

They watched in silence as he was zipped into a body bag, loaded into the back of an ambulance and driven away. A post-mortem would tell them more.

In the meantime they needed to find out who he was.

THREE

Rachel flung her backpack into the boot of her car and made a mental check of its contents. A bar of chocolate, an orange, a flask of coffee, a couple of layers in case her waterproof trousers and jacket weren't enough, a compass and water. She wasn't going to be that person who needed rescuing. Even in the height of summer, Scotland's weather was notoriously fickle, veering from rain and wind to clear blue skies often during the same morning. Having climbed Scottish mountains since she was three, Rachel had learned to always be prepared, no matter how good the weather, how clear the summit looked.

The drive as dawn broke had lifted her battered spirits. There were hardly any vehicles on the road, although that would change as the day progressed. In the meantime she took advantage of the lack of traffic, steering her car around tight bends, only slowing down to watch a herd of roe deer run into a wood on top of a hill. On the other side of the road the sun bounced off a small lochan, bringing back happy memories tinged with sadness. She used to go fishing in lochs just like these with her father and Peter, her godfather, when she was

young. It had been a while since she'd been fishing. She made a
mental note to call Peter and suggest they go soon.

The sun was fully risen by the time Rachel pulled into the
car park at the foot of Ben Macdui. The only other vehicle in an
otherwise deserted car park was a burnt orange VW camper
van. It was difficult to say if it was occupied as the curtains in
the back windows were drawn. Sometimes, serious climbers
slept in their cars. It was the best way to get a head start. All the
more reason for Rachel to get going before the day-trippers
arrived. She wanted the mountain to herself.

She tied her bootlaces and hefted her rucksack onto her
shoulders. About four hours to the top, she reckoned, thirty at
the summit taking in the view, and ninety minutes back down.
An hour's drive home. She'd be back in Inverness late
afternoon.

The still morning air contained a hint of the warmth to
come, the silence, apart from the sporadic calling of birds and
the scrape and tumble of rocks underfoot, was total. She
revelled in the quiet as well as the way her muscles stretched
and flexed as she scrambled up the stony path. It had been years
since she'd felt like this. As if she could climb two Ben Macduis
and still have something left in the tank. And she felt good.
Strong. In control. With every step the stress of the previous
weeks melted away.

If she continued to make this rapid progress, she'd reach the
summit sooner than planned. This was a mountain that
required care when covered in ice in the winter but was relatively easy to climb in the summer. Which was not to say she
wasn't aware of the low-lying cloud at the top. It always caught
the tourists out. From the foot of the mountain on a summer's
day the climb would look like a piece of cake, but inexperienced
hikers often discovered the walk in was further than they'd
anticipated, and for those wearing sandals and flip-flops it
would get more uncomfortable by the minute. Sadly, it wasn't

uncommon for visitors to be that unprepared. It wouldn't be long before they found themselves in difficulty. Lost or hurt, they'd regret not having thought to bring water, let alone a compass. Regret not having informed anyone where they were going, and having forgotten to charge their phone. Too many tourists died on the Scottish mountains every year.

Rachel was halfway up the mountain when she got the uneasy feeling someone was following her. She stopped, took the water bottle from her rucksack and used the action to pause and casually look around. A buzzard circled lazily, its shadow a crucifix on the pale green grass. Apart from that, she was alone. She was just being paranoid. Events of the last few months had unsettled her, that was all, made her more aware than ever that the world was not a safe place. What danger could there be out here? Who was going to pursue her up a mountain? If anyone was planning to waylay her, there were much easier places to do it.

She returned her water bottle to her rucksack and set off again. She wasn't going to let her paranoia spoil her climb. The mist that had been drifting in from the west was beginning to blanket the summit and roll down towards her. She glanced behind her as a rock tumbled down the mountain – not one she'd dislodged. Her unease returned. She glanced behind her. No one there. She continued to climb as the mist swirled around her, fine droplets falling on her skin.

She had just passed the snow tunnels when she heard a sound she'd recognise anywhere – the muffled crunch of boots on stone – coming from close behind her. She spun around, her heart in her throat as a ghostly hooded figure emerged from the mist. Legend had it that a mystical grey man lived on the mountain. Several serious climbers claimed to have seen him.

As the figure drew closer, his features became more defined and Rachel realised she recognised him. Eric Hunter. A mountaineer and journalist and a recent thorn in her side.

'What the hell are you doing here?' she demanded. 'Have you been following me?'

He pushed his hood down. 'Not exactly. I was heading here for a climb – I was going to take the Braeriach route but when I saw you park up, I turned around. You were already a good bit up the path but I knew I'd easily catch you up. I wanted to speak to you.'

'You and I both live in Inverness. We have phones. You could have called me and asked me for a meeting.'

'Would you have agreed?'

'It would have depended on what you wanted. But unlikely.'

He gave an amused smile. 'You know, looking into your past is like peeling an onion. You get more intriguing with every fact I uncover. I heard about your hand-to-hand combat in a disused operating theatre with a serial killer. You seem to attract trouble the same way cowpats attract flies. I thought your job was to try people in court. Not to do the police's job for them.'

'You know damn well it's my job to investigate sudden deaths and, if they look suspicious, to work with police to make sure the perpetrators end up in court.' God, she sounded such a twat – as if she was reading from a job advert.

Eric held up his hands, palms out. 'Hey, I'm one of your admirers.' His expression turned serious. 'Nevertheless, while I was digging into your past, I found stuff I never expected to find. Something about you that hasn't appeared in any of the media reports about you – has never been in the public domain.'

A chill swept across Rachel's skin.

'What do you mean?' she asked, trying to keep the panic from her voice. There was no way he could know. 'What stuff? There's so much.' She forced a laugh which, even to her own ears, didn't sound very convincing.

'Don't panic,' Eric said. 'Your secret is safe with me. At least for the time being.'

Was that a threat? A precursor to blackmail? 'I have no idea what you mean,' she said stiffly. As she continued up the path, Eric turned so that he was walking backwards in front of her. He searched her face before giving a wry smile.

'To be honest, I don't give a shit about your past. Don't get me wrong, I admire anyone who can have a career in the law with a convicted murderer as a father. That has to take a bit of chutzpah in anyone's books. He gave her an admiring glance. 'But it's what you've got up to since you started with the fiscal's office that really intrigues me. You've brought down a drug ring and solved several murders, including catching Inverness's first and let's hope final – serial killer. I gather that, if it wasn't for you, he might have killed more women before he was caught. That's what I put in the op ed piece I did on you? Have you read it?'

'No. I'm not interested in anything you lot have to say about me.' She'd had enough media attention to last a lifetime and had no wish to read anything more about herself. 'And while I quite like thinking of myself as outwitting the local criminals single-handedly, I can assure you that wasn't the case.'

Eric gave her a lopsided smile. 'I know. But I also know that as far as both the investigations were concerned, you were a terrier that didn't know when to let go. Furthermore, you're clearly not in anyone's pocket. No one could accuse you of being a people pleaser.'

He stopped in the middle of the path. She could either walk around him or push past. She held her ground.

'Let's just say you are the case study that just keeps giving,' he continued. 'I've been reviewing the trial records of the sex-trafficking ring – the one your mother was expected to testify in.'

'Why?' Rachel asked, immediately curious.

'I heard they'd been requested by your pet lawyer. *Now why would that be*, I thought to myself. *Is she following a lead?*'

He fell into step beside her.

'Who told you that?' she said, annoyed. It was like having a ferret rooting around in her past. More importantly, how had he found out? Where was he getting his information from? The mist was thickening. In a few metres she and Eric would be encased in it, cocooned together as if they shared a cell.

'So you're not denying it?'

'Would there be any point?'

She continued up the track. He was beginning to freak her out with his questions.

There was no chance she could outwalk, let alone outclimb Eric Hunter. Neither would she give him the satisfaction of turning around and going back down. He wasn't going to spoil her plans for the day. She increased her pace. He kept up with her easily.

'Why are you looking into the trial your mother was supposed to testify in before she went missing?' he continued.

'It's got nothing to do with you.'

'On the contrary, I think it might have. I looked into the case when the men were first arrested. I was a rookie reporter at the time.'

Rachel's interest level upped a notch, as he must have known it would .

'Everyone knew the men on trial were bottom feeders,' he continued. 'Small cogs in a well-oiled team headed up by some of the most evil men you'd hope never to meet.'

'Go on,' she said, when he hesitated.

He took his time before continuing. 'Looking back at the trial reignited my interest in organised crime. I was curious to know what had happened to them in the decade or so since the trial. I was shocked to learn organised crime in Scotland is much more widespread, more sophisticated and much more diversified than I could ever have imagined. The stuff they were doing eleven years ago was child's play compared to what they get up to these days. It scares the bejeezus out of me.'

He had Rachel's full attention now. 'Tell me more.'

'These gangs initially started in London but spread to other cities, places like Liverpool. Now they are in Inverness, operating under our noses, using our home town as a route into the rest of the Highlands and Islands.' Clouds covered the sun for a moment, the sudden shadows mirroring his expression.

'These are men who don't care what they do to make themselves rich. They kidnap, traffic vulnerable and desperate people prepared to risk everything in hope of a better life. They kill, sell weapons, use kids to run drugs for them, and don't give a fuck who gets hurt in the process. They'll do anything as long as it makes them money. And there is a shitload of money to be made these days.' He shook his head in despair.

'You know what really gets to me? These evil fuckers could be your or my neighbour, a respected member of the business community, on the school board or a quango. They're bloody experts at distancing themselves from the stuff that makes them rich. You'd never imagine these people are heads of Organised Crime Groups – their kingpins.'

'Have you identified any of these "kingpins", as you call them?'

'I'm working on it. As I'm sure Police Scotland are. It's one matter finding the bastards though, another proving it. Linking them to the money they make from their illegal activities is crucial. The problem is, they accumulate all this wealth but can't really spend it. They have to find a way to launder it. People – the police in particular – tend to notice if ordinary folk start to splash cash around. The police are getting better at tracking the money, but the crooks are getting better at hiding it. Bitcoin has been a godsend to criminals.'

They'd reached the plateau now and began to emerge from the cloud.

She still wasn't sure what, if anything, this had to do with her mother's murder.

She said as much to Eric.

'I'm coming to that. I think the people who ran the sex-trafficking ring a decade ago are the same ones now running the whole shooting match north of Glasgow. The people convicted in the trial in which your mother was due to testify were low hanging fruit and totally expendable. The question I have is: did she suspect or even know one of the people at the top?'

Rachel's heart gave a sickening jolt.

Recently, when she'd visited her father in prison, the first visit since he'd been convicted, he'd told her to stop looking into the sex-trafficking ring. He'd said it could be dangerous for her and for him. Did that mean there was some truth in what Eric was suggesting?

She needed to go back over the files. Find time to listen to all the police interviews. Speak to the firm of advocates who had defended her father. Maybe approach Angus, her childhood friend, who had been devilling – the Scottish term for training to be an advocate – with the firm at the time. Maybe even speak to her father again. If there was any truth in what he'd told her – that he'd gone to prison to protect her – was it from these people? And were they, as Eric suggested, hiding in plain sight?

Could her father have been framed? By someone in organised crime? If so, why? For something he knew was the obvious answer.

No, that was grasping at straws. Her mind ran over the trial – every point of evidence, the inexorable steps to the truth, the eventual conclusion that he was guilty. Her father was a liar. There was no getting away from the fact he'd known her mother hadn't gone off on her own accord, and he'd kept up that lie for years. What reason would he have to do that, other than covering up his crime?

Yet. Yet. As long as there was the slightest doubt, she had to keep an open mind. She owed it to him – and her mother.

'Do you think one of these OCGs murdered my mother?' she asked Eric bluntly. 'And framed my father?'

'I wouldn't rule it out. Your father was a criminal solicitor. What if he worked for an OCG? Gave them legal advice? Represented them, even? Knew who some of the top guys were? What if your mother found out and he told them?'

Silence fell between them as Rachel grappled with what this might mean.

'Someone must know who they are.'

'I'm getting there,' he said. 'But this is not just about names – it's about finding out that something else I've been told is true. If it is, it's possibly the most terrifying thing I've discovered in all my years as a journalist. But I need more proof. My source could be bullshitting me. To be honest, I hope they are.'

'How are you going to prove it? You really should keep the police in the loop.'

'I have a plan. I'm not ready to give it away yet, but I promise I'll go to the police as soon as I'm ready to publish.'

'Will you let me know if you find out anything?'

'As soon as it's appropriate,' he said, so emphatically Rachel knew there was no point in pressing him.

By the time they reached the summit, the mist was moving to the west. It would clear before long.

They sat against rocks and opened their backpacks. Eric had brought two rounds of sandwiches to go with his flask of coffee, as well as crisps and biscuits.

As the last of the mist drifted away, they were silent again as they took in the view over the hills and glens.

'Doesn't this make you believe in God?' Eric said. 'This is free, God's gift to us. And do we appreciate it? No. We put owning material things above all else. We allow having a new car, or a bigger house than our neighbour to determine our worth. These crime bosses only care about what shit they can buy during their short lives. Nothing else matters, least of all the people whose lives they ruin. That's why I love what I do: unearthing them for prosecutors like you to bring to justice.'

Rachel got what he meant. Every person had the right to be defended from exploitation. It seemed the world was increasingly divided into the powerful and the powerless. Her role, and maybe Eric's, was to stand between them, to ensure that evil was not allowed to thrive.

'That's why I decided not to expose what I learned about your past,' Eric continued. 'I couldn't see what purpose it would serve, except to ruin your career.'

He knew, she realised with a plummeting heart. 'How did you find out?'

He turned so he could look at her. 'You know I can't reveal my sources. But, as I said earlier, your secret is safe with me. Particularly as I have something to ask in return.'

Here it was. The quid pro quo.

'I always felt that my children would be safe in Scotland,' Eric went on. 'But it doesn't feel at all safe now. Worst of all, I worry I might be putting my family in danger when I should be doing everything possible to protect them.' He stared into the distance, stroking his beard, before continuing. 'I owe my wife everything. Ella and I were young when we married. I was twenty-one, Ella twenty. We were both at university but when she got pregnant she dropped out, so I could continue.' He bit into an apple and chewed before continuing. 'Ella came to London with me when I asked her, even though her family were in Inverness; we had two kids by then and life would have been much easier for her had we stayed. I uprooted her again to come back here. I found I couldn't live so far from the mountains. She never complained. Never moaned. She's given up so much for me and my career. I'd do anything for her. Anything to protect her, including keeping her in the dark. But someone needs to know what I've uncovered. When I saw you pull up in the car park, I knew immediately it should be you. I know you don't like these evil fuckers either. One day, maybe sooner than I'd like, I might need you to do something for me.' He held her gaze. 'I don't mean to freak you out, but in case the worst happens, I have to make sure the story I'm investigating doesn't die with me.'

It was as if a ghost had walked over Rachel's grave. She had a very bad feeling about this and, judging by Eric's expression, he did too. Despite his light tone, Rachel saw real fear in his eyes. If Eric, the most fearless climber she knew, was frightened, he had to have good reason.

'You think someone might kill you? Jesus, Eric! In that case you definitely have go to the police. Immediately. Tell them what you know and let them investigate.'

He raised his eyebrows in exaggerated incredulity. 'What? Like you do? You should practice what you preach.' His expression grew serious again. 'I can't. I'm not ready – not yet. I don't want to just chop the head off the group, I want to dice it into tiny bits so there's nothing left of it.' He gave her a strained smile. 'Don't worry, as soon as I have proof I'll go to the authorities.' He grasped her wrist. 'I want you to promise that if anything happens to me, you'll be on the case. Take what I've discovered to the police.'

'How will I do that when I don't know what it is?'

'Trust me, you'll know.'

FOUR

When she got home, Rachel poured herself a diet tonic and took it into the garden to drink. May was her favourite time of year, the winter mostly past, weeks of summer on the horizon. The sun had stayed out and glinted off the sea. Runners and walkers were out in force on the canal path and the distant Braeriach appeared tantalisingly close.

Her mind flashed to Angus, as it always did when she looked at that particular mountain. Last week she'd seen a photo of him with his new woman on the inside pages of the Edinburgh newspapers. Amanda Logan was typical of Angus's girlfriends, tall and willowy with not a hair out of place, an advocate specialising in human rights. Not in a hundred years could Rachel imagine her pulling a knife on anyone, let alone getting into a brawl with a murderer, no matter how lofty the reason. She sighed. Amanda was not someone Rachel could ever compete with. Taking Rachel on would be a challenge for anyone, let alone an ambitious advocate with an eye on becoming a KC. Just as well Rachel liked her own company then.

She turned her thoughts to a challenge she might be able to rise to.

She'd been unable to get her conversation with Eric out of her mind. It wasn't just the fact that he'd stumbled on her secret – there was little she could do about that, except trust that he was telling the truth when he said he'd keep quiet. What he'd said about the growth of OCG groups in Scotland had alarmed and dismayed her. She hoped he knew what he was doing. Eric was a risk-taker. That's what made him one of the best mountaineers she knew. But taking risks got people killed.

Not that it would stop her digging too. The possible link between a powerful and expanding OCG and her mother's death needed to be thoroughly investigated and either upheld or dismissed.

She thought about the boxes of files in her hall. Would she discover the truth in there?

The boxes hadn't been touched since Angus, a leading criminal advocate as well as her childhood friend, had delivered them a few weeks earlier. So much had happened since then, she hadn't had a chance to look at them. What information could her mother have learned that might have made it imperative that she did not testify at trial? More importantly, did it have anything to do with her murder?

There was no getting away from the evidence that had convicted her father. 1) Her mother's rings, passport and bank cards had been found in his possession. 2) He'd used her mother's debit card around the country in an attempt to prove she was alive and had left of her own volition. 3) His insistence she'd left after confessing to an affair, despite the police finding no evidence to support his allegation.

Although her father had always claimed the cards and passports belonging to her mother had been planted in his safe, that didn't explain the ATM withdrawals he'd made with his wife's card. Despite the weight of evidence against him, he'd refused to plead guilty. When the trial had started, he'd seemed confident he'd be acquitted, but as the trial progressed and the evidence against him had mounted, he'd become increasingly subdued, his bluster diminishing with every day that passed.

Rachel shook her head, frustrated. Why go down that dead end again, tormenting herself with the fantasy that her father was innocent? She should leave it alone. But even as the thought passed through her mind, she knew she wouldn't. Not as long as there was the slightest chance he'd been wrongly convicted.

Although she'd attended the trial most days, she hadn't sat in every single day. She'd had lectures and seminars to attend, so she might have missed something.

Furthermore, her mother had been frightened of something – a work-related issue she'd told Rachel's grandmother. Even if it had nothing to do with her death, discovering what that had been had become an itch Rachel just had to scratch.

She couldn't keep putting it off. It was time to start scratching.

An hour later, Rachel sat cross-legged on her sitting room floor, one of the boxes in front of her, a large yellow legal pad and black Biro to the side. Usually, she used her phone to take notes, more for speed than anything, but she'd always found writing on paper in long hand better when she wanted to make sense of something. It was particularly useful for drawing mind maps, making connections.

She selected Taylor Swift's new album on her Sonos sound system and opened a packet of tortillas and guacamole dip. Honey, the cat she shared with her neighbour, crawled into her lap, made a couple of circles and settled.

The first box contained a wad of files and a few dozen cassettes. Looking at the labels, Rachel confirmed that they were a combination of witness statements and police interviews. She started by scanning through the papers, not sure of what she was looking for except that it was something others might have missed, particularly as she was coming at it from a different angle and more than a decade had passed.

The first file contained pages and pages of notes from police officers who had been involved over the years with the burgeoning spread of organised crime across the area. As Eric had said, it had started insidiously, with drugs becoming increasingly common as Inverness had grown. Over the years leading up to the trial, the gangs had diversified into the many forms of human trafficking, including sex trafficking.

Rachel stood to stretch her legs. She crossed over to the patio doors and looked out to sea. Young women were in particular demand for the sex industry. Most, if not all, believed they'd be working in hotels, the hospitality sector or care homes, and handed over their passports in good faith, believing they'd be returned on their arrival in the UK. But instead of being taken to a hotel or B&B, they were taken to a house, or flat, sexually abused and told they'd be used as sex workers until they paid off an impossible sum of money. They'd be warned that going to the police would result in their arrest and imprisonment, deportation at best.

Which was exactly what had happened to Monika Troka, the woman who had through her ingenuity and courage escaped and brought the story of her ordeal to Rachel's mother's attention. Monika was originally from Albania. She had been befriended online and lured to the UK with promises of clothes and trips abroad and, more enticingly, love. The reality had been entirely different.

Rachel retuned to the boxes and sifted through the cassettes until she found the one marked with her mother's name. She'd taken a cassette recorder from the office a couple of weeks ago and, drawing a steadying breath, she slid the tape into the cassette player.

Her throat closed as she heard her mother's soft island accent for the first time in over a decade. As her mother repeated her name, Mary Ann McKenzie, and her date of birth and address, Rachel was transported back in time to an image of herself in her mother's lap in front of an open fire. Rachel must have just recently got out of the bath as her mother was towelling her hair while singing along to a Gaelic Runrig track.

Rachel closed her eyes as longing vied with guilt and regret. The last months she'd spent with Mum she'd disappointed her in every way a daughter could disappoint a mother. If only she'd known how little time they had left, and that she'd never have the chance to make it up to her.

She straightened her shoulders and pushed the image away. Self-pity achieved nothing. She couldn't change the past, but she could change the future. She needed to concentrate on what was being said rather than the sound of her mother's voice.

Her mother was being interviewed by DI Jason Bright and DC Eilidh Souter. DI Bright was asking her mother to take them through how Monika Troka had made contact with her.

Mary Ann explained that Monika had pretended to be suffering with severe abdominal pain in order to get admitted to hospital. She'd been accompanied by one of the men who guarded the brothel. He tried to pass himself off as her husband, there to speak on her behalf. When they'd finally, with the greatest reluctance, agreed to take her to hospital, Monika had been warned not to speak and to pretend she couldn't understand English.

Luckily for Monika, an on-the-ball nurse had become suspicious. The 'husband' was at least two decades older than his wife and hadn't appeared to know very much about Monika's history, was even unsure of her age. The nurse had managed to get Monika on her own by insisting she needed to provide a urine sample and following her into the patients' toilet. A terrified Monika had revealed that she was one of a number of women kept prisoner in a house and made to have sex with up to a dozen men a day.

The nurse had called the Social Work Department and had got through to Mary Ann, who had been the on-call manager that day. Rachel's mother had wasted no time coming to the hospital and, with the nurse's help and collusion, managed to get Monika on her own. Monika had explained what had happened to her, that she was a prisoner, made to provide sex to pay off a debt her captors claimed she owed, though she'd no idea how she incurred it. She'd begged Mary Ann for her help.

There had been nothing else of note in her mother's statement. Only that the Social Work Department had known for some time that there were brothels operating in the area and had worked with the police to try and shut them down on several occasions. Frustratingly, the gangs had always been one step ahead of the police raid, moving out before they arrived.

On this occasion, the police moved exceptionally quickly, organising a raid on the property without alerting Monika's minder. This time they had arrived to find the house occupied: six victims, two clients who'd been let go, and another three gang members – two men and a woman – responsible for keeping the women under guard.

The conditions the women had been kept in had been shocking – mattresses on the floor, dirty blankets, a single shower. The female gang member refused to testify. Once a prostitute herself, she'd graduated, for lack of a better word, to a position of authority over the women, guarding them for the same people who had once trafficked her. A form of Stockholm syndrome, perhaps.

Rachel slid the recording of the first interview with Monika Troka into the cassette player.

Monika's voice was hesitant at first as she gave her name

and date of birth, but she'd become increasingly confident as the interview progressed and she took the officers through what had happened to her. She'd been fifteen when she'd met Dave, as he'd called himself, online. He'd spent time grooming her until, lonely and vulnerable, she'd believed everything he said about being in love with her and had accepted his invitation to visit him in the UK. He'd promised to pay for everything.

Instead, the man she thought loved her had become her jailer and pimp. After he'd dumped her at the house, she'd never seen him again.

So far, so banal.

Rachel made a note on her pad. Had the man calling himself Dave ever been identified?

Three men, identified as Kevin Solomon, Toby Storr and Murray Wild, had rotated with the female gang member so there was always someone at the house to stop them from seeking help. The women couldn't even leave the house to go to the shops.

The DI and DC took turns pressing Monika for details. Names, dates, who had come to the house and when. Monika was clearly doing her best to supply as many details as she could which were frustratingly few.

'These men who came for sex didn't bother with names,' Monika said, sounding exasperated. 'They came and went. Often the same ones over and over. Most of the time I didn't know where we were. They kept moving us. Sometimes we stayed in the same place for six weeks, other times it was only two or three. We never knew how long we'd be staying. They would come just before we were to start work, or in the middle of the night, and order us to pack our things. They would be impatient, beat us if we took too long.'

Anger burned like acid behind Rachel's ribs. If there was one thing she couldn't stomach, it was men being violent to women.

'Once I kicked one of them in the balls,' Monika continued. Rachel heard the smile in her voice. 'They beat me badly that night. But I didn't care.'

Way to go, Monika! Rachel cheered out loud, earning a startled look from Honey.

Then Monika said something else that made Rachel's skin prickle.

'Once,' she said, 'a woman came.'

'What woman?' DC Souter asked sharply. 'Do you know who she was?'

'She was one of them.' Monika spat the words.

'Can you describe her?'

'No. I didn't see her. I was passing the sitting room on my way to the toilet, and the door was open just a little bit. She was talking to the man I called big nose, the one who came with me to the hospital. I couldn't make out what she was saying, but her voice was educated, more fancy than the men who took me, much more fancy than the woman who guarded us. I could tell from the way the men spoke to her that she was someone they respected.'

'Did they see you?' the DC asked.

Monika gave a sour laugh. 'No. These people never saw us. We were not like human beings to them. Just things to be bought and sold, like toys in a shop.'

The police officers continued to press Monika, but she was adamant she hadn't seen the woman, had never heard her voice again or heard a name, that really she had nothing more to add.

Statements taken from the other women had thrown no light on the woman's identity. None of the others had seen or heard her.

Monika's testimony had been the basis for the prosecution of the three men. The female gang member – deemed as much victim as offender – had not been prosecuted. The gang leaders – the kingpins – had proved elusive. The three accused men had insisted point-blank that there had been no one else involved, although this had been blatantly untrue. They had also categorically denied that a woman had been one of their bosses. Apparently they'd laughed derisively at the notion, claiming they would never take orders from a female.

Rachel switched off the cassette recorder and thought for a while.

What had happened to Monika? Where was she now? Was she alive? What about the other witnesses? Why hadn't any of the neighbours noticed there was a brothel in the neighbourhood?

Something else struck her. She rewound the tape until she found the point again. Monika had said they were moved at random intervals, sometimes weekly, sometimes after six weeks. Why was that?

She went back over the police notes. When the police or social workers believed a brothel to be operating in an area, they would meet and decide a time to raid. The Social Work Department was included as they would be required to care for the victims in the aftermath of the raids.

None of these raids had been successful. Each time they'd found the premises empty, no evidence to suggest who was running the brothel or where they'd gone. But the raid that followed Monica's hospital visit had been hastily put together without the usual planning meeting, taking place a couple of hours after Rachel's mother alerted the police.

Had someone inadvertently given the planned raid away to the wrong person? Or had there been an informer within the group – someone in the police or Social Work Department?

Rachel's heart began to race. Was this the information her mother had discovered that had made her fear for her life? If so how could Rachel find out who was involved in the planning meetings? The fiscal in charge of the case had died a couple of years ago following a stroke. Rachel had gone to his funeral.

Where was Detective Inspector Jason Bright, the senior investigating officer on the case? The name wasn't familiar to Rachel. A quick google came up with a piece about him retiring eight years ago after twenty-five years of distinguished service. If he was still alive, would he be prepared to speak to her? And what about DC Eilidh Souter? Where was she? Rachel googled her too. And came up with zilch, apart from a photo she'd been tagged in by a friend. Having no social presence to speak of was weird. Rachel peered at the slightly out of focus photo. In it, Eilidh had her arm around another woman with thick dark hair clearly visible under a mortarboard, as if she'd been at a graduation ceremony. The photo had been taken outside Marischal College, which was part of Aberdeen University – the same university Rachel had attended.

Finally, Rachel googled Monika. Nothing on her either.

Was Eilidh Souter still with Police Scotland? Would she speak to Rachel about the case? If there was something missing from the files, she was bound to know.

One way or another, Rachel was determined to find out what wasn't in the files as much as what was. In the meantime she couldn't resist googling the article Eric had mentioned he'd written about her. It summarised her role in two recent cases, revised her personal history, but it was the last paragraph that caught her attention.

There is a lot more to say about Miss McKenzie. Her private life and her backstory make fascinating reading. If you'd like to know more, read next week's Inverness Record *where I'll be taking a deep dive into a life that contains more surprises and revelations.*

Rachel groaned. Fuckity Fuck. Would she never be free of her past?

FIVE

Rachel was going through the trial transcripts again the following morning when she realised where she might get the information she needed. Nora Goodall had worked with Rachel's mother around the time the brothels were under investigation. In fact she was the one who had told Rachel that her mother had been worried about the case. She might have met Monika, might even know what had happened to her after the trial, if she'd had friends, any support. And if Nora didn't know, she might be able to direct Rachel to someone who did. She sent her a text asking if she could come and see her again, and Nora texted back inviting her to drop by after lunch.

It was a perfect Scottish afternoon, clear skies, warm sunshine and only the lightest of breezes, as Rachel drove the seven kilometres of windy, tree-fringed road to the affluent village of Beauly on the banks of the River Ness.

Nora, wearing a V-neck T-shirt and loose linen trousers, with bracelets up a freckled arm, met her at the door. Just like the last time she'd visited, the older woman suggested they have tea in the garden.

After Nora had passed Rachel her tea, she leaned forward.

'What can I do for you, Rachel? I trust you aren't on the trail of another serial killer. I read the article about you in the *Inverness Courier*.'

Rachel winced internally. 'No, nothing like that.' She breathed in the heady scent of roses before continuing. 'The last time I came to see you, you mentioned there were two cases my mother had been involved in that worried her.' Having looked into it, Rachel had ruled out the case involving the sudden death of a child from meningitis when he'd been in care and under Mary Ann's supervision. The birth father who had threatened her mother had moved to New Zealand with his wife.

'I'd like to ask you about the sex-trafficking case. In particular about Monika Troka. She was the woman who led the police to the brothel.'

'I don't know how helpful I will be, but fire away with your questions and I'll do my best.'

'After she was rescued from the brothel, do you know what happened to her?'

Nora thought for a few minutes. 'Well, after the police finished interviewing her, she would have been put in a place of safety. She and the other women would have been taken to hospital to be checked over – as long as they agreed, of course. A social worker would have given them emotional support – most likely your mother, as she was the one who had the relationship with Monika. I imagine a police officer would have supported her in the lead-up to the trial.'

'Could the police officer have been DC Eilidh Souter?'

'I don't think I ever knew,' Nora said. 'It wasn't my case.'

'What was the Social Work Department's involvement prior to the raids?'

'One of our managers – your mother, at that time – would meet with the DI in charge of the case, or his DC. Either we would tell them we'd identified a brothel, or they would let us know that a confidential informant had tipped them off. The police would plan a raid and let us know when it was to happen so we could arrange for one of us to be there.'

'Is there any way to find out who was at these meetings?'

Nora thought for a while.

'In those days there might have been a minute-taker from the department. Leave it with me. I'll see if I can find out.'

'That would be really helpful.'

Nora walked Rachel through the garden to her car. 'I'll see what I can find in the minutes, if I can find them – I'm not sure I'll be able to – and then get back to you.' She regarded Rachel with concern. 'I just hope you know what you're doing.'

SIX

Rachel went for an early-morning run before showering and dressing in her signature work outfit of tailored black trousers and white shirt.

As she cycled along the canal, the quickest way to get to her office, her thoughts turned to the day ahead.

Apart from deciding whether sudden and unexplained deaths should be investigated, a major part of her job was preparing cases to prosecute in court when another party was thought to be responsible for a victim's death.

Last week there had been a two-car multiple fatality on the A9 – two brothers and the driver's girlfriend in one car and an elderly woman in the other. Rachel had meetings that afternoon with the parents of the brothers – one of whom had been the driver of the Audi that had caused the crash. Although speaking to relatives of the deceased was an important part of her job, one she tried to do with kindness and tact, she was not looking forward to this particular interview. The family had made it clear that they didn't believe their son had been at fault, insisting the toxicology was incorrect, adamant that their son never consumed alcohol if he planned to drive.

Before the meeting, she had another court case to prepare for as well as her John Doe – the body in the graveyard – to follow up on.

As usual she was the first to arrive in the office. She made herself a coffee and, knowing that Dr Alison Halliday, one of the forensic pathologists based at the hospital, was always in early too, phoned the pathology department. She was put on hold for a couple of minutes before being connected.

'I thought it wouldn't be long before I heard from you. I was about to call you, if not.' Alison Halliday's tone was warm. Rachel had worked with her before and liked and respected her. 'We have a backlog of PMs building up, so I came in on Saturday to do your John Doe's PM. Didn't have anything better to do, if I'm honest.'

Rachel and Alison clearly had something in common.

'Does that mean you have something to tell me?' Rachel asked.

'Yes and no. I don't have a definitive cause of death. We are going to have to wait until his toxicology comes back for that. Some drugs, cocaine in particular, can occasionally cause cardiac arrest in young people. So I can't rule out death by natural causes or suicide at this point.'

Rachel took a sip of her coffee, welcoming the immediate hit of caffeine.

'I gather he's not been identified yet,' Alison continued.

'Not as far as I know.' Rachel flicked through her emails. Nothing from the police. 'Nope. Afraid not. But it's early days.'

'I thought that might be the case, so I took a sample of DNA from the cartilage in his knee and sent it off to the lab so they can check it against the PNC to see if they come up with anything.'

Alison was referring to the Police National Computer. Whenever someone was arrested on suspicion of committing a crime, a sample of their DNA was taken and entered on the database, as well as NDNAD, the UK's National DNA Database. The problem was, a person had to have been arrested in order to appear on the police database. If he'd never been arrested, Rachel's John Doe wouldn't be on there.

'If we don't get a hit, we can upload it onto GEDmatch,' Alison continued.

'GEDmatch?' Rachel asked.

'It's the best chance of getting a hit when we don't get one on the police database. Look, why don't I put you in touch with someone I think you'll find helpful. Not just for this case but maybe others in the future. He's a genealogist, name of Greg Berkeley. He lives in Inverness and I'm sure he'll leap at the chance to speak to you.' She rattled out a mobile number which Rachel took down.

'I'll try and get Gartcosh to fast-track your John Doe's DNA.' Gartcosh was Scotland's national crime campus which housed multi-agency teams and a forensic laboratory. 'I happen to have become friendly with one of the scientists there,' Alison continued. Rachel heard the smile in her voice. 'And I think he'll be happy to help.'

Rachel could hear the clicks of a keyboard as Alison typed something into her computer. 'By the way, I did discover something that might be useful in helping to trace our John Doe in the meantime.'

'Which is?'

'He had a plate in his forearm. He must have suffered a complex unstable fracture at one time.'

'What's that?'

'It's where the bone breaks so badly that the sharp end of the bone pierces the skin. A sort of inside-out wound, if you like. It usually only happens if severe pressure is applied or if a person had weak bones – and there was no evidence of that in our John Doe. The wound needed a number of stiches, and a steel plate was fitted to help the broken bones knit together.'

'Could it have happened in a car accident?' Rachel asked.

'That's possible. Although for a break as severe as this, I would have expected other injuries.'

'What about a physical attack? As in deliberately done?'

'Yes. But not necessarily.'

'If we had a name we could search hospital records,' Rachel said. Although that would take time. Hospital records weren't as joined up as people liked to think.

'That was what I was calling to tell you. This plate should help us get a name for our John Doe.'

Rachel's pulse gave a kick of excitement. 'How so?' She spun around in her chair. While she'd been talking to Alison the others had dribbled in and phones had started ringing. Suruthi held up a coffee mug and raised questioning eyebrows. Rachel pointed to the half-full mug on her desk and shook her head.

'Every mechanical part that is placed in a person – pace-makers, breast implants, just to name a couple of examples – is manufactured in a factory somewhere and stamped with a serial number which identifies where the part was manufactured. That way if a number of parts seem to develop a fault or turn out to be substandard in any way, the patients can be recalled for review before they start experiencing symptoms.'

'How does that help?'

'Because if we know where the part was made, we can find out where it was sent to. Which hospital and even which patient had it implanted.'

'So if we trace the serial number it will lead us back to the patient and we'll have a name?' Rachel asked.

'That's the idea. But it might take some time, depending how quickly the manufacturer supplies us with the relevant information. They might insist on a court order before they'll do so.'

'Luckily that's my area of expertise. If you can establish the manufacturer, I'll take it from there. See if I can nudge them along.'

That was positive. Once they had a name, they'd be a good way along the road in finding out about their John Doe and what happened to him. His people would be able to reclaim him. If they wished. She pushed away the depressing thought that they might not. She'd cross that bridge when she came to it.

'Preliminary thoughts about our John Doe?' Rachel asked, unwilling to let Alison go without knowing more.

Alison sighed. 'You're always in such a rush, Rachel. I'm not going to speculate until I get the toxicology results. Did that once and it came back to bite me, so never again. On first glance he looks like a well-nourished, healthy male. Heart and other organs all looked normal. But you know as well as I do that doesn't mean buttons at this point. Aside from the historical breakage to his arm, there were no injuries to other bones. I couldn't see any obvious needle tracks – recent or historical. I noticed the soles of his feet were soft, his nails manicured. He was someone who clearly cared about his personal appearance. Oh, and he had a tattoo of Scotland – including the islands – on his upper arm. I'll send you a photo of it, if you like. Lividity suggests he died in the sitting position. That's about it for the time being. If we had a name, I'd be able to check if there was any significant history in his past which would help.'

Rachel thanked Alison and disconnected. Time to check in with Selena, find out if the police had made any progress.

She had a favour to ask her too.

SEVEN

Rachel met Selena in the shared courtyard outside the Ministry of Justice. The spacious, modern purpose-built building housed Police Scotland on one side and the Crown Office and Procurator Fiscal Service on the other. Previously the court had sat in Inverness Castle in the town centre, but the layout hadn't allowed for physical distancing between victims and accused – a situation which often resulted in outright brawls.

The sun was beating down and they agreed it would be a sin to waste a chance to bask in it. They chose a bench furthest away from the traffic and, more importantly, out of hearing from anyone entering or leaving the court. Rachel had bought sandwiches from M&S Food on the opposite side of the road. Selena supplied the coffee, a black Americano for Rachel, a flat white for herself.

They spent the first few minutes catching up. Selena had recently moved from Uist to Inverness and had been in short-term accommodation while she looked for something more permanent. Last week she had found a flat to rent close to the police HQ. She was thrilled with it.

'It's five minutes away from here on the other side of the

river and less than a hundred yards from the church. I can roll out of bed at nine thirty on a Sunday morning and still easily make the service.'

Rachel hadn't known that Selena was religious. Despite being thrown together in some tense and frightening situations in the short time since they'd met, they were still getting to know each other.

'There's an Aldi around the corner and even a chiropodist if I need my bunions seen to,' Selena continued. 'Best thing is that it overlooks the river. I like to be able to see the water from my window. It reminds me of home.'

There it was again. The shadow in her eyes. The flash of pain across her face.

'I move in at the weekend,' Selena said. 'You'll need to come around as soon as I get some furniture organised. At the moment you'd have to sit on the floor.' She gave Rachel one of her broad smiles. Once again, it didn't reach her eyes.

Something wasn't quite right with the new detective constable, although Rachel couldn't quite put a finger on it. Maybe it was the dark circles under her eyes or her new habit of nibbling at the nail on her right middle finger.

Taking on a new, challenging job in an unfamiliar city had to be tough, particularly when it meant leaving family – and Selena was close to hers – and friends. On the other hand, Rachel knew the police constable was tougher than she looked.

Selena had brought a two-litre bottle of water with her and swigged from it at regular intervals. 'I don't drink enough water, according to NHS Scotland. If I up my intake, it will improve my brain power. Apparently.'

Rachel's concern deepened. The self-deprecating humour was new too.

They were quiet for a moment as a tattooed man emerged from the ministry, a young woman with a similar number of tattoos and a harassed, pleading expression following close behind. It sounded as if she were berating him. When she grabbed his arm in an attempt to get his attention, he shrugged her off with a snarl.

'Wish I could tell her to leave him,' Rachel said, looking after them until they'd crossed to the other side of the road. 'If she thinks he'll change, she's going to be disappointed.' Another woman in danger from the very person who was supposed to love and protect her. Like Rachel's mother had been. Another reminder her father was a very bad man and as guilty as hell.

'You can't save everyone, Warrior Rachel,' Selena said softly.

'Please don't call me that,' Rachel said, more sharply than she'd intended. She was uncomfortable with Selena's admiration, especially when she knew she was about to exploit it.

'Hey.' Selena looked puzzled at Rachel's reaction. 'At least it's better than being called Wise Selena.' She was referring to her own Gaelic nickname.

'Sorry,' Rachel apologised. 'I've got something on my mind. I'll tell you about it once we've got business out of the way.'

Selena bit into her half of the egg-and-cress sandwich and spoke around a full mouth. 'OK. Got to admit I'm dying to know what it is. In the meantime, as I said, Du Toit asked me to bring you up to speed with cemetery man.' Rachel had worked with Detective Inspector Kirk Du Toit before and liked and respected him, even though she knew he didn't entirely approve of the way she involved herself in cases. She'd had to remind him on more than one occasion her role in the Crown Office and Procurator Fiscal Service gave her overall responsibility for any sudden or unexplained deaths. So, although he didn't welcome Rachel's interference with police investigations, he recognised her right to do so. As long as she didn't get in the way.

'That's decent of him. Tell him I appreciate it.'

'I'm afraid we're no closer to identifying our John Doe,'

Selena continued. 'We didn't get a hit on the PNC. So it's not likely we'll get a match on the national DNA site either. I also checked missing persons UK. No matches. I've been liaising with local forces over Scotland, but no luck there either. No household, guest house, hotel, hostel or even campsite has reported anyone matching his description as missing.'

'Nothing in his pockets? A bus ticket? A receipt?'

'Not a thing. More reason to think he, or someone else, didn't want him to be identified. We've checked the CCTV at Inverness bus and train stations. Also no joy. We will need to have more before we can justify hours trawling through weeks of airport footage, never mind CCTV across Scotland. Particularly as we don't have even rough dates as to when he might have travelled.

'As you suggested at the cemetery, he could be from anywhere. Perhaps he was a tourist and his people back in his home country haven't noticed he's missing yet. Not everyone checks in with family or friends every day. If we'd found his phone,' Selena continued, 'it would have been fairly straightforward to identify him. Apart from his contacts we could have used the GPS on his phone to track where he'd been in the hours before his death. And there's no way of checking his social media without a phone, which is annoying. Assuming Meta let us access his messages and WhatsApp, we'd know everything about him by now. I know Dr Halliday is chasing up the serial number of the plate she found in his arm. Fingers crossed that leads somewhere.'

They fell silent as a motorbike opened its throttle and roared past.

'So in short we haven't been able to trace an address,' Selena continued, 'or figure out what he was doing in the graveyard or how he got there. Or, to be honest, anything useful at all.'

'What about access to a GP – attendance at a hospital?' Rachel asked.

'Again, we'd need a name before we could follow up. Without one it would be like looking for a needle in a haystack.'

Because of the case Rachel and Selena had recently worked together, both knew more than they wanted to about hospitals and how their records systems worked. They were a rich source of information, but to access a record they required a name and date of birth as a minimum.

'The plate in his arm is currently our best chance,' Selena said.

'There's another possibility if we don't get a hit on the police DNA database,' Rachel said. 'Alison suggested sending his DNA to GEDmatch.' She explained what she'd learned about the site. 'She's given me the name of a genealogist who might be helpful. He knows ways of tracing people using their DNA, even if they're not on either database. I've arranged to meet him next week.'

'That will give us a fallback position if we don't identify him soon,' Selena replied. 'We have a couple of other possibilities up our sleeve. We traced his shirt and trousers to Hugo Boss. Unfortunately there are dozens of stores across the UK that stock the brand. The shoes are a different matter. There can't be too many places that sell Prada shoes in a size nine, so that's another possible line of enquiry. I'm phoning around suppliers. I only have a dozen or so to go. Hopefully, given how expensive they are, he used a credit card to buy them.'

'Dental records?' Rachel asked.

'Not much help if we don't know where he lived. Maybe the forensic dentist will have something useful to tell us. Even so, that will take time. It looks like getting a hit on his DNA might be our best bet.'

They stopped chatting as a group emerged from the ministry, likely from the same court as the man and woman who'd just walked past. Judging by the cheerful demeanour of this group and the pats on backs, matters in their case had gone their way.

'It's the lack of ID that I keep thinking about. Did he purposefully not have anything on him, or did someone else take it?' Rachel said.

'It's possible he didn't want to be identified. Maybe he abandoned a life he no longer wanted. Perhaps he was depressed and didn't want loved ones to know he'd found life unbearable. Or maybe he was high and confused,' Selena mused. 'So he left wherever he was staying and wandered off.'

'If that were the case, I imagine someone would have reported him missing by now,' Rachel said. 'Anyway, all that's conjecture. Remember the ABC of any investigation,' she continued with a smile.

Selena smiled back. 'Assume nothing. Believe nothing. Challenge everything! Fair enough. In the meantime, we'll continue with our enquiries while we wait for his DNA results and the results of the toxicology.'

'What about door-to-door enquiries at the houses near the graveyard?' Rachel asked. 'Did anyone see anything? Hear anything?'

'Nope. Makes me think he went there in the small hours when everyone was in their beds.' Selena shivered. 'Odd place to go in the middle of the night, whatever the reason.'

'But a good place if he didn't want to be seen.' Rachel shook her head. 'Once we have a cause of death, we can decide what to do next. He could have died from any number of causes. His death doesn't have to be suspicious.'

But there was already enough to make Rachel think it was. The question was, were they looking at an accidental death or the cover-up of one. Or even murder?

'I need a favour,' Rachel said, turning to the matter that had been keeping her awake at night.

She explained about the case files from the investigation into the sex-trafficking ring.

'It was as if the gang had prior knowledge of the raids. It occurred to me that it would be useful to know who was on the team when they were planned. A Detective Inspector Bright was in charge of the investigation. I gather that he's retired. I don't suppose you can find an address for him? And contact details for Detective Constable Eilidh Souter while you're at it? I'm hoping she's still with the force.'

Selena frowned. 'I'm not sure I should be looking for information like that, far less passing it on.'

'I don't want you to do anything criminal. I only want to speak to them.'

'In that case, why don't you ask Du Toit?' Selena asked.

She had a point. Selena knew Rachel better than she liked.

'Because the last time I spoke to him he made it clear he was up to his eyes.' More significantly, she remembered with a guilty pang that when Selena had joined his team he'd warned Rachel against treating the new detective constable as her personal police officer. Which she was uncomfortably aware she was doing right now.

Selena sighed. 'There's a couple of officers who have been in the division forever. I'll ask them if they have an address or contact details. But that's it. If I don't come up with anything, it's back to you.'

'Fair enough.'

They were quiet for a moment.

'You OK?' Selena peered at Rachel. 'You look like shit, if I'm honest.'

'Thanks for that,' Rachel said, not admitting that she'd been thinking the same about Selena. 'Not the boost to my ego I was looking for.' But her attempt to laugh it off didn't wash with Selena. She knew what Rachel had gone through over the last few months.

'Look,' Selena said, 'I know you like to keep your cards close to your chest, but don't you think it's better to talk? If not with your friends, maybe a professional. Coming face to face with a serial killer would do anyone's head in.'

Rachel didn't want anyone's sympathy. Even Selena's. 'I know you mean well, Selena, but there's nothing wrong with me that a few days off won't fix. Actually, I'm thinking of going to Uist later in the summer, catch up with my grandfather, maybe spend a day or two on Skye climbing the Cuillin.'

The two women had met on Uist when Rachel had gone there to investigate a suspicious death. Both had family on the island.

'Sounds like a good idea. I'd go with you like a shot if I had leave owing. Which I don't.' Selena gave another deep sigh before continuing. 'In the meantime, if ever there's a woman who needs a night out dancing, it's you.'

Selena might have a point. It had been weeks since Rachel had had an evening out. Maybe it *would* make her feel better. She'd been feeling down lately, more so after their John Doe had been found. It had triggered memories she'd rather have kept suppressed.

'I don't suppose you have cowboy boots. Or a Stetson?' Selena continued, screwing up the empty cardboard sandwich packet and tossing it in the bin.

Rachel shook her head, bemused. 'I have black ankle boots,' she said, 'but no one could describe them as cowboy boots.'

Selena stood and grinned down at Rachel. 'They'll have to do. I have a spare Stetson you can borrow. Do you have plans for Saturday evening?'

'No.'

'In that case, leave everything up to me. I'll meet you outside Tomlins at eight on Saturday.'

Before Rachel could protest, Selena's phone pinged. 'Thighearna's a Dhia, is that the time? I'd better get back to the office or the sergeant will be sending a search party for me.'

EIGHT

After work Rachel was looking through a pile of camisole tops in Victoria's Secret for a birthday present for Suruthi when a familiar badly dyed red head caught her eye. Red Mags, her neighbour and a part-time prostitute, was swiping through a rail of silky pyjamas. Mags was wearing leggings and an over-sized white blouse with one button too many left undone. Despite the woman's profession and her mode of dress, Rachel was fond of Mags. She had a big heart, even if she tried her best to hide it.

Rachel was about to go over and say hello when the older woman, after a furtive glance to where two shop assistants were chatting and another to the security guard who was looking at his phone, ducked down, opened a drawer, reached in, grabbed a handful of flimsy garments and shoved them in her handbag. She stood, a satisfied smile on her face.

The shop assistants were engrossed in conversation so, keeping one eye on the security guard who had looked up from his phone and was conducting a visual sweep of the room, Rachel hurried over to the older woman, placing herself between the line of sight of the guard and Mags.

'Oh, hello, Hen,' Mags said. 'I didn't notice you. Buying anything nice?'

'Put them back,' Rachel hissed.

'Put what back?' Mags said, widening her eyes.

'I saw you. If you don't return the underwear you put in your bag to the drawer you took it from, I'll hand you over to the security guard myself.' She darted a glance his way. Happily, he'd turned his attention towards two teen girls who had entered the store, arms linked and giggling.

Mags hesitated before reading Rachel's expression correctly. Pouting, she opened her bag and handed Rachel the panties. Judging by their size – a UK 8, no match for Mags's ample girth – the stolen underwear wasn't for herself.

'Is there anything else in that bag of yours that shouldn't be there?' Rachel demanded, keeping her voice low. With another quick glance at the security guard, she hunkered down and shoved the garments back into the drawer she'd seen Mags remove them from.

'No,' Mags replied grumpily.

Rachel wasn't sure she believed her but wasn't about to tip the contents of her neighbour's bag on the floor to check. Instead, she grabbed her by the elbow and marched her past the belatedly suspicious gaze of the security guard. Relieved when no alarm sounded as they emerged onto the street, she tugged her neighbour into a doorway and confronted her.

'What were you thinking, Mags? Do you want to go to prison? You weren't even being very subtle about it. And I saw the size on the label. No way would they'd fit you. Were they to be a present or did you plan to sell them?'

Red Mags, despite being on the wrong side of fifty, still worked the streets occasionally. Rachel wished she wouldn't. Not because she had a moral objection, but because it was dangerous work – as both of them knew to their cost.

'No, as it happens. It's just that I'm bored out of ma skull.

Since Ashley and Jody I cannae bring myself to go back on the street.'

Rachel's heart ached for her. 'That's a good thing, Mags,' Rachel said. 'Are you short of money? Is that why you were shoplifting?'

'It's not that. I've got Bill's pension.'

'Are you still going to No. 79?' No. 79 was a refuge for prostitutes, a place where they could get medical care, advice or could even do a load of washing.

'Aye, but it's no the same without Ashley or Jody.' Mags's face crumpled. 'I cannae help but think I should have been able to stop them being kilt. It was ma job to take care of them.' Mags had always taken a maternal role with the younger prostitutes.

'Oh, Mags, it wasn't your fault. You must know that.'

Mags sniffed loudly and wiped her nose on her sleeve. 'All I know is nothing in this world makes sense to me any mair. Ahm too old and too ugly to work the streets even if I still wanted to. These days ahm nothing but a waste of space.'

'Come on, Mags! This isn't like you. You're still needed down at 79 – the women trust you. They need to be able to talk to someone who understands what they're going through.'

'S'pose,' Mags muttered, clearly unconvinced and with a noticeable tremble of the lips.

Rachel's heart went out to Mags. Her neighbour looked uncharacteristically vulnerable.

'No suppose about it.' Rachel indicated the street with a tip of her head. 'Come on, Mags. I'll walk you home.'

'I don't want to go hame. There's nowt to do there and no one to talk to. Ma local is near here. Come with me. I'll buy you a drink.'

Rachel thought of all the chores waiting for her at home, the unfinished reports, her plan for an evening run. But it was impossible to ignore the plea in Mags's eyes. She smiled. 'Lead the way.'

Mags was unusually quiet as she led Rachel along up the main street in the town before ducking into an alley. She turned. 'It's along there.' She pointed to what looked to Rachel like a tenement door to a block of flats. A heavyset man, his arms and neck covered with tattoos, stood outside. 'You have to promise me you'll keep schtum aboot this place. I don't want you telling anyone. Particularly Selena. Police aren't welcome here.'

Tattoo man greeted Mags by name and she slipped him a note. He didn't ask who Rachel was and Mags didn't tell him. He held the door open for the two women. Rachel followed Mags up a flight of stairs into a large room with a bar at one end, tables along three sides and two pool tables in the centre.

There were no windows and the low lighting was disorientating. It could have been any time of day or night. Rachel sniffed the unmistakable scent of grass and cigarette smoke. Clearly the law didn't apply here. Apart from three men standing at the bar, the other customers were all women, mostly young.

Although it was early evening, the place was buzzing. People moved around playing pool and drinking. Music played beneath the voices. The room had the atmosphere of a party in full swing. Convivial and relaxed.

Rachel spotted Chrissie, a prostitute Mags had introduced her to, by the pool table, a cue in her hand. The woman sketched a wave in their direction.

'We need a pub to go to too, you know,' Mags said belligerently. 'Same as we do our shopping, go to the pictures, sit in the park, just like other folk. Not all of us spend all our time out of our box, not knowing what day it is.' She shot Rachel a challenging look, as if she had disagreed with her.

Silence fell. Rachel was acutely conscious of curious stares from the other customers. A spurt of laughter came from the corner. And conversation started again.

'Mine's a pint.' Mags nodded towards the bar.

When Rachel returned with a pint for Mags and a vodka and tonic for herself, they took a table facing the bar and sat side by side.

'There's something I want to tell you. Now, I want to make it clear that I'm no snitch, but when I see something that's no right...' Mags took a long gulp of her beer and hitched up her breasts with her forearms.

'I'm all ears.'

'See him over there?' Mags pointed to one of the men at the bar – a rake-thin man with scraggly hair and a wispy beard. The waistband of his trousers hung so low Rachel could see most of his underpants.

'What about him?'

'He's a lad I've known for years. I went to school with him, more years ago now than I care to remember.' Mags sniggered. 'Or ahm able to remember, come to that.'

Rachel waited for Mags to continue. She'd learned that the older woman didn't respond well to being rushed.

'I worked with his gran when I was married to my Bill. I gave up the game when I got married, you know, and got a proper job. Ian's gran was the school cook; I was the cleaner back then.'

She looked back to the man at the bar.

'We called him Skinny Ian at school because he was always just skin and bones. I'm not sure he got enough to eat at home. His mam was spaced out on drugs most of the time and left the kids to fend for themselves. That's why he lived with his gran. Others who weren't as kind called him Half-Shilling Ian' – she pointed to her temple – 'on account of him not being all there, if you know what I mean.'

Rachel nodded. Poor thing. Her heart went out to him.

'Back then Inverness was a much smaller town. We had the odd tourist passing through on their way up north or in search of the Loch Ness monster, but mainly it was just us locals. Everyone knew Ian and what he was like. Folk helped out by keeping an eye on him.'

In a lull in the music, the crack of a ball being hit dead centre with a snooker cue rang through the room, followed by a thud as it dropped into the pocket.

'First his mam died, then his gran, leaving him alone,' Mags continued. 'His brothers and sisters had cleared off as soon as they could support themselves. Social services got involved then. It was clear he wasn't going to manage on his own, so they put him in a unit they had for his sort. Then someone had the bright idea that everyone should be living in the community, whether they wanted to or not, so they shut down the unit and gave Ian a wee council hoose down at Harbour View. It was an all right sort of place back then,' Mags said. 'It's only in the last twenty years or so that it's gone downhill.'

She stared into her pint as if she could see a happier past in its golden depths.

'Anyroad, someone told me – doesn't matter who – that a couple of drug dealers have moved in with him and they're using his place to deal from. Now' – Mags held up a hand as if to stop Rachel from disagreeing, although she hadn't been about to – 'I have nothing to say about people buying and selling drugs, as ahm sure you know. Not people buying and selling for their ain use, at least. But these men who've moved in are scaring Ian shitless. They aren't locals – they're up from England, maybe Manchester, or Liverpool – somewhere in the north. They're bad people and none of us want them here. Someone needs to rescue Ian from their clutches afore Ian gets caught up in their shit.'

Rachel was familiar with what Mags was describing. Cuckooing was when drug dealers took over the home of a vulnerable person in order to use it as a base for drug dealing, storing firearms and other criminal activity. It was a fairly recent phenomenon.

'It's not just a few grams of drugs they're selling. They have bricks of coke hidden in the house, so I'm told. What's worse they're using kids to deliver them.'

'Has anyone reported this to the police?'

Mags looked at her as if Rachel had suggested flying to the moon on a broomstick. It was the reaction she'd expected.

Rachel hid a sigh. Something else to add to her ever-growing to-do list.

As a couple of women came over to sit next to Mags, Rachel finished her drink. 'Thanks for letting me know, Mags – I'll look into it. In the meantime, I'll let you get on with your evening.'

NINE

The next morning Rachel was in the office, catching up on paperwork. Reaching for her coffee mug and finding it empty, she glanced over her shoulder at Suruthi, who was staring at her phone, a frown on her face.

'Rachel, did you know that Eric Hunter, the journalist, is missing?'

'Missing? In what way, missing?' Rachel asked, shocked. She spun around in her chair until she was facing Suruthi. They were alone in the office. Linda had gone to see Mainwaring, Plover and Alastair had buggered off without saying where they were going.

'A police officer pal just let me know. Apparently he left on a trip on Sunday and apart from a call that evening, his wife hasn't heard from him since.'

A sickening shot of adrenaline coursed through Rachel. 'I saw him on Saturday! Is he usually good at keeping in touch?' she asked, hoping for an answer she already suspected would not be forthcoming.

'According to the wife, she might not hear from him for a day or two if he's up a mountain and can't get a signal, but he always calls her when he gets down to let her know he's OK. It's unusual for him to be out of touch for so long. She'd tried to call his mobile several times, left texts but he's not returned her calls. She thinks his phone might be dead.'

'That definitely doesn't sound good.' Rachel's mind raced as she sought a simple explanation for Eric's disappearance. There had been snow on the mountains over the last couple of days as well as low-lying cloud which would have made the ascent more treacherous than usual. That wouldn't normally bother a climber of Eric's calibre. But accidents could happen to anyone. On the other hand, Eric would never let his phone run out of battery. He of all people, given his role with search and rescue, would know how important it was to keep his phone charged, particularly when climbing. Her anxiety jumped a level as her mind leapt to the conversation they'd had on the mountain and Eric's sense of foreboding – his fear that his life might be in danger. Had Eric fallen while climbing, or was there a more ominous reason for his disappearance?

'His wife said he took his climbing gear but hadn't decided where he was going to climb. She didn't think it was Glencoe, although he has a bothy there. Apparently the police checked it out anyway. It didn't look like he'd been there recently. He could be anywhere,' Suruthi continued. 'If he's hurt it could take forever to find him.'

The Highland and Islands Police division covered an area which made up one third of the whole of Scotland, a sixth of the size of the UK in total, and covered with glens, rivers, mountains, forests, cliffs. There were hundreds of places people could get lost. Not Eric, though.

'Whatever the reason he's not been in touch, it's got to be serious,' Rachel said. 'Eric is like a mountain cat, one of Scotland's best climbers, so if he went up a hill and didn't come down again, that can't be good. Something must have happened.

A fall, most likely. Eric is too experienced to get himself lost. Jesus, fingers crossed they find him soon and that he's OK.'

It was ironic that Eric, who'd been involved in dozens of search and rescue operations as a team member, was now the subject of one.

'Again, according to his wife, although he took his climbing gear and camping stuff, she didn't think the main reason for the trip was to go climbing. Apparently he'd arranged to meet someone.'

'Fuckity Fuck. Now I'm really worried.'

'Why?'

'I met him on Ben Macdui the day before he left on his trip. We didn't bump into each other by accident. He spotted me and followed me.' The fizz of anxiety had solidified into a knot of dread as she replayed the conversation they'd had on the mountain. She needed to speak to Du Toit.

Suruthi raised her eyebrows at Rachel.

'I didn't know Ben Macdui was a mountain. Sounds more like the name of one of those men who do yoga in kilts – although, come to think of it, don't they film themselves on Scottish mountains?'

'Eric?' Rachel prompted, to get Suruthi back on track.

'Yeah, sorry. It was the thought of those kilts and what might be under them that distracted me. I did know Eric was a journalist. Didn't he have quite a lot to say about police handling of those horrible murders? And your involvement.'

'Yes, and very little of what he said was complimentary about Police Scotland. He'd been researching me, found out about the trial my mother was supposed to testify in before she was killed, realised an OCG was involved and ended up going down a rabbit hole about OCGs in Scotland. What he discovered frightened him to the extent he thought his life might be in danger.'

'Christ! I can see why you're worried. Do you honestly think that's connected to him going missing?'

'I don't know. I'm not sure what's worse: him missing because he's had a fall, or him missing because he was investigating OCGs.'

'Let's not get ahead of ourselves. We don't know for sure that anything has happened to him,' Suruthi said. 'Fingers crossed, he pops up hale and hearty in the next few days.'

Rachel hoped so too. But her gut was telling her otherwise.

'I assume you are going to tell Du Toit what you told me,' Suruthi continued.

Rachel got out of her seat. 'I sure am.'

Having passed through security at the entrance of Police Scotland's part of the building, Rachel took the elevator to the first floor, walked through the open-plan office between the desks occupied by police officers until she reached DI Du Toit's door. The wall facing the main office was made of glass and through it she could see he was on his computer. She tapped on the door and he waved her in.

The detective inspector looked tired. His brown eyes had bags underneath them and his shirt was crumpled as if he'd slept in it – possibly on the office floor. There were stacks of paper on either side of his computer. A map of the Highlands and Islands took up most of one wall. His office had a view of the river and, if he had a rope, he could practically belay down to the Innes Bar.

'You OK?' she asked.

'Yes. Just busy,' he said, glancing up from his computer, his voice unusually curt.

He leaned back in his chair, hooked his arms behind his neck and stretched. 'What can I do for you, Rachel?'

'Do you know about Eric Hunter? That he's missing?'

'I'd heard. My colleagues in uniform are leading the search.'

'Any joy?' Rachel asked.

'Not as far as I'm aware.' He leaned forward, his brown eyes curious. 'What's your interest?'

'I'm worried,' Rachel said, taking a seat on the other side of Du Toit's desk. 'I think something might have happened to him.'

'If he was climbing, that's an entirely possible scenario.'

'Yes. But I think there's another possibility.' She told him about Eric following her up the mountain, the hints that the story he was about to break might put him in danger.

'Did he tell you what the story was about?' Du Toit asked.

'Just that it was a big one. Something to do with an OCG in Inverness. And that his life and the lives of his wife and children might be threatened because of it.'

Du Toit drummed his fingers on his desk as he turned this new information over. 'Unless we know what the story was, that doesn't take us much further forward. We've put in a request to his network provider, but we're still waiting for them to come back to us. When they do, we'll get a better idea of where he is and what he's up to. But, given there's no evidence he's not just got lost and that he's only been missing just over thirty hours we'll have to give my colleagues and search and rescue time to find him.'

'That's not good enough,' Rachel said, aware of the edge in her voice. 'I can't be the only one who thinks that the search for a missing journalist on the trail of a big story should be investigated with speed and urgency. Can you at least find out when and where his phone last pinged and let me know?'

Du Toit got to his feet. 'I have the greatest respect for your instincts, Rachel, so I'll pass your concerns on to the appropriate officer. But you have to leave investigating to the police. To me. I have other cases on my plate that I won't get into here and I have to decide where the use of my time – and that of my team – is most beneficial.' He looked at the door and lifted his pen. 'As soon as you have anything more for me, feel free to get in touch.'

TEN

Rachel was about to leave for work the next morning when Mags appeared at her gate.

'There's someone you need to talk to.'

'Hello to you too,' Rachel said. 'Who? And when?'

'We call him Gentleman Tim – that's cos no one knows his name. And because he speaks like someone in an old movie. Sometimes I wonder if he remembers it himself.'

'And where would I find Gentleman Tim?'

'I'll take you to him. Now. If you're ready?'

'Can I at least ask what it's about?' She'd planned to get to work early. Find out if there was news about Eric. The niggling sense of anxiety about him hadn't gone away overnight. She knew it wouldn't until he turned up safe and sound.

'Oh, for God's sake, can you just come! It's only a wee walk away. Trust me, you'll want to talk to Tim.'

Rachel locked the door behind her. She and Mags walked to the canal path, keeping to the right side. The rain of the last couple of days had stopped, there was only a light breeze and the sun was shining. A perfect morning and the dog walkers and runners were making the most of it. They continued past the empty buildings that had stored cargo when the canals were in their heyday. A little further along they crossed Clachnaharry Road and followed a private road upwards.

They passed a large house on their left and a little further along reached the end of the road and an empty building that might have been a school or council offices at one time. Now the windows and door were boarded up with reinforced steel. Rachel followed Mags around to the back of the building. At the foot of a fire escape was a small door that looked as if it might lead to a cellar.

Although it was closed, the padlock that had once secured it was broken. Mags took out her phone.

'I'll text him. Let him know we're here.'

They waited for a while and Rachel was beginning to wonder whether Tim wasn't there or had changed his mind about meeting them when the hatch opened slowly to reveal a thin face covered by a bushy, unkempt beard.

'You brought her then?' the head asked.

'Aye. You coming out or are we coming in?'

'You're coming in.' Sharp green eyes raked over them. 'If the pair of you can manage? There are wooden stairs but some of the planks are missing. There's a rope you can use as a handrail, but you might be better jumping. It's not far.'

Mags went first, sitting on the lip of the opening and letting go, landing on the floor with a soft thud. Rachel did the same. Although she landed easily and lightly, she was surprised how high the opening was. At least five feet off the ground. A challenge, surely, for the emaciated elderly man in front of her. And Mags.

'Sex work keeps you in shape,' Mags said with a smirk, reading Rachel's admiring look correctly.

Rachel peered into the semidarkness. Slivers of light illuminated the dirty, dusty cement floor. A pile of coal lay in one corner. Dismantled iron beds took up the rest of the space,

along with old computer monitors, kettles and toasters. The
wind whistled through the open hatch, not quite drowning out
the sound of distant traffic. Gentleman Tim stretched up to
close it. He was tall, well over six feet, so he could reach it
easily. The cellar was plunged into darkness. Tim flicked a
switch and a single bulb suspended from the rafter in the ceiling
illuminated the room. It took Rachel's eyes a few moments to
adjust. Once they had, she appraised Tim properly.

Rachel guessed he was in his seventies, although it was difficult to say with any certainty. He was wearing trousers held up
with a piece of string, a stained too-small-for-him jumper with
holes in the sleeves. He had a bulbous nose, hollowed-out
cheeks, and knobbly ankles that stuck out from his too-short
trousers. Despite his bedraggled appearance, his upright
bearing made Rachel think he had been someone in authority at
one time.

On one side of the cellar, partly hidden by some of the junk,
was a grubby sleeping bag. Next to it was a half-burnt candle
stuck on a saucer, an open tin that looked as if it had once
contained beans and sausages, a tin plate, a fork, as well as a
small camping stove. A cheap, broken chair, obviously rescued
from someone's bulk items left out for recycling, completed the
sleeping space. On top of the chair were two books: a Jack
Reacher, and a well-thumbed copy of *Twenty Thousand
Leagues Under the Sea*.

There was no evidence of drug paraphernalia, no confusion
in Tim's eyes.

'You live here,' said Rachel, stating the obvious.

'Most of the time,' Tim said. 'For the last year, anyway.' His
accent was soft, maybe from the Borders but his voice sounded
croaky as if he hadn't used it for a while.

'What about the house we passed on our way up the driveway?' Rachel asked as an opening gambit. Mags had clearly
brought her here for a reason. It looked like she was going to

have to winkle it out of them. 'It's clearly occupied. Are they happy with you staying here?' Rachel pressed. In her experience, most people didn't tolerate squatters in buildings near their homes.

'The one halfway up the hill? It's used as an Airbnb,' Tim said scathingly. 'The people who own it don't even live in Scotland. It's managed by a letting company, and they don't care as long as no one complains. But, to be on the safe side, I try to keep my comings and goings to a minimum. I don't want some nosy parker local reporting me to the police or the council.'

'Why are we here, Tim?' Rachel asked, deciding it was time to go the direct route.

'Before I tell you anything, I want you both to promise me you won't tell anyone about this place.'

'I'm afraid that will depend on why we're here,' Rachel said.

'If I'd wanted to tell anyone else I'd have done it afore now,' Mags told Tim. She indicated Rachel with a nod of her head. 'You can trust her. She won't do or say anything to get you in trouble. But she needs to hear what you have to say.'

Tim thought for a moment, clearly still unsure. 'Very well,' he said eventually. 'It's about the body that was found in the graveyard.'

'What about him?'

'He was here.'

A tingle ran up Rachel's spine.

'When?'

'A couple of nights before his body was found. I came in from my evening stroll and saw the padlock was broken. When I went inside, I heard footsteps coming from the floor above. I wasn't best pleased, I can tell you. I didn't want to share with anyone who was off his mind on drugs. I've had those sort find their way here often enough.'

'Did you speak to him?'

'I thought about it. I went up the stairs quiet as you like. I used to be in the army, so I know how to move without being heard. He was in one of the rooms on the first floor. Sitting in a corner, hugging his knees and shivering like he was four years old instead of a grown man. It was obvious he was scared. I nearly went to him, to ask if he needed help, but I changed my mind. I didn't want to get mixed up in anyone else's trouble. I just wanted him gone. I certainly didn't want him bringing people here.'

As she had so often over the last few days, Rachel thought about Louis. Her heart ached for both him and their John Doe. She knew how awful it was to have nowhere to go to feel safe.

'Are you sure it was the same man who was found in the graveyard?'

'Who else could it have been? I heard the body in the grave-yard was about the same age and was wearing light brown trousers and a white shirt, same as he was.'

Why had their John Doe taken refuge here? Did he live nearby and have local knowledge of the area? Was that how he'd known there was a deserted building in the vicinity? How had he gone from here to the cemetery? And why? To meet someone? Were they looking at a drug deal gone wrong?

'Did you tell the police?'

'No. I told Margaret. She said I had to tell you.'

'Mags was right. I have to call it in. The police will want to talk to you.'

Tim looked at Mags, aghast. 'I thought you said I could trust her!'

'I need to inform the police, Tim. You must know that,' Rachel said gently. 'You won't get in trouble, I promise.'

Rachel couldn't get a signal on her phone so she and Mags risked the rickety stairs, making use of the makeshift handrail to go outside, blinking as they emerged in the bright sunshine.

Mags sat on a bench, reached into her copious handbag, and produced a packet of digestives and a flask of tea. She offered them to Rachel who refused both. She'd had a bad experience involving a toenail clipping when she'd last accepted a drink from Mags.

Mags had just finished her tea when a police car came to a halt in front of them in what must have been the car park when the building was legitimately occupied.

Selena stepped out of the driver's side. She was accompanied by DS Audrey Liversage.

'I never imagined it would be so busy here in Inverness,' Selena said. 'The work's non-stop. Makes me wonder what Glasgow or London would be like.'

Audrey shot Selena an impatient look. 'Can we get on?' she said. 'We need to get back to the office.'

Selena had a habit of speaking her thoughts out loud that didn't always go down well. Although Rachel found it refreshing, she wasn't sure it was the best trait for a police officer to have.

Audrey turned to Rachel. 'Would you mind telling us how you happen to be here, Miss McKenzie?'

Mags poured herself another cup of tea while Rachel brought the police officers up to speed.

'You're confident it was our John Doe?' Audrey asked.

'As confident as I can be,' Rachel said, 'without Tim visually identifying our dead man or in the absence of matching fingerprints.'

'I brought a photo of him,' Selena said. 'It's in the pocket of my jacket.'

'Where is Tim?' Audrey asked, just as he emerged from the hatch, his face pinched with anxiety.

'This is Detective Sergeant Liversage and Detective Constable MacDonald, Tim,' Rachel introduced the police officers. 'Would you mind repeating what you told me?'

Tim had little to add. He concluded his story: 'He was hiding in a room on the first floor.'

'What makes you say he was hiding?' Audrey asked.

'It was obvious. He was huddled in a corner. As I told Missy here' – he indicated Rachel – 'I was in the army and I can tell when a man is in fear of his life. He was scared witless.'

'Hiding from who?' Audrey asked gently.

Tim shrugged. 'He didn't say and I didn't ask.'

'We really need to find out if the man whose body was found in the graveyard and the man who stayed here are the same person,' Selena said in her soft island accent. She reached into her back pocket and brought out the photo of their John Doe. Rachel caught a glimpse of the head and shoulders of the waxen-faced man from the graveyard, a sheet just visible below his collarbones.

Selena showed the photo to Tim. He took a moment before replying. 'Aye. That's him. I thought it must be when the body was found. Poor bugger.'

'Did he have anything with him? A change of clothes? A bag?'

Tim shook his head. 'I don't know. I only saw him for a moment. There was nothing there, and I had a look round after he left.'

'What about food or a wrapper from something he might have eaten?' Selena asked. 'A coffee cup even.'

'Not that I saw.'

'When did he leave?' Rachel asked.

'No idea about that either. He wasn't here when I got up the next morning. He'd gone, taking any stuff he might have had with him.'

'How long was he here? When did he arrive?' Selena asked. She was busy scribbling notes as she spoke.

'No idea of that either. As I said, he was here when I came back and gone when I went out in the morning.'

'When was that?'

'About seven.'

'How do you know he wasn't here when you left?' Selena asked. 'It's a big building.'

'Because the first thing I do when I wake up in the morning and before I go to sleep at night is to check I'm alone. The army taught me that too. I lock the cellar, but someone is always breaking the padlock open, so I don't rely on it.'

'We're going to get a couple of our colleagues out here,' Audrey said. She turned to Selena, 'There's always a chance it wasn't our John Doe.' She turned back to Rachel as Selena spoke on the radio. 'While we wait, we're going to search the building.'

'Thanks for your help, Tim,' Rachel said, before turning to the police officers. 'You'll need to excuse me – I have to get to the office.'

'We'll take it from here, Miss McKenzie,' Audrey said. 'Tim, I'll have to ask you not to go anywhere.'

As Rachel turned to leave, Mags came up to her. While the police officers had talked to Tim, she'd remained on the bench, eyes closed as she soaked up the sun.

'Well?' Mags asked.

'It looks like the visitor might be the body we found, yes.'

'You'd never have found out about that man being here if it wasnae for me.'

'Then I thank you.' Rachel smiled. 'I said you weren't a waste of space.'

Mags's smile grew wider. She held up the plastic cup of her thermos. 'Cheers! I'll see you at home later.'

After Rachel left, Selena asked Gentleman Tim to wait outside with Mags, explaining they would need to take fingerprints from him. He didn't look overly happy at the need to come down to the station.

While they waited for the scene examiners to arrive, she

and Audrey searched every room in the building – all twenty of them: ten on the ground floor, six large ones and four smaller ones on the first – for any evidence of their John Doe's stay. There were no obvious signs of a scuffle, although it was difficult to be sure amongst the discarded drug paraphernalia on the floor of every room. Hearing the crunch of tyres on gravel heralding the arrival of forensics, they went back outside. Gentleman Tim was still sitting on the bench next to Mags. Audrey approached them and hunkered down next to Tim.

'You can't continue to stay here, Tim,' she said. 'I'm going get DC MacDonald to speak to social services for you. They'll be able to find you a place to stay. It might be a hostel at first, before they find you somewhere permanent.'

Tim scowled. 'No. That's not what I want. I told the lady lawyer that.'

'It's not up to her, Tim,' Audrey said.

'That's what I get for helping the police, is it?'

'You did the right thing telling us,' Selena said.

'I'm not doing anyone any harm,' Tim protested. 'Look at this place!' He indicated the empty building behind them with a sweeping gesture. 'No one cares about it. It's going to fall down in a couple of years anyway.' He was probably right, judging by the missing tiles on the roof and the broken floorboards in several of the rooms. 'You can't tell me the council are ever going to repair it. They'll sell off the land eventually for so called luxury homes.'

'I might agree,' Audrey said, with a tight smile, 'but as a police officer I have to uphold the law, and the law says this is private property and anyone who doesn't have the right of entry is trespassing.'

'We might be able to get you into sheltered housing,' Selena entreated, recognising a stubborn look when she saw one. 'You'll be warm and dry, and you might even be able to get meals on wheels. What's not to like?'

Tim turned his furious gaze on her. 'That's for people who can't look after themselves – and I'm perfectly able to look after myself. Don't either of you confuse choosing to live in a different way to most of the population with something that has to be fixed.'

Rachel's neighbour, Red Mags, had folded her arms across her chest and was also glaring at Selena and Audrey.

'I'm sorry, Tim,' Mags said. 'I should've guessed that the polis wouldn't be able to help themselves. They just don't know when to do nothing. Look, you two, he's right – he's not doing anyone ony harm. If he hadnae agreed to help you, you'd never have known that man had been here. Or Tim himself, for that matter.'

'But we do know now,' Audrey said. 'After the scene examiners are finished, I'm going to have the entrance Tim's been using secured so no one can get in. Apart from anything else, those stairs are dangerous.'

For a moment it looked to Selena as if there was going to be a stand-off between Audrey and Red Mags. She was about to intervene when Mags gave a loud, theatrical sigh. 'You can stay at mine,' she said to Tim, 'until you find somewhere else. There will be plenty of places, maybe not as quiet as this but private enough. Come on. Let's get the hell out of here.'

Selena waited until they were out of earshot before turning to Audrey. 'Couldn't we just have turned a blind eye to him dossing down here? Once the scene examiners are done, of course. He's right. Would the council even care?'

Her sergeant pursed her lips and frowned. 'DC MacDonald, do I need to remind you that you are an officer of the law, not a social worker, and the top line of your job description is the upholding of that law. It seems to me you have far too much reverence for Miss McKenzie and her modus operandi. DI Du Toit did warn me this might be the case, so I'm going to suggest to you that if you wish to forge a career as a detective constable, you remind yourself of the law and commit yourself to upholding it. Do I make myself clear?'

And with that she turned on her heel and marched over to the police vehicle, leaving Selena gasping with shock.

So her growing sense over the last couple of months was correct. The team didn't see her as one of them. They thought her inexperienced and naive. She took a deep calming breath. OK, maybe she was inexperienced, but she was also a fast learner and determined to forge a career in the CID. Bugger the lot of them, she would just have to find a way to change their view of her.

ELEVEN

It turned out that DI Jason Bright was indeed alive. He'd retired eight years earlier and was living in Alness on the Black Isle – neither black nor an island, but a peninsula just north of Inverness. Selena had emailed his number and address to Rachel, adding that the DI was fondly remembered by the colleagues who had worked with him. A good boss and a bit of a laugh, apparently. As yet, she hadn't come up with anything on DC Souter, except that she had left the force years ago.

The retired DI was happy to speak to Rachel and they'd arranged to meet at his home after Rachel finished work on Thursday.

Rachel had taken her car to work so she could drive to Alness. Her route took her across the Kessock Bridge to the other side of the Black Isle and up the East coast to where the town lay, near the mouth of the River Averon and the Cromarty Firth.

In one of Scotland's usual mercurial swings in the weather, last night's heavy rain had cleared away, and Rachel's thirty-minute journey was bathed in sunlight.

Jason Bright lived in a seventies-style bungalow close to the bank of the river. The garden at the front had been slabbed over, either by its current occupant or the previous one. Pots of geraniums bracketed the door, adding a splash of colour to the white pebble-dash walls.

A man with a gaunt face, prominent cheekbones and a pronounced stoop answered the door to Rachel's ring. He looked much older than his actual age. Police officers were permitted to retire when they were sixty. Although they weren't compelled to, most did. In that case the DI couldn't be older than his late sixties. She wondered fleetingly if he was ill.

'Miss McKenzie, I assume,' he said with a warm smile. 'Please come in.'

He ushered her into the kitchen. 'That way we can talk while I make us a cup of something. Tea OK?' When she nodded, he waved her into a chair at a pine table, pushing a pile of papers to the side. The kitchen was simple: pine cupboards, and laminate worktops, with a number of cookbooks on a shelf. Rachel had been correct about it having a view of the river. She could see it from the large kitchen window.

Something wet and cold nuzzled Rachel's palm. She looked down to find a cocker spaniel gazing up at her with hopeful eyes.

'Alba likes to say hello. You don't mind dogs, do you?' Jason said, with the utter conviction of a dog owner who adores their dog and assumes that everyone else will too.

'I like them.' Rachel reached down and scratched behind Alba's silky floppy ears. Alba gave a sigh of pleasure and rested her head on Rachel's knee.

While they waited for the kettle to boil, he asked how her journey had been, what the traffic had been like and how was Inverness these days? He hadn't visited for a number of years but had heard it was continuing to grow. He seemed in no rush to get to the reason Rachel was there. While he chatted, she glanced around for evidence of a partner. Did he live alone? It was impossible to tell.

Finally, after they both had mugs of strong tea in front of them, he gave her another warm smile. 'I'm curious why you wanted to see me. Not that I don't welcome a visit from a pretty young woman, particularly a fiscal. I'm assuming it's in connection with a case I was involved with when I was still a copper.'

Rachel smiled back. Despite his frail appearance, there was no doubting the intelligence in his alert brown eyes. Although he had to be a decade younger than Rachel's grandfather, in some ways he reminded her of him.

'My mother was Mary Ann McKenzie,' she said, certain there was no point beating around the bush with this man.

'I guessed as much. I remember the case. I also remembered she had a daughter called Rachel who would be around the age you are now.'

'Were you involved in the investigation into her murder?'

'No. But naturally I knew about it. Back then there were two DIs covering the Highlands. Your mother's murder was DI Rule's case. He died five years ago. Lung cancer.'

'What about before her body was found? Were you, or any of the coppers you knew, involved in investigating her disappearance?'

He frowned. 'If I remember correctly, I don't think your mother's disappearance was ever really investigated. I believe the police sergeant at the time was satisfied with your father's explanation that she'd left of her own free will. Many in the force knew your father. Didn't like him, to be honest. But coppers never care for lawyers who defend criminals, and your father could be brutal when questioning an officer.' Rachel's father had been a solicitor advocate, which meant he could defend criminals in court. 'So it seemed entirely possible that she'd left him, especially when there appeared to be evidence she was alive. When her body was found and it was clear she'd been murdered, I imagine they felt terrible. Some of them would have met your mother.' His frown deepened. 'Is that why you're here?'

Alba nudged her palm again, reminding Rachel that she was still there.

'In a way. I want to ask you about the case my mother was supposed to testify in, had she not disappeared before it came to court. The one involving Monika Troka and the sex traffickers.'

Judging by the small jerk of surprise in his eyes, he did remember. He took his time before replying. 'That was a number of years ago. I'm not sure I recall every detail, my memory isn't so great these days. Look, if you tell me what you'd like to know, I'll give it my best shot and we can take it from there.'

Rachel gave Alba's ears another tickle as she thought about what to say.

'When my mother disappeared, did it cross anyone's mind that it might have something to do with her scheduled court appearance?'

He considered the question for a while before replying. 'If I remember correctly, there were a few weeks between your mother's disappearance and the trial starting.'

'About five,' Rachel conceded.

'Again, if my memory serves me right, her testimony, while it would have been helpful, wasn't crucial. We had the men, caught literally pants down in the house, we had Monika's identification of the men who had essentially kidnapped her and kept her prisoner. We also had statements from four of the other women who were kept with her, although in the end they were too scared to testify.'

'Why? Were they threatened?'

'Not as far as I'm aware. But they were understandably scared of these men.'

'Weren't they under police protection?'

'We didn't have the necessary resources. They were offered flights home. With the exception of Monika, they all took up the offer.'

'What about the man Monika knew as Dave? Did you find him?'

'Unfortunately not. I imagine he gave Monika a false name. The Facebook site he'd used had been deleted. Facebook wouldn't agree to give us access to the data.'

'Do you know where Monika Troka is now?'

'I understand she died.' He shifted in his seat.

'Died? How? When?'

'She drowned herself in the River Ness about a month after she testified. She'd twice the legal limit of alcohol for driving in her blood. I expect she was pissed and fell in. Or maybe she threw herself in.' He shrugged. 'Who knows? It's the sort of thing that happens with these women.'

Rachel was beginning to dislike former DI Bright intensely. 'Wasn't she being protected?'

'Protected?' he said, incredulous. 'What world do you live in? We've barely enough officers to investigate crime, let alone watch vulnerable women who don't want to be watched. She was offered a free ride back to Albania. In any case, there was no evidence of foul play. No trace evidence on her body.'

'So her death was investigated?'

'Yes. Of course.'

'Do you have names of any of the other women? Addresses?'

'Of course not.' He was becoming visibly more irritated. He pushed back his chair. 'We're talking about events that happened more than a decade ago.' He leaned forward. 'Why are you asking, anyway?'

'I gather none of the gang bosses were arrested. Did you have suspects?' Rachel asked, dodging his question.

Jason gave a resigned shake of his head. 'We never even got close. These people tend to keep themselves far removed from the men they pay to do their bidding. As far as we knew, they didn't even live in the UK. They might have done once, but many of them moved abroad to control their empires from there.'

It was the same thing Eric had said. If they knew so much about these people, why couldn't they catch them?

'In one of her interviews with you, Monika mentioned a well-spoken woman who came to the flat where she was held. Any idea who that might have been?'

'No. She never saw her and the woman apparently never came back. All she could tell us was that she sounded educated. And Scottish.'

'So not the prostitute working with the gang then?' Rachel asked.

'Definitely not.'

'What happened to her?'

'Again, no idea. We didn't charge her. She was as much a victim as the others.'

Although his tone remained pleasant, he wasn't being very forthcoming. Perhaps he genuinely didn't remember. Maybe that was the source of his irritation and not her questions? Perhaps DC Souter, if she could locate her, would be more helpful. But Rachel wasn't finished with Jason Bright yet.

'When did you first start watching the brothels?' Rachel asked.

'Back when we heard a rumour that they were popping up all over Inverness.'

'Over what period did you watch them?'

'Roughly eighteen months.' He looked bemused to be on the receiving end of her questions. A bee buzzed against a window. Jason ignored it.

'How many officers were on your team throughout the time you were conducting your investigations?'

She watched his reaction closely. His expression remained blank.

'It varied. Usually around six. Not enough to watch the brothels all the time, unfortunately. But enough to know what was going on.'

'Did you have an informant?'

'I'd rather not answer that question.'

'I'm going to assume you did. Did he, or she, know when the raids were scheduled to take place?'

'Of course not.'

'From what I've gathered, every time there was a raid planned on one of the brothels your team had been staking out, by the time your team got there the brothel had been cleared out, moved somewhere else. Except for the last time, obviously, when matters moved too swiftly. Did it occur to you that someone in the planning team – or someone close to them – might have been giving the gang warning they were about to be raided?'

'Absolutely not. I'd worked with all the officers involved over the years. I trusted each and every one of them.' He sighed. 'Look, I wasn't naive. I did look into it. But not one of them was at the pre-raid meeting every time. So unless two of them were in it together-' he shook his head 'which in my view is out of the bounds of possibility, for reasons already stated.'

'But you would be there for every meeting, I assume. As the officer in charge. What about DC Souter? Was she?'

'Young lady, I don't care for what you are insinuating,' Bright said with a belligerent thrust to his jaw. His chair scraped on the tiled floor as he pushed away from the table. Hearing the anger in her master's voice, Alba growled softly.

Rachel got to her feet too. 'I'm not insinuating anything. I just want to get to the truth. If someone in the force was informing or engaging with organised crime and this had anything to with my mother's murder, then I have the right to ask any questions I feel appropriate.'

Jason Bright's face was flushed. 'And I don't feel the need to answer them.' He narrowed his eyes at her. 'Are you here in a professional capacity?'

Rachel shook her head. No point in lying. It would take him a single phone call to find out she wasn't. 'I'm asking as one professional to another.'

'What could any of this possibly have to do with your mother's murder?'

'Don't you think it's odd that she was murdered before she could testify? Particularly since another witness, Monika Troka, died soon after?'

'If the gang bosses wanted to stop Monika testifying, they would have had her killed before the trial.'

'Tell me, was she offered police protection *before* the trial?'

DI Bright glared at Rachel. 'I don't know where you are going with this. Your father was convicted of your mother's murder. I have no doubt they got the right man. If you have any more questions you should address them to the team who investigated your mother's murder. Now, if you'll excuse me.'

It was clear that he was done talking to Rachel. He took a step towards her. He didn't look nearly as frail now. She found herself escorted out of the kitchen and propelled out the front door.

'I gather DC Souter has left the force. Do you happen to know where I might find her?'

'If I did, I wouldn't tell you.' He looked at her, his expression grim. 'You're young and you are supposed to be on the same side as the police, so I'm going to give you some advice you'd do well to heed.' Of course he was. 'Leave well alone.'

He clearly didn't know her. Nothing he'd told her had brought her any closer to the truth. So she'd keep digging.

'Thank you for your time,' Rachel managed to say, before the door was firmly closed behind her.

TWELVE

As soon as Rachel got into the office the next morning, she searched the digital files for the report on Monika's death. Whenever there was a sudden death, the police sent a report over to Rachel's office, where it would be logged on their system. One of the fiscals, more often than not Rachel these days, would decide whether the death required further investigation and inform the police of her decision.

Overnight, her fury at DI Bright's casual indifference to Monika's death had grown, as had the suspicion that someone in the know had been informing the gang. She didn't really think DI Bright was the informer, but wasn't ready to rule him out either. Her next move would be to speak to DC Souter. Pushing aside the unwelcome thought that she was guilty of doing the very thing Du Toit had warned her against when Selena transferred to Inverness, she resolved to ask her friend to help track Souter down.

To her frustration, she couldn't find a report on Monika's death on her computer. She looked over to where the Linda, the office manager, was logging on to her computer. Linda had worked in the unit longer than anyone, even Douglas. And as far Rachel could determine, he'd worked here forever.

'Linda, any thoughts on why I can't find a police report in our files?'

'From when?' Linda asked.

'About eleven years ago. I don't have an exact date.'

'It must be among those we haven't got around to digitising yet,' Linda said. 'We only started putting the paper copies onto the computer about eight years ago. Douglas was never a fan. He always preferred paper versions. Although he stonewalled, he was ordered to get on with it. Unfortunately, it was never a priority for him so we still have a backlog. And now that Clive has left I can't see that changing anytime soon.'

'Where are the unlogged paper copies?' Rachel asked.

'In storage.'

'And where's that?'

'At the castle. In one of the basement rooms.' She reached into a drawer, pulled out a stapler and placed it on her desk. She was always accusing her colleagues of taking it and losing it. 'Why don't you ask the police? That might be quicker.'

An excellent idea. However, the police report wouldn't name the fiscal who had dealt with it and it wouldn't say why they'd decided not to carry out further investigations. When a report of a death came in, the fiscal who received it would review it, decide what action if any was required: 'No Pro' meant no further proceedings; a 'view and grant' meant a post-mortem wasn't required. If he or she had cause for concern, the fiscal would pass it back to the police for further investigation.

It was something else to ask Selena to help her with.

THIRTEEN

The Innes Bar – a favourite watering hole for police officers – was buzzing at six thirty. Rachel had phoned Selena and suggested they meet there for an after-work drink. It had been a week since graveyard man had been found, more than forty-eight hours since Gentleman Tim had told them about the man who'd found refuge in his temporary home, and they were no further forward in identifying him. Worryingly, five days after Eric had last been in touch with his wife he still hadn't been found and Rachel's fear something bad had happened to him had continued to grow. Du Toit had rung her to let her known that Eric's phone had last pinged off a mast north of Fort William on Sunday afternoon and the search had moved to the mountains and lochs there. Given he could have been heading in any direction, it was an enormous area to comb. Literally like looking for a needle in a haystack – even with the help of a heli-copter fitted with heat-seeking equipment. She'd not lost hope he'd be found alive, but it was fading with every day that passed. She was increasingly sure his disappearance was linked to the story he'd been investigating. Eric had promised to let

Rachel know what it was but so far nada. All she could do was to continue to follow up the sex trafficking trial and trust it would lead her to him.

Rachel bit into the burger she'd ordered while waiting. She should really have ordered a salad. But she'd convinced herself that her blood sugar was low, causing her energy levels to drop, and a burger and chips would sort her out. In a sudden surge of remorse, she removed her burger from the bun. That would subtract a few calories as well as some processed carbs.

Selena flopped into the chair opposite her and pinched a chip from Rachel's plate.

'I'm hoping you're going to tell me you've discovered who our John Doe is,' Rachel mumbled around a mouthful of beef patty.

''Fraid not,' Selena said, signalling the waiter. 'We didn't get a hit on the police DNA database. Or on our criminal history system either.' She was referring to the database of convictions and cautions. 'The good news is that the fingerprints we found at the building matched those of our John Doe. Forensics have gone over the abandoned building with a fine toothcomb, but there's so much rubbish – including used syringes – it will take time for them to test everything for DNA.'

Selena paused to order a BLT from the app on her phone. 'On the other hand, we didn't find evidence of a struggle,' she continued when she was finished with her order. 'There was no obvious indication anything was cleared up either – no evidence of bleach, for example. So we don't think anything happened to him in the building.'

She nicked another chip from Rachel's plate.

'Although we haven't completely ruled out that he was a local, we don't think he was. Otherwise someone would have come forward to report him missing. A man like that had to have a job and friends, if not family. The fact that he was there at all seems to fit with the idea that he was hiding from someone and didn't want to be found. If so why? From who or what?' She sighed. 'So many questions and so few answers. Did Alison forward his DNA to GEDmatch?'

'So I believe. I'm meeting with the genealogist next week. I'm hoping he'll have something for me. She's still trying to track down the plate in his arm. I'm hoping both or either will give us an ID. She's still awaiting toxicology to rule out an overdose accidental or otherwise.' Rachel took a final mouthful of her burger and wiped the grease from her lips with a napkin. 'Therefore no need to pass it over to Alastair just yet. I'm going to hang on to the case until we know more. Until we do, his death should still be treated as suspicious. Possible murder.'

'Agreed. We'll continue to try and find out what we can about him,' Selena said. The waiter brought her BLT. She took a bite and chewed for a while. 'You know, as much as I find tracing dead bodies interesting, I wish Audrey and Du Toit would give me something more complex to get my teeth into.'

'I thought you might have had your fill of murder,' Rachel teased.

'I wouldn't have become a detective if I had. Not that I want people to get murdered just to keep me happy,' she added hastily. A blush spread across her face. 'God, Rachel, that was a crass thing to say, given what happened to your mother.'

'Look, Selena, we are almost certainly going to work together for a very long time. You will never be able to *not* mention murder around me.'

'OK. Got it.' Selena gave a relieved smile.

'That brings me to the other reason I wanted to meet,' Rachel said. She repeated what Mags had told her about Skinny Ian. 'If they are dealing drugs from his house, you guys need to do something about it. Could you pass that on?'

'I'll phone it in, soon as we're done here.'

'One last thing. I need a favour.'

Selena gave Rachel a questioning look.

'I went to see DI Bright,' Rachel said, after swallowing a chip she'd been unable to resist. 'He told me Monika Troka, the woman who testified in the sex-trafficking case, drowned a month after she testified.' She decided not to mention that Bright practically threw her out.

Selena's eyebrows shot up. 'And...?'

'He said her death wasn't deemed suspicious. That she either fell in and drowned because she was drunk and stoned. Or else took her own life. Either way he wasn't very interested. I wasn't happy with that so when I got to the office I looked for the death report. There was nothing on the computer. It's possible it hasn't been digitised yet. When I get a chance, I'll go to where the old records are stored and check, but in the meantime, could you look up the police report on your system?'

'I could try. But why don't you ask Du Toit?'

'Because I know how busy he is.' Rachel felt a familiar stab of guilt, knowing that wasn't entirely true.

'Fair enough. I don't see why I shouldn't be able to get it.'

'I also want to know who, apart from Jason Bright and DC Souter, was at the meetings about the people-trafficking rings.'

Selena frowned. 'I don't know where to find that info. But leave it with me. I'll see what I can find out.'

'One last thing, could you get me an address for DC Souter?'

Selena rolled her eyes. 'Anything else?'

Rachel smiled. 'That's it for the time being. Thanks – I owe you.'

As she walked home Rachel wondered if she was guilty of manipulating Selena – using someone she liked and respected to further her own agenda. Someone she was aware liked and respected her too. The thought was repugnant but had to be considered. When she wanted something she knew no other way than to keep at it. Regardless of who or what got in her path. Not for the first time she wondered if she was more like her father than she cared to think.

FOURTEEN

Rachel gritted her teeth and, ignoring the screaming of her biceps, pulled hard on a bar attached above her spare room door, before dropping back to the floor. That was three sets of ten. Not bad. She had another five in her. She was getting stronger – physically anyway. Most nights she had nightmares, sometimes waking herself up by crying out in her sleep. Last night's had been another particularly grim one. In it she'd been running through the cemetery in almost complete darkness when Louis had appeared from the woods, his decomposing arms stretched out to her, his mouth an open O of anguish. She'd been rooted to the spot in terror, unable to cry out or run away. She'd woken up with her heart racing and tears on her cheeks. She'd leapt out of bed and gone for a run. Physical exercise was the only way to forget her demons for a while.

She eyed the pull-up bar. If she wanted to get back to the level of fitness she had when at university, she needed to regain the upper body strength she had when she used to climb regularly.

As the strains of Britney Spears' 'Work Bitch' faded away,

she forced her aching muscles to do ten more pull-ups before dropping to her feet.

As she wiped herself down and poured a glass of iced water, there was a loud banging on her door. She wasn't expecting anyone. Her plans for the day were unexciting: she was going to burn some more energy with a climb after taking a load of washing to the laundrette. Her machine had broken and the new one she'd ordered hadn't arrived yet.

She opened the door to find an almost unrecognisable Red Mags on her doorstep, looking pleased as punch. Mags had two usual modes of dressing – one for work: vertiginous heels, a short, tight skirt and a boob tube; and one for home: leggings and sweatshirt or T-shirt, covered, when inside, with a nylon overall and, more often than not, her feet shoved into her dead husband's slippers. Today, though, she was wearing trousers and a blouse, and her flat shoes wouldn't have been out of place on a schoolteacher – or in an office. Her usual bright red lipstick had been swapped for a more subdued coral, and her previously flaming red hair had been dyed a more subdued auburn.

'Any tea on the go?' Mags asked. 'And close your mouth afore a fly flies in.'

Speechless, Rachel stepped aside to let her neighbour enter.

'I want to talk to you,' Mags said, walking into Rachel's kitchen. 'I've been thinking about what you said the other day.'

'Take a seat and I'll make the tea.'

Rachel switched on the kettle and got two mugs down from cupboard. Honey, the cat that had adopted them both without being loyal to either, had snuck in behind Mags and wound itself around Rachel's ankles.

'As I told you, I've been feeling I'm nae use to onyone these days. I'm no used to doing nothing. There's life in me yet. I'm only fifty-two, for God's sake. Too young to be sitting aboot doing nothing. And I want my daughter to stop being so ashamed of me she can't bring herself to visit. Yes, I'll keep going down the centre, help the lassies like, but I got to thinking, I could help you too. Like I did when I helped you catch that madman.'

She was referring to the man who'd killed two women Mags had kept under her wing.

'When I had information I knew was important – like when Annie telt me aboot her sister – I brought Annie to see you and that helped you catch the killer, didn't it?'

'Yes, it did,' Rachel had to concede.

Mags stooped to stroke Honey before continuing. 'And I took you to see Gentleman Tim too, although I'm no very pleased about what the polis did. Anyroad, I've been thinking since I took you to ma local...'

'Go on,' Rachel encouraged, not having a clue where Mags was going with this.

'You know the other prostitutes trust me more than anyone else. Same goes for the others who live on the wrong side of the law – the street dealers, the robbers. They're small-time, so I'm no interested in getting them into trouble, but they tell me things. Things that might be useful to you. If I'd been younger, I might have set myself up as a private detective. I'm too old to do that now.' She treated Rachel to one of her hard, fierce stares, before burping long and loud. 'As I said, people speak to me,' she continued. 'They know I'm not going to tell the polis or say anything that might get them in trouble. And if I don't hear it from the horse's mouth, I hear the chat eventually.'

Rachel continued to listen, still unsure where Mags was going with this, but intrigued.

'I'm not sure I follow.'

'Look, you're pretty street smart, I'll give you that. When I first met you I thought butter wouldn't melt in your mouth, but I've come to learn there's a lot more going on under the surface.

You're not like other posh folk.' She gave Rachel an appraising look. 'You're tough as boots. More like us than you'd you likely want to believe. And that's OK. Following the rules never got anything done.' Mags's expression softened. 'I know what happened to your mother. That's bound to toughen a lassie up.'

Of course, Mags was bound to know. Was there anyone in Scotland who didn't?

'You might be tough and smart, but you're still wet behind the ears. You need to learn how to ask the right questions, the ones that get you the answers you need. Even then, people won't talk to you the way they talk to me. They don't trust you. At least not at the moment. They think you're one of those lawyers that want to put everyone in jail if they sneeze without a hanky. But if they see you hanging oot with me, they'll learn they can trust you. You should come back to the pub with me. The mair folk see you with me, the mair they'll know you're OK.'

'I'm still not sure what you're getting at, Mags.'

The expression in the older woman's eyes changed to one of exasperation.

'You don't need to pay me or anything like that,' she said. 'You don't even need to hang out with me that much, 'cept when I take you places I think you should go, or when you take me to Tesco – you still have to do that, whatever you decide.'

Mags didn't own a car so depended on Rachel to take her to the shops every couple of weeks to do a 'big shop'.

'And I could go to places with you. See, I can dress up, not look out of place with the posh folk, if you need a bodyguard like. I know you pulled a knife on those men,' she said, referring to the occasion when Rachel had been approached by a couple of drunks and had used her fish-gutting knife to see them off. Definitely not her finest hour. 'But didn't you think they could have just as easily used it on you? Or they might have had one of them zombie knives down the back of their trousers. What good would your wee knife have been then?'

Mags had a point. But to suggest Rachel needed a bodyguard! Rachel suppressed a smile. Furthermore, the role that Mags was suggesting was really that of a police informant.

'Don't you think it's Selena or Detective Sergeant Liversage – the officer who was with Selena at Tim's – that you should be approaching?'

'Oh God, not her. Not any of the polis. They never get it right. You're the one I trust. It has tae be you or naebody.'

It was quite a proposal, but what harm could it do? It had its advantages. Besides, Mags appeared determined to offer her services regardless of what Rachel said.

'No violence,' Rachel warned. She'd had enough of that to last her a lifetime.

Mags grinned, showing her nicotine-stained teeth. Rachel grinned back.

'And no smoking when we're together.'

They chinked their mugs of tea.

'Then if we are agreed,' Rachel said, 'could you ask about the man in the graveyard. Does anyone know who he is? Seen him before? Supplied drugs to him?'

Mags puffed out her chest and grinned. She all but saluted. 'I'll go now then. I'll report back as soon as I know anything.' She stood. 'Onything else, while ahm at it?'

'Yes, as a matter of fact. Could you ask around, see if anyone knows of or met a Monika Troka. She was a trafficked sexworker. It's going back more than ten years, but someone might remember her. She was Albanian.' It was a long shot, Rachel knew, but worth a punt. 'Or anyone who worked in a brothel either voluntarily or against their wishes back then.' It was just possible someone knew who the 'bottom bitch' – the slang term for the female gang member – was and where she was now.

Rachel ignored the nagging voice telling her that even if they did, they might not be able – or willing – to tell her anything new. Still, don't ask, don't get.

'Okey-dokey,' Mags said getting to her feet. 'The younger ones wouldn't know her, but the old yins – them as are still alive – might. I'll ask around.'

FIFTEEN

The last thing Rachel felt like doing on Saturday evening was going out, let alone dancing. After Mags left, she'd driven to Ben Wyvis, having set herself the goal of getting up and down quicker than the time before. Now her muscles ached and all she wanted was a long, deep bath, and then to curl up on the sofa and watch a film. But that was not an option, so she'd headed out to meet Selena as promised, at Johnny Fox's. She'd worn her ankle boots and jeans as instructed but was none the wiser as to where they were going dancing.

She'd arrived first so ordered a vodka and tonic for herself and a small white wine for Selena.

There was a flurry of activity as the old-style bar doors swung open and a hen party spilled into the pub. One of the group was holding aloft a 'Wicked Willy' inflatable penis, while other members of the party held blow-up flamingos and palm trees.

Selena followed in their wake. She was wearing blue sparkly Levis, low on the waist and secured with a thick diamanté-encrusted belt and tucked into the most magnificent mid-calf leather boots Rachel had ever seen. They had twin flames emblazoned on the outside of each boot. A checked shirt tucked in at the waist and a wide-brim cowboy hat completed the ensemble. She had another hat in her hand. Oblivious to the amused stares of the other customers in the bar, Selena sauntered across to Rachel, the heels of her boots clicking on the stone floor.

Rachel passed Selena her wine with a grin. 'Howdy, pardner,' she drawled in the best American accent she could manage. 'Where did you blow in from?'

'I just came in on the last stagecoach,' Selena drawled back.

'It feels as if I should have ordered you two fingers of whisky and had the bartender slide it along the counter,' Rachel added.

Selena raised her glass and tapped Rachel's. 'Just you wait. We are going to have the best night ever.'

'Where are we going?' Rachel asked.

'Have you ever been to the Grand Ole Opry in Glasgow?' Selena asked.

'Can't say I have.'

'But you like Country and Western music, right?'

'It's not karaoke, is it?' Rachel said, alarmed. 'There is no way I'm getting up and singing Dolly Parton in front of people.'

Selena grinned again. 'It's not karaoke and no one is going to ask you to sing. But that's all I'm going to tell you until we get there.'

An hour later Rachel was watching Selena, in a horizontal line with a number of similarly dressed cowboys and girls, all strutting their stuff as they performed a series of synchronised, choreographed moves. Selena had allowed Rachel to sit out the first couple of line dances – in order to get a feel for the moves, she said – but now she did a sideways shuffle over and hauled Rachel, protesting, onto the dance floor.

Rachel felt ridiculous as she did as Selena instructed, right down to hooking her thumbs in her jeans. She let Selena direct her moves, but she was as stiff as a cardboard cutout, no matter how much she tried to let herself go.

Having given a couple of dances her best shot, her clumsy choreography not without incident – which included stepping on people next to her, behind her, and in front of her – Rachel excused herself and left the dance floor.

Sipping her drink she watched enviously as Selena, a beaming smile on her face, threw herself into the dances with abandon, ogled by several cowboys.

How would it feel, to be like Selena? To be free and uninhibited without needing to be tanked up on vodka. Had it made a difference that Selena had grown up in a secure, loving and tight-knit family and community? The polar opposite of Rachel's life from her teens on. No wonder she'd spent years building a protective shell around herself, trying not to show her feelings – not always successfully. Sometimes she wished she could let go too.

A cowboy sidled into position next to Selena. He'd been paying her a lot of attention throughout the evening, dancing next to her, speaking into her ear, making her laugh.

When the dance finished, Selena grabbed Rachel's hand and dragged her to the ladies. 'What do you think?' Her face was flushed, her eyes glittering. 'Are you having fun?' she asked. She perched on the vanity counter and swung her legs.

On the other side of the room, Rachel peered into the mirror to apply fresh lipstick. Behind her, Selena had stopped swinging her legs. Thinking herself unobserved, her expression had gone from happy to sad and contemplative.

'OK.' Rachel turned to face her friend. 'Give it up: what's going on?'

Selena sighed. She slipped off the counter and checked under the doors of the closed stalls.

'It's work,' she said with a sigh when she was content they were alone. 'I don't think my colleagues like or rate me much.'

'I'd be gobsmacked if that were true. Everyone likes you.'

'They think I'm a numpty. A wee girl from the islands who got the job because Du Toit put a word in for her. Some of them hint that I'm his pet. Worse, that we're sleeping together.'

'That's ridiculous! 'Sides, I always assumed he was married.' Rachel realised she knew very little about the DI's personal life. Only that he'd been brought up in South Africa by his Scottish mother and right-wing Afrikaans father, from whom – because of their different political beliefs – he was estranged. Although he'd never mentioned a wife or girlfriend or partner, Rachel had assumed one existed.

'I don't know what his marital status is! And anyway, that's not the point!'

'Sorry, I know it isn't. Come on, Selena, the last thing you are is a wuss. It strikes me your colleagues are jealous because you helped bring down a drug ring, rescued a girl from drowning and passed your detective exams first time.'

'I doubt they know about the exams.'

Rachel raised an eyebrow. 'I'd be surprised if Du Toit didn't tell them.'

Selena shook her head and swayed slightly. She was drunker than Rachel realised. In her experience, Selena wasn't much of a drinker. 'They treat me like I'm a child.' She drew her hand over her head. 'That's why I cut my hair.' She gave Rachel a defiant look. 'Thought it would make me look more sophisticated. Pathetic, eh?'

So Selena wasn't as confident and carefree as she came across.

'Anything I can do to help?' Rachel asked.

Selena slipped off the counter. 'No thanks. I'll work it out. I just feel a bit out of my depth sometimes. They'll get to know me eventually, realise I'm not a country bumpkin. Things will settle down then.'

She didn't sound very certain.

'Have you discussed this with Audrey or Du Toit?' Rachel asked.

'Thighearna's a Dhia, no. The others would call me a snitch. I'd be well and truly screwed then.'

Two women burst into the toilet, laughing and staggering, preventing further conversation.

Rachel gave Selena a quick hug and they returned to the main hall where dancing was still in full swing. Selena got back in line and the same cowboy joined her. She smiled up at him as she started to dance.

The conversation in the ladies had unsettled Rachel. She'd keep an eye on Selena, check how she was doing in a couple of weeks. If things hadn't improved by then, she'd consider having a word with Du Toit.

Rachel was thinking about leaving when Selena brought her dancing partner across to their table. 'Hey, Rachel. This is Joe. He's a copper too.' Joe was good-looking in an unremarkable way. Just under six foot, solid and reassuring – everything most women's mothers wanted in a boyfriend. Rachel, who was drawn to work-obsessed former friends, could neverthe-less see that Joe was everything you wanted in an officer of the law.

'Selena tells me you're a lawyer with the fiscal's office.' He had a local accent and there was something familiar about him.

'Joe Adamson, right? We were in school together,' Rachel said, finally locating him in her memory bank.

'Were we?'

'Yes. You were a couple of years above me. You were in the track team. If I remember you were really good. A potential for the Scottish under sixteens back then.'

Joe looked pleased – if a little bashful – that Rachel remem-bered him. She warmed to him. Some natural suspicion when it came to meeting new people was self-preservation, but her levels were bordering on the extreme.

When Joe excused himself to go to the toilet, Selena leaned into Rachel.

'So, what do you think?' she asked in a conspiratorial whisper.

Rachel had only vaguely remembered him from school and that had been years ago. In the few minutes they'd talked this evening she'd had no time to form an opinion.

'He seems nice,' she said.

Selena gave a little puff of happiness. 'I know it's early days but I really like him. I'm sorry about earlier – in the ladies – I think I've just been feeling a bit homesick. And lonely. I'm also worried about my mam. I don't think my brothers are doing enough to look after her. Mam's been getting a bit forgetful. I phone her every day, but it's not the same as seeing her.'

She blinked and her expression cleared. 'I'm just being a worry wart about everything. I'll be OK. Everything will work out.' She gave Rachel a wry smile. 'If not, I'll just ask God to give me a bit of help.'

SIXTEEN

It was after one o'clock in the morning when Rachel got back to Clachnaharry. She'd walked along the canal, avoiding the shortcut through the park. She could look after herself, no matter what Mags said, but she'd no wish to come across anyone having illicit sex in the bushes.

Selena had stayed in town to have another drink with her police constable. Their brief chat in the ladies appeared to have cheered her up. Or else the PC had.

As she approached her door, the hairs on the back of Rachel's neck stood up. It was wide open. She'd definitely locked it. Instead of doing the sensible thing and phoning the police, Rachel crept around the perimeter of the house, looking in the windows. When she came to the back, which faced the sea, she saw the glass in her kitchen door had been smashed. Simultaneously she glanced through the patio doors and her heart jumped to her throat as she caught sight of the bottom half of a prone figure. She'd recognise those slippers anywhere: Mags.

Rachel picked up a garden fork she'd left stabbed in the

ground in her front garden. It wasn't much protection but was the best she could do.

She nudged her kitchen door further open with her foot. In the movies the killer would be hiding behind it, ready to pounce on her as she came in. So she did what any heroine worth her salt would do: she took a deep, silent breath and slammed the door open with all her strength. To her relief there was no grunt of pain, no expulsion of breath, only an almighty bang as the door hit the wall.

Rachel edged inside. A groan came from the hall. Her neighbour was lying on her side, a gash on her temple and a pool of blood under her head. Rachel chucked the garden fork aside, crouched and checked the pulse in Mags's neck. It was weak and rapid.

'Mags, can you hear me?' Rachel asked, keeping one ear cocked for sounds of activity in the rooms. She couldn't be sure whoever had attacked Mags wasn't still in the house.

Mags groaned again and her eyelids flickered.

'It's OK, Mags. I'll get help.' Rachel stabbed 999 into her phone and asked for an ambulance.

Mags brought her hand up to her head.

'Try not to move,' Rachel said. 'An ambulance is on the way. Are you hurt anywhere apart from your head?'

Her question elicited another moan. A quick glance around was enough for Rachel to realise that whoever had attacked Mags had also ransacked her home. In the sitting room books had been pulled from shelves, the contents of the boxes containing the trial notes scattered on the floor. Worst of all, her mother's record player, the only possession Rachel had of hers, had been thrown on the ground, all the records smashed.

Rachel held the older woman's hand as the sirens in the distance grew closer. Whoever had attacked her had knocked one of her front teeth out. Close up, every wrinkle was visible, particularly the smokers' lines on her top lip. As was her thinning hair, the loose crepey skin around her arms and the once fierce jawline. Mags was tough but no gym bunny. She might have been able to see off a punter with a few words or, in a pinch, with a closed fist, but those days were gone. It hadn't helped that whoever had attacked her hadn't been messing around. Rachel prayed Mags hadn't been hurt because she'd taken the desire to act as Rachel's bodyguard to heart.

'Rachel?' Mags moaned.

'It's OK, Mags. You're going to be fine. Can you tell me what happened?'

'Want to sleep,' she mumbled. Her breathing deepened. Rachel squeezed her fingers.

'You do that,' she said softly. 'I'll keep watch until help arrives.'

When the paramedics rushed through the door a couple of minutes later, Rachel stood aside, leaving them to make their assessments. Her hands were coated with Mags's blood, her blouse smeared with it.

'Let's get a drip in,' one of the medics shouted to his colleague.

At that moment Selena appeared. She'd ditched the Stetson but was still in her sparkly jeans and cowboy boots. She seemed to have sobered up. She glanced around the house.

'Are you OK?'

Rachel nodded.

'And Mags?'

'I don't know. Not great.'

One of the EMTs looked up. 'She's stable for now, but we're going to take her to hospital for a full review. I expect they'll want to keep her in at least overnight.'

'How come you're here?' Rachel asked Selena, as the paramedics lifted Mags onto the stretcher and out of the house.

'When I got home I heard the call over the police radio,

recognised the address and Ubered over. Thighearna's a Dhia, Rachel. I thought it was you.'

Selena glanced around, clocked the TV still on the stand, Rachel's Sonos speakers, the scattered papers. 'Looks like your intruder was looking for something,' she added.

Just what Rachel had been thinking.

Selena took her phone from her pocket. 'I'm going to phone Du Toit. We need crime scene examiners over here.'

As she dialled, she looked at Rachel, who hadn't been able to hide a shiver. 'You're coming to mine.' She held up a finger. 'No arguments. God knows when the examiners will get here, let alone when they'll finish. I'll tell them to call me when they're about to wind up and I'll come and lock up for you. Then tomorrow I'll help you put everything to rights.' She held up her finger again as Rachel opened her mouth to answer. 'Dhia mise, if you even try and refuse, I'll pick you up and put you in one of the patrol vehicles when they come and tell them to take you to mine, blue lights and all.'

Rachel had no doubt Selena meant what she said. Anyway she didn't have the energy to fight her.

'Only if we can go via the hospital. Check what's happening with Mags.'

This time it was Selena who hesitated. 'Fair enough. I want to know that she's OK too. But you should change your top first.'

Rachel glanced down. She hadn't given the blood a second thought after she'd first noticed it. Luckily Selena was here and could vouch for her, otherwise the patrol officers who had just arrived, lights flashing, might be tempted to take Rachel into custody.

'Call an Uber,' she said to Selena. 'I'll wash up, grab my toothbrush and some clean clothes and we can swing by the hospital on the way.'

· · ·

It hadn't been long since Rachel had last been in Inverness General Hospital and the memories still freaked her out.

They found Mags on a trolley in the corridor of A&E, a police constable by her side. Rachel's neighbour's head had been bandaged and her face was swollen. Her eyes were closed, her face devoid of colour. Sensing someone leaning over her, she opened her eyes and smiled weakly. 'Fuck's sake. My heid feels like someone took a sledgehammer to it.'

A nurse bustled over and lifted the back of the trolley so Mags could sit up. She helped her take some water. 'We're going to keep her overnight to observe for concussion. If everything seems OK, we'll discharge her in the morning.'

Rachel felt a gush of relief.

'I want to go back to ma hoose,' Mags protested.

'Absolutely not,' the nurse said firmly. 'We don't know how long you were unconscious for.'

'Can you tell me what happened?' Selena asked Mags.

'I'd just come hame. I'd been to the pub. I saw someone was using a torch, moving around your sitting room.' She looked at Rachel. 'I know dodgy behaviour when I see it. Your curtains were closed and I know you never pull your sitting room curtains – you should, by the way. There are a lot of weirdos out there who get their kicks watching wummen, especially when they don't know they're being watched.'

Rachel thought back to the evening she'd thought she'd seen a shadow move outside her window. Had it not been her imagination after all?

'Why didn't you phone me – or the police – instead of investigating yourself?'

'Because I didn't know you weren't in there and not in trouble, did I? I promised you I'd look after you, didn't I. And I'm no feart of anyone.'

Rachel's heart tightened. It pained and touched her that the older woman felt Rachel needed protecting.

'Maybe you should be,' Rachel said. 'God, Mags, you could have been killed.'

'I got him a cracker on his face with my fist,' Mags said with satisfaction. 'Broke ma nail doing it.'

'Did you get a look at him?'

'No. He'd a balaclava and gloves on. I tried tae pull it aff – that's how I broke my nail – but he coshed me over the head with sumthin'.'

'Do you know what it was?'

'Naw. It was dark, wasn't it? Could have been a hammer. It was bloody hard at anyroad.'

'Oh, Mags. You shouldn't have done it, but thank you. You get some rest now,' Rachel said. 'Let me know when you're being discharged and I'll come and get you.'

In their second Uber of the night, Selena asked Rachel for her thoughts. The driver had the radio on so they couldn't be overheard.

'I don't know what to think. Maybe a passing crook taking a chance. My house is secluded. Maybe they saw me when I left to meet you.' She hated that someone had been in her home, poking through her stuff, touching it. It made her feel violated and exposed.

Opportunistic burglaries were up across Scotland. As if the small-time criminals realised Police Scotland didn't have the manpower to do anything about the large majority of them. And they were right. The Scottish government had all but said that, in an attempt to reduce the numbers of people in prison, they were going to concentrate on serious crime. Housebreaking, when no one was hurt, didn't come into this category.

Except someone *had* got hurt. Mags. The intruder could have killed her. It was time Mags forgot about her mission to become Rachel's sidekick. It could only lead to more trouble.

A thought struck Rachel. Was it possible Mags had been the target all along and the intruder had broken into the wrong house? Maybe someone didn't like her blossoming relationship with Rachel and, by association, the law? Maybe they didn't like Mags connecting Rachel to the homeless man and thereby the body found in the graveyard. Rachel's unease deepened. Maybe someone had learned that Mags was asking questions on Rachel's behalf and wasn't happy.

Or could it have something to do with her visit to ex-DI Jason Bright? It was a bit of a coincidence the break-in had happened shortly after Rachel had gone to see him – shortly after she'd asked Selena for the police report. But how would he know she had requested it? Unless he still had contacts in the force.

Was the break-in linked to Eric's disappearance – and the story he was following? She sat back on her heels and ran through their conversation on the mountain.

He'd promised he'd find a way of letting her know what he'd discovered. He hadn't. He'd trusted her to work it out. He hadn't given her much to go on.

He'd said that he'd been digging into OCGs and his interest had been sparked when he was looking into Rachel's past. He'd requested transcripts of the sex-trafficking trial. Had he chased up the same leads as her?

The only way of knowing was for her to continue to follow that story and hopefully his tracks. A shiver ran up her spine. He'd been concerned his questions were putting him in danger. Had he found the name of one of the OCG bosses? Had they found out and put a stop to him and his questions. Would they try and do the same to her?

In any case, she wasn't about to stop. According to Sir Thomas Bingham, the greatest judge of his time, the responsibility of the official responsible for conducting an inquest was to ensure the relevant facts were fully, fairly and fearlessly investigated. It was a motto that Rachel tried to follow.

So she would continue. Fully, fairly and fearlessly.

SEVENTEEN

Selena's flat was on the second floor of a sandstone tenement overlooking the River Ness. As she'd told Rachel, it was sparsely furnished, mainly with furniture the last owner had left, presumably because it didn't fit with their new place. A chair. A coffee table. A bed for each of the two bedrooms. The sofa was stained, the chair worn at the edges, and the coffee table had a wobbly leg.

'I've decided to wait until I have a permanent place before I send for my stuff,' Selena said, as if seeing it through her visitor's eyes. 'I know I could make it look more homely in the meantime, but I haven't got around to it. Plus the landlord is thinking of putting it on the market. If the price is right, I might buy it.' She smiled at Rachel. 'As I said before, the location is perfect. And the house has good bones, I think. Would you like to see the rest?'

'I would.'

'Obviously this is the sitting room.'

In daylight – not far away now – light would stream through the south-facing windows making the already spacious room feel more so. Stripped pine floorboards were, unusually, mainly intact. The kitchen required updating, but as it was small that shouldn't be too expensive. The bedroom Selena had chosen as hers was also south-facing with the same original sash windows and stripped floorboards as the sitting room. As well as the bed, on top of which sat a Winnie the Pooh teddy, there was a free-standing pine wardrobe.

The second bedroom was north-facing and smaller than the master. The bed was made up ready for guests.

'Mam taught me to always be ready for unexpected visitors,' Selena said. 'It's always been a part of highland hospitality to offer a place to sleep and a meal to anyone in need.' She grinned at Rachel. 'I'm afraid you're going to have to do without the meal though. Unless you'd like a bowl of cornflakes?'

'That's OK. I'm not hungry.'

'Cup of tea then? Or straight to bed?'

Rachel gave in to Selena's ministrations. She was still too wired to go to sleep and if she were honest, it was quite nice being looked after. Every now and again. As long as it didn't become the norm.

'A cup of tea would be good.' She followed Selena into the kitchen.

'I've asked Clive to lock up and drop your key off when the forensics are done,' Selena said. 'He texted me to say he was on the callout.'

Rachel was glad her ex-colleague, formerly one of the Death Unit administrators, was on the case. If she had to have people poking around her home, she'd rather it was him.

Selena made tea and gave Rachel hers with a plate of biscuits.

'Go on, eat up. Sugar is good for shock.'

Obediently Rachel bit into a milk chocolate digestive. It had indeed been a shock, finding Mags on her floor. For a terrifying moment she'd thought the older woman was dead.

What do you think the person who broke into your house

was looking for?' Selena asked. The same question had been running through Rachel's mind.

'I don't know. Maybe nothing. As I said earlier, maybe they picked my house at random.' But her gut told her otherwise. Her mind went to the trial notes. Was it something in there? In which case, why not take them? Unless they hadn't wanted to draw attention to them, knowing Rachel could request more copies anyway. Or perhaps Mags had interrupted them before they could. 'Maybe they just wanted to scare me.'

'Why would they want to scare you, though? They hurt Mags, Rachel. What if you'd been there?'

'If they'd wanted to harm me, they didn't need to break into my house to do so.' But the thought was scary. Her mind circled back to her last conversation with her father. When she'd asked him about the human-trafficking case he'd warned her not to look into it, suggesting it might be dangerous if she did. Well, she had been looking and someone didn't like it.

Could Jason Bright be behind the break-in? Had it been a warning for Rachel not to look too closely at him? She told Selena about her visit to the retired detective.

'You should let Du Toit know,' Selena said.

'There's no point. I've no evidence Bright was involved.'

At that moment her mobile pinged with an incoming text. Thinking it might be Mags, Rachel looked at it. She didn't recognise the number. The text was short and to the point.

Next time it will be you.

'What the fuck?' Rachel yelped.

'What is it?' Selena asked.

Rachel passed her phone over. There was no mistaking now that the break-in had been a warning to Rachel.

'Rachel, that's the same as the text you got a few months

ago, isn't it?' Selena replied with a shocked look on her face. 'What did that one say exactly?'

'*Stop looking or you will go the same way as the others.*' Rachel said, stunned. The cogs in her brain were slowly turning, thinking about the murderer she helped catch. It couldn't be him. He was in jail. She crossed to the window and looked out. Was someone out there watching her? She shuddered. The shadows were where monsters lived – waiting to pounce. Her mouth was dry, her heart crashing against her ribs. She took deep breaths to force the terror away. She needed a clear head to think.

Most inmates had illegal access to phones, some flown in by drones along with packages of drugs, others smuggled in the orifices of friends and relatives. Prisoners were a creative, innovative bunch.

But why break into her house? If in prison, he would have had to persuade someone else to do it on his behalf. Maybe to threaten and intimidate her, to stop her from testifying against him? *Fully, fairly and fearlessly*, she reminded herself. She wasn't doing so well on the fearlessly right now. She felt like cowering under the blankets.

'I'll get that mobile number traced,' Selena said, 'but I don't hold out much hope. The last one came from a burner, as I recall.'

She came to stand next to Rachel at the window. 'Look I was going to leave this until Monday, but I think I should tell you now.'

'Tell me what?'

'I found the police report on Monika Troka.'

'What did it say?'

'It's not very helpful, I'm afraid. Her body was retrieved from the River Ness on the morning of September the fourth. Her toxicology report showed high levels of alcohol and benzodiazepines, and it was assumed she either fell or jumped

in. According to Bright – coincidentally the senior investigating officer – Monika had been under a great deal of stress
leading up to the trial. There were no witnesses and unfortunately no working CCTV cameras in the area, so the date she
went in wasn't known. No one had reported her missing so no
one was looking for her. Because she'd been dead for some
time it was impossible to know if the injuries she'd sustained
were from being bashed around in the water. The pathologist,
who has since passed away, found water in her lungs,
suggesting she went into the river while still alive. Any trace
evidence had long been washed away. Based on the toxicology, he determined the cause of death to be accidental or
suicide.'

Although that aligned with what Bright had said, Rachel
wasn't convinced. She found the timing hard to explain. Why
would Monika wait until after she'd testified to kill herself?
Surely the months leading up to the trial, possibly in fear for her
life, would have been the most stressful time.

'Do you have a copy of the police report?' she asked.

Selena opened a drawer and pulled out a sheaf of papers.
She handed them to Rachel.

As far as she could tell, the investigation into Monika's
death had been perfunctory. A couple of her acquaintances said
she was looking forward to starting over, possibly in England or
Wales. She had been anxious and stressed leading up to the
trial but hugely relieved when it was over, although disappointed and concerned that the top dogs hadn't been identified.

DC Souter had been the detective carrying out the investigation, reporting to DI Bright who had signed the report. Investigation closed. Was that usual? Shouldn't they have been more
suspicious?

'Why wasn't Monika given police protection?' Rachel
asked.

'I don't know. It's not in the police report. Maybe she

refused it. Not everyone wants to disappear and start over in a place where they don't know anyone.'

'She didn't know anyone here,' Rachel snapped. 'Except a couple of her fellow captives and the people who had imprisoned her and abused her!' She took another deep, steadying breath before continuing: 'Didn't it cross anyone's mind to investigate? She'd recently testified against some serious criminals.'

'I wasn't around then, Rachel. Neither was Du Toit.'

'But DI Bright was,' Rachel said. 'He of all people must have had his suspicions.' She leaned back in her chair. 'He was DC Souter's supervisor. Have you found anything more about her?'

Selena sighed. 'I looked up her records. I'm not sure that's allowed, so I want you to appreciate I'm going out on a limb here for you, Rachel. I didn't want to ask around because the team would want to know why I'm interested, and I think it's better they don't.'

'And...?' Rachel prompted.

'She took left the force about six months after the trial. She was only thirty at the time.'

'I wonder why. That's young to get burnout.'

'That's what I thought. She relocated to Skye. Maybe she found a job she liked better there. I looked up the electoral records and found an address for her. She lives a couple of miles further on from Borreraig which is a small hamlet about eight miles away from Dunvegan in Skye. I used Google Earth to check it out. Her place is at the end of a road to nowhere. There's nothing but moor and sea surrounding her. Even by island standards, it's practically off grid.'

'What does she do now?'

'No idea.'

'Did you happen to find a contact number for her?'

Selena hesitated, looking uncomfortable. 'I can't give you

that. The address – fair enough, that's in the public domain, but her personal telephone number...' She shook her head. 'Sorry, Rachel. No can do.'

As yet Linda, who had offered to look when she got a moment, hadn't been able to find a copy of the report. The Death Unit was legally required to be notified by the police of sudden or unexpected deaths and Monika's death definitely fell into this category. Rachel needed to find out which fiscal had received the report and why they hadn't asked for it to be investigated further.

And if it wasn't, why not.

One way or another, there were more questions that needed to be answered.

EIGHTEEN

When Rachel woke up the next morning it took her a moment or two to remember where she was. She'd slept badly, waking up on several occasions, her senses on full alert. It was unnerving to know she was in someone's sights. She was more convinced than ever the clue to her mother's murder lay in the trial transcripts – and very likely Eric's disappearance too.

She dressed quietly and quickly. She'd wait until she was home to shower. She splashed her face and brushed her teeth before following the smell of coffee and bacon through to Selena's kitchen.

Selena was dressed in last night's jeans and a T-shirt with an image of the Blues Brothers on the front. 'Eggs and bacon OK for you?' she asked.

'Perfect.'

'Help yourself to coffee.'

The doorbell rang and Selena went to answer it, but not before she checked who it was through the security system. Rachel should really think of getting something similar.

Selena pressed the buzzer to release the front door. 'It's Clive with your key,' she told Rachel. Clive, his white T-shirt emphasising his muscles and contrasting with his ebony skin, breezed into Selena's flat with a smile.

He dangled Rachel's keys before tossing them to her.

'All done. You can go back whenever you like.'

'Not till she's had breakfast,' Selena said firmly.

Selena seemed to have developed a bossy streak since she'd become a detective, but Rachel didn't have the energy to argue with her. Especially as she was certain Clive would side with the police officer. The clincher – she was starving.

'If there's any breakfast going spare, count me in,' Clive said, taking a chair at the table. 'I got a glazier out,' he told Rachel, as Selena cracked eggs into a pan. 'He's boarded up the broken glass in your kitchen door. He'll be round this afternoon to replace it.'

'Thanks, Clive. I appreciate it. Did you find anything?'

'Nothing. Except a piece of fingernail. Selena told me it belonged to the victim. Mags, isn't it? It's bagged and in the lab. Might get some DNA from it, although I suspect it won't be top of the list for getting tested. Unless' – he looked at Rachel – 'you push it?'

She intended to.

'We also found some prints,' he continued. Selena plonked a mug of coffee and a bowl of sugar in front of him. 'Selena's will be on file, but we will have to get yours and Mags's too, for elimination. But I'm not hopeful. We think this was a professional job.'

'Mags said the person who attacked her was wearing gloves and a balaclava,' Rachel said, 'so I suspected there wouldn't be much to find.' Her stomach growled as the smell of bacon drifted into the room.

'I didn't say it was hopeless, just that we weren't optimistic.'

· · ·

Rachel called the hospital while she drank down the rich dark coffee Selena had made her, Mediterranean-style, brewed in a coffee pot before being poured into a cup the size of a bowl with warm milk added. Selena told her how she had been on a trip to France with her cousin from Uist and the B&B had served it like that in the morning; she was now addicted to having her morning coffee that way.

Mags had had a good night according to the nurse who had answered the phone. But they hoped to keep her in for another twenty-four hours. 'Just to be on the safe side.'

'Is she allowed visitors?' Rachel asked. She didn't like to think of Mags being alone.

'She has one with her right now. I believe it's her daughter.'

'Then let her know I was asking after her. If she needs anything, she can call me.' If Mags's estranged daughter had come to be with her mother, something good had come from last night's events.

'I should go home,' Rachel said to Clive and Selena when she finished the call. She looked around for her jacket.

'I'm not sure that's a good idea. Not until we catch whoever broke into your house. You know you can stay here as long as you want,' Selena said.

'I don't intend to be hounded out of my home,' Rachel said firmly.

'In which case,' Clive said, 'you need to make sure that, if someone tries to break in again, you know about it. That means an alarm and more outside lights.' He turned to Selena. 'I have footie this morning but as soon as I'm done, Suruthi and I will meet you at Rachel's.'

'No. Please. You don't have to. Enjoy your Sunday. I'll be fine,' Rachel protested.

'No way,' Clive said. 'That's what friends are for.'

'She thinks she doesn't need friends,' Selena chipped in.

Clive gave a look of pretend hurt. 'Do you mean to tell me

you've been using me all this time just to have someone to go clubbing with?'

Rachel laughed. Colleagues or friends, friendly colleagues, whatever, she felt better around them.

Selena and Rachel walked back to Rachel's. Feeling weird about having everyone come over, Rachel had tried again to persuade Selena that she didn't need her help. Selena was having none of it. 'As we said back at mine, that's what friends are for. They help each other.' She smiled. 'Anyway, I like helping people. That's why I became a police officer.'

Rachel felt a pang. No one could doubt Selena's good heart. On the other hand, Rachel sometimes wondered if *she* were driven more by anger than kindness.

'You going to see Joe again?' Rachel asked as they turned into the park that would take them to the canal path and Rachel's house.

'I hope so. We exchanged numbers. If he doesn't text me later then I'll text him.'

Rachel felt a prickle of unease but wasn't sure why. Joe was a few years older than Selena but she didn't think that was it. She thought back to her schooldays, trying to recall what she'd known about him. Nothing, was the answer. Apart from him being a good athlete.

She shook her unease away. Just because she was in someone's target range, she couldn't spend her life being suspicious of everyone.

As Clive had said, the window of the back door to Rachel's house was boarded over. Rachel wondered what the rest of the village of Clachnaharry made of the first break-in at their village for decades, and if it would help or hinder Mags's reputation within the community. The house looked the same as it had last night – upturned drawers, papers flung over the floor, the drying pool of blood in the hall – except for the boarded-up door and the fingerprint dust that covered almost every surface.

'Anything missing?' Selena asked.

'Not that I can see. Except my laptop.'

'Was it an expensive one?'

'You could say that. It's a MacBook Air. Cost me over a thousand pounds.'

'Work stuff on it?'

'Thankfully nothing that hasn't been saved to the cloud and protected with passwords. It has a programme that can delete the hard drive remotely. I did that before going to sleep last night.'

'I'm thinking whoever did this wants to know something they think *you* know,' Selena said.

Rachel thought so too.

'I'm going to look into your past cases, just to be on the safe side. We both know how powerful a motive revenge is,' Selena said.

Rachel picked up the record player from the floor where it had been tossed. As she did, she noticed there was a record still on the turntable, not one she immediately recognised. Curious, she removed it and looked at the label. Her blood ran cold. The title of the record was 'Everybody Has Secrets'. It was definitely not one from her mother's collection. Rachel had looked through it several times since she'd retrieved it from the house. Someone, presumably the person who had broken into her home, had left it. It was clearly meant as a warning. More chillingly, did it mean they knew her secret? If so, how the hell had they found out?

'You know as well as I do that the force isn't going to spend more time and energy investigating, not when they've been told break-ins aren't a priority,' Rachel said through stiff lips as her mind whirled. She wasn't going to tell Selena about the record. She didn't want her to know there was something in Rachel's past almost no one knew. But Eric had found out. So it was possible others had too. Her head throbbed.

'I'd bet my life on it that this wasn't a bog-standard burglary,' Selena was saying. She had her back towards Rachel, so hadn't noticed her reaction. 'Of course it will be investigated. Du Toit will make sure of it. He of all people has your back.'

Before Rachel could collect herself and respond there was a knock on her door. This time Clive was in baggy shorts and a double layer T-shirt. He had a black eye and split lip, which he immediately explained as having happened on the football field that morning. Suruthi was her usual stunning self in a floaty skirt and a white, embroidered blouse, her fingernails and toenails painted scarlet.

Clive emptied a carrier bag on the table. 'Three cameras – two for the front, as it's not overlooked, and one for the back – as well as four lights that are motion sensitive. That should have you covered.'

'You didn't have to do that,' Rachel said. 'I would have got those later.'

Clive raised an eyebrow. 'No time like the present. Point me to your toolbox and I'll get them up.'

As Clive installed the cameras and lights, the others set about putting Rachel's house back in order: righting boxes, refilling drawers, asking Rachel where things went and tossing items to each other to put away in the right place. As Suruthi gathered up the scattered papers, she paused to look at them.

'Why do you have copies of this particular trial?' she asked, flicking through the pages. 'It's one of the cases I currently have under review. The police are still hopeful they can get to the gang bosses. Have you had enough of pinching Alastair's cases so you're going to pinch mine?'

It was said lightly enough, but there was an undercurrent of frost in Suruthi's tone.

Clive, having finished with the lights, had come inside in

search of a cold drink. Rachel's three colleagues looked at her, enquiring expressions on their faces.

Rachel hesitated, fighting her deep-seated reluctance to discuss any aspect of her past. 'It's the case in which my mother had been due to give evidence before she was killed,' she said finally.

The others exchanged knowing glances.

'I still don't understand,' Suruthi said. 'What are you looking for?'

'I'm not sure. I just hope I'll recognise it when I find it.'

'Someone sent Rachel a threatening text after the break-in last night,' Selena told Clive and Suruthi. 'Warning her she'd be next. I sent it to a colleague to see if he can trace the number, but I'm guessing it will be from a burner phone.'

'How long have you been looking into this case?' Suruthi asked, still clutching the sheaf of papers.

'Not long. A few weeks. More seriously over the last week. I asked an advocate friend who worked with the firm that defended my father about it. He got me copies of the trial transcripts.'

'But why are you reviewing it now?' Suruthi asked.

Rachel wasn't ready to give her friends the whole story, but she decided they should know the part that was relevant.

'I think the group had an informant back then. Either a police officer or someone affiliated with the Social Work Department,' she said reluctantly.

Suruthi was appalled. 'Rachel! For God's sake! Leave that to the police to investigate.' She tossed Selena one of the Diet Cokes she'd retrieved from Rachel's fridge. 'I'm sure you agree,' she said to Selena. 'If an OCG has you in its sights, that's really, really not a good thing. These are serious criminals who think nothing of getting rid of anyone who gets in their way.'

Exactly what Eric had said. Eric who was still missing. And had been looking into OCGs. Rachel swallowed hard. 'We can't know for sure this has anything to do with an OCG,' she said. 'Selena is going to look into my past cases. It could easily be someone with a bone to pick with me.' The fiscals regularly got threats from the criminals they prosecuted, and right now she'd rather that was the answer.

'If we get a DNA hit from the nail we found, that might help,' Clive said, also looking worried. 'But it could take weeks – months even supposing there is any.'

'In the meantime, do as the text said and stop looking into OCGs,' Suruthi said. 'Leave that stuff to Selena and her colleagues. We wade knee deep in shit while we're at work – why go looking for it? Someone tried to kill you once before; you've no reason to think someone else with bigger fish to fry won't do the same.'

It felt as if a net was floating over Rachel's head. Something dark and oppressive, closing in on her. But wading in shit *was* her job.

'That's what we signed up for isn't it? To catch the bad guys and get them locked up. Anyway you don't have to be in law enforcement to have your life threatened. Look at the politicians – particularly the women. If we back off because we're frightened, it will only embolden the pricks.'

Clive and Selena were staring at Rachel, concern and doubt writ all over their faces.

'Listen to Suruthi,' Clive urged. Selena nodded in agreement.

In sudden panic, Rachel picked up her house keys. 'Come on, everyone, food and drink at the inn – and I'm buying. And I'm not taking no for an answer.'

NINETEEN

As soon as everyone had left for their respective homes, Rachel, who had made sure not to drink, got into her second-hand MG and headed in direction of the Black Isle. She hoped that on a Sunday afternoon Jason Bright would be at home. If not she'd come back.

If he was responsible for the break-in and the attack on Mags, she wanted him to know that she suspected him. And to challenge him about Monika – why her death hadn't raised alarm bells. She also wanted to ask if he remembered who in the Death Unit had signed off on it.

When she arrived at his home she was pleased to find his car in the driveway, but when she knocked on the door, there was no reply. Perhaps he'd taken Alba for a walk. Rachel glanced around. She could see a faint path by the river. If she had a dog, that's where she would go.

It was Alba who caught her attention first. The spaniel was bounding along, a tennis ball in her mouth. DI Bright, his stooped figure in a tweed jacket, emerged from the woods a few minutes later. He was holding a plastic ball launcher.

When he noticed her he frowned. 'Miss McKenzie. I didn't expect to bump into you out here.'

'I have a couple more questions if you have a moment?' There was no point in pretending this was a chance encounter.

He sighed. 'I thought I'd told you I had nothing more to say to you.'

'Why didn't you order DC Souter to investigate Monika's death more thoroughly?'

'It *was* investigated. She either took her own life or fell in because she was pissed.'

'That's not at all certain. Although the pathologist marked the cause of death as a possible suicide, had I been the fiscal to receive the police report and the PM I would have insisted Monika's death was properly investigated. Who signed it off at the Death Unit?'

'Your boss.' The response came without hesitation and with the addition of a smirk.

'Douglas?' Her heart gave a thunk.

'Yes. He was in charge back then.' Bright gave a wry smile. 'Seems he's always been in charge. He agreed further investigation wasn't necessary. A No Pro. No further proceedings required. How is he, by the way? I can't imagine he'll approve of your continual accosting of me when he finds out.'

'I haven't been able to find a police report, let alone the fiscal's summary,' Rachel countered, without answering his question. She couldn't see Douglas signing off on one without asking for further investigation.

DI Jason shrugged. 'That's your problem, not mine.'

She let that go. He was right. Until she had the report – and Douglas's response to it – she was on shaky ground. Especially since she couldn't be sure that it hadn't been misfiled or lost.

'Why did DC Souter leave the force?' she asked, changing tack.

Bright puffed his cheeks out. 'You'd have to ask her.'

'I intend to. You don't have a number for her, by any chance?'

'No. And if I did, I wouldn't give it to you.'

'Did you arrange for my home to be broken into last night?'

He was either a very good actor or genuinely surprised. 'For God's sake, woman. Are you aware you have just accused a senior police officer of a criminal act?'

'I simply find it odd that my home was broken into a couple of nights after I came to see you. Whoever it was attacked my neighbour when she came to investigate and left me a warning to stop looking.'

Alba dropped a stick at Rachel's feet. She picked it up and threw it for her.

'What about Eric Hunter?' she asked. 'Did he come to see you?'

DI Bright shook his head. 'Go home, Miss McKenzie. I looked into you after your first visit. I understand some horrible things have happened in your life and that you're not stable because of it. Now, I strongly suggest that you stick to the job you are paid to do and leave the police to do theirs.'

'Getting to the truth *is* my job,' Rachel muttered, before turning on her heel and walking away.

TWENTY

Du Toit, in jeans and jumper, was pacing as he waited for Rachel to arrive. A knot of anxiety lodged behind her ribs. In the past the detective inspector had been a support and an ally. Judging by the furious expression on his face, right now he was neither.

Her phone had rung just as she'd pulled up outside her house. It had been Du Toit demanding that she meet him outside the Ministry of Justice. She stepped out of her car and into the drizzle.

'What the hell were you thinking, Rachel?' Du Toit said when she was in earshot. 'No, let me guess – you weren't thinking at all.'

'Bright called you?'

'The minute you parted ways with him. He was livid. Understandably. Does Plover know what you were up to?'

'I had a couple of questions for him, that's all.'

He frowned at her. 'Don't take me for a fool. It is never that simple with you, Rachel.'

'Don't you think it's odd that I go to see him to ask about the case my mother was involved in and two days later my home gets broken into? The intruder was clearly looking for something. What if it was information in the trial notes? Remember it was the same case that Eric was interested in?

'He'd said he was planning to meet someone, possibly a source. He was worried his investigation was putting him in danger. He's missing. I'd been looking into the same case. My home was broken in to. My laptop stolen and I've been warned off. The two events have to be related. Perhaps he went to see Bright too? Although, of course, Bright denies it.'

Du Toit's expression turned blacker. 'Listen to yourself, Rachel. You are all but accusing a senior police officer of breaking and entering, as well as serious assault, and involvement in a journalist's disappearance.'

'You and I both know, to our cost, there are corrupt police officers in every part of the force,' Rachel shot back.

'Fok, Rachel. Have you lost your mind?'

While they'd been speaking, the steady drizzle had turned to rain. 'Let's continue this conversation in the bar.' He handed her his raincoat. She put it over her head and led the two-minute dash to the Innes Bar.

As it was early on a Sunday evening, there were fewer police officers in the bar than usual. One or two smirked in their direction before returning to their conversations and drinks.

Du Toit insisted on buying the drinks and as she sat at the table waiting for him to return, she thought about the conversation to come. She'd crossed a line. She knew that.

He looked tired, Rachel reflected. He was juggling several cases at once and his workload was clearly taking its toll.

And now she was about to add to his headaches.

She waited until he returned with drinks – a Guinness for him and a Diet Coke for her – before she began to speak.

She took him through what she had gleaned from the trial transcripts.

'I'm convinced somebody was tipping off the gang in

advance of the raids. I think it was either one of the police officers involved in the team or someone very close to him or her.
As far as I can tell, DI Jason Bright was there every time.

'Furthermore, the main witness was found drowned a
month after testifying. DC Souter, DI Bright's sidekick when
they were investigating the brothels, left the force only a few
months later. Have either Bright or Souter ever been investigated?'

'For what?'

'For corruption.'

Du Toit gave her a blistering look. 'That's quite an allegation you're making, Rachel.'

'Doesn't mean there might not be truth in it.' She leaned
forward. 'Couldn't you ask Selena to look into it? Check if
either DI Bright or DC Souter was there every time a raid was
planned.'

'You can't really be suggesting Jason Bright was a stooge for
a sex-trafficking ring?' Du Toit's voice was ominously quiet. 'I
understand your desire to prove that your father was not
responsible for your mother's murder, but this is going too far.'

Rachel took a sip of her Diet Coke before continuing, taking
the moment to maintain her composure. 'What if my mother
came to the same conclusion? What if she discovered who that
person was, and was killed because of it? What if the same thing
happened to Eric?'

Du Toit was said nothing for a few long minutes, exasperation written all over his face.

'The crime scene investigators found skin underneath your
neighbour's fingernail, right?' Du Toit said.

'Yes. They sent it to the lab.'

'I'll get it expedited. In the meantime, keep away from DI
Bright. It was all I could do to persuade him not to complain to
Miss Plover about you. I explained you'd had a couple of diffi-
cult months, and that you'd faced down a couple of murderers

because of your admirable need to get to the truth, but that sometimes you get carried away. I promised to have a word with you.'

A warm flush of anger swept over Rachel. 'Is that what you think? That I get carried away?' she said through gritted teeth. 'Jesus, Kirk, you might as well have told him I'm unhinged. Nothing but a hysterical woman.'

She felt both wounded and offended. 'I know I don't always stay in my lane, as Douglas likes to put it. I prefer to call it getting to the truth, without fear or favour. Isn't that our – the police and the legal profession's – joint responsibility?'

'Bright has looked into you. Your career. Past cases. Your background, personal history. He wants to know why you weren't charged with carrying a concealed weapon on Uist. He suggested I'd been involved in a cover-up. To be fair, he has a point.'

Oh, Fuckity Fuck. 'It was my fishing knife. I'd forgotten it was in the pocket of my jacket. If I hadn't had it on me, I might have been killed.'

'I'm aware of that.' Du Toit said tightly. 'That's why I didn't make a big deal of it.'

'How did DI Bright find out?' Rachel asked.

'He used his connections – apparently he's friendly with the chief superintendent – to access my report.'

What a weasel. 'I'm sorry, Kirk. The last thing I wanted was to drop you in it.'

Thank God no one knew about the other time she'd pulled a knife. Except Mags. Jesus, what if Jason Bright found that out too? Was that behind the hidden message on the record player?

A cold sweat broke out across Rachel's skin. What if he was determined to continue digging into her past? Eric had hinted he'd uncovered her secret. What if Bright had too? In which case she was screwed. Her career would be over before it truly got off the ground.

'Any news regarding Eric Hunter?' she asked.

'No. My colleagues are still looking.'

'It's been too long. He needs to be found. How can someone in an orange camper van disappear from the face of the earth? Are they checking ANPRs for his registration?'

'My colleagues know what they are doing,' Du Toit said edgily. 'Of course they've checked for sightings of his number plate and vehicle.'

'It's not enough! There must be a way of pinpointing the story he was following. He was a journalist. He would have kept notes.' In her heart she knew the outcome was not going to be good, but she wasn't going to give up until she knew for certain what had happened to Eric.

'You know as well as I do, we can't access his internet without probable cause.'

'I think Eric is dead,' she said, uncomfortably aware of the ache in her voice. 'And I don't think it will be as a result of a fall. Someone broke into my house and ransacked it, attacking Mags along the way. I think the same people might have harmed Eric. What happens if they target Eric's wife, Ella? Her kids? You have to offer them some protection.'

Du Toit gave a regretful shake of his head. 'You know as well as I do, we simply don't have the officers to spare. Even if we had, there's no good reason to think she's in danger. The best I can do is to ask a patrol car to go past every now and again.'

Rachel wasn't satisfied. She stood, preparing to leave.

'One more thing before you go,' Du Toit said. 'Where did you get DI Bright's address? Think before you reply.'

'I can't tell you,' Rachel said.

'Let me guess. DC MacDonald.' He gave a disapproving shake of his head. 'When Selena joined CID, I warned you against using her as your personal officer. She's having difficulties settling in. Don't drag her down with you.'

Ouch. 'That isn't fair. I'd never do anything to harm her career.'

'Don't pretend to be naive. That offends me. Your actions have consequences for the people who love you or want to protect you. Be careful you don't sacrifice us on the altar of your personal crusades and obsessions.' He drained his pint and set his empty glass on the table with a thunk. 'I suggest you think on what I've said. You have to leave this alone. If you won't, I'll have to go over your head and speak to Miss Plover.'

Rachel struggled to contain her fury. She held his gaze until he turned to leave.

'And I suggest you listen to me and think seriously about getting Ella Hunter and her children under police protection,' she said his back. Du Toit stopped and shook his head before continuing out the door.

TWENTY-ONE

Feeling as if she'd had the crap beaten out of her, as soon as she got back to her cottage in Clachnaharry, Rachel changed out of her jeans and T-shirt, dragged her duvet onto the sofa, plonked a bottle of vodka, some tonic and a packet of tortilla chips on the table and curled up to watch her current favourite video on YouTube. It was one of those train videos she'd discovered recently. There was something soothing about the clickety-clack of wheels on rails, the view from the driver's cockpit, the monotony of the passing landscape. And she needed soothing as well as something to divert her from going over that afternoon's events.

She'd never seen Du Toit so livid. He'd always been courteous and respectful of her position. That afternoon, he'd spoken to her as if she were a badly behaved spoilt child, and it smarted. Particularly as she had silently agreed with him that she'd crossed a boundary. Done what everyone was always accusing her of doing – allowed her heart to rule her head. Maybe, like he'd suggested, she *was* reckless, playing fast and loose with the lives and careers of people who cared about her.

She took another swig of her vodka, enjoying the burn as it

slid down her throat, hitting her bloodstream with a pleasant buzz a few moments later.

As for accusing her of exploiting Selena, recklessly pursuing her own agenda...

She splashed more vodka into her glass.

If she were honest, there was at least a smidgen of truth in what Du Toit had said. She *was* emotionally involved.

The last two cases she'd been involved in had taken their toll. Had made her question herself. The first case, the one in Uist, where she'd pulled her fishing knife on someone, wasn't the first inkling she'd inherited her father's violent nature. But she'd been able to explain it away to herself. She'd feared for her life. A murderer, who'd killed before, his last victim right in front of her, had planned to kill her too.

But pulling the knife on the drunks? That was different. That was breaking the law. If it ever came out, it might cost her her career. And given her past record, it might even put her in prison. What had she been thinking, going back to see Bright. Had she just made a prize ass of herself? Very bloody likely. It was as if there was a wind-up motor in her chest, propelling her forward, constantly stopping her from relaxing. Her heart was racing even now, making it difficult to breathe. She took several slow inhales and exhales to get it under control.

The last time she'd faced off with a murderer, there had been a moment, albeit a split second only, when she'd realised she would have let him be killed by the mother of the child he'd kidnapped if it had led to finding the little girl before she'd drowned. Thank God she'd drawn back from the brink at the last minute.

Was psychopathy genetic? Was something inside her hardening? Lately it felt as if she were growing a shell, like a bloody crab, ready to retreat into it if anyone got too close. Maybe that was a good sign. The harder the shell, the less the pain. But was it what she wanted?

Her inability to form close relationships – with men and women – the feeling of being an outsider – being on the periphery of her life – an observer rather than a participant, was a lonely place to be. She had a deep longing for connection. And that was the problem. Take Uist, for example. She'd almost fallen for a guy who turned out to be a murderer!

Great instincts. Not.

But, she told herself, she had good points too. Any moment now she'd remember what they were. Right now she felt too sleepy to think clearly.

Rachel jerked awake from her usual nightmare. In it she'd been injected with a paralysing agent before being flung into the river. She'd been underwater – completely and horrifically powerless, staring into the empty eyes of a corpse.

Now someone was banging at her door.

She'd dozed off with the video still streaming on her phone. A shaft of sunlight split the room in two, landing on her face and almost blinding her when she opened her eyes. She groaned and squinted at her phone. Seven o'clock. In the evening. Still Sunday. She peered at the coffee table. No wonder her head ached. She'd polished off the best part of half a bottle. It had been a while since she'd craved the oblivion of alcohol and she was paying for her lapse. Her mouth felt like a camel's armpit. She must have been sleeping with it wide open. She staggered to the door and opened it, only just remembering to check the feed on her phone before she did.

Angus! Of course it was. She groaned. The man had a genius for pitching up unannounced when she looked like shit. Sometimes she imagined a neon sign floating over her house with flashing lights in the shape of a pointed finger encouraging everyone in the area to pop in to see the sad single woman.

Perhaps there should be one saying visitors only welcome by appointment?

She knew she looked a state. The baggy joggers she wore as pyjamas sagged at the bottom as well as the hips, and her T-shirt was paint splattered. Her mascara was bound to be all over her face and she was barefoot. There was no disguising her bruised and battered toes. Her hair was screwed into a messy bun at the top of her head, her eyes in all probability bloodshot. She smothered another groan.

On the other side of the scale, Angus was a sight for sore eyes. She squinted at him through one eye. This was the off-duty Angus – not the professional, dark-suited, white shirt and polished brogues one. He was wearing a fitted white T-shirt that emphasised his lean frame and broad shoulders. Jeans worn low on his hips emphasised his long legs and thighs toned from years of climbing. His tousled hair and stubble made him better looking in Rachel's eyes – less perfect, less model like. It wasn't fair, Rachel thought, that her childhood friend could look so good without apparently even trying. She'd known Angus since she was six and he nine, they'd gone climbing and fishing together with their fathers.

Aware of how she looked in contrast, her approving appraisal turned to irritation. She'd half a mind to close the door on him. That might encourage him to let her know when he was coming.

'Have you heard of phone calls – or texts even?' she snarled. Why was he here anyway? 'You might as well come in.' She spun on her heel leaving him to follow – or not.

'Good evening to you too!' he said, following her into the sitting room. 'But I did text you from Edinburgh. Said I was coming to see you. Didn't you get it?'

She checked her phone. There it was. It must have arrived when she was passed out. Her embarrassment deepened as she took in the crumpled duvet on the sofa, the crumbs of tortilla chips on the coffee table, the half-full glass of vodka.

It was too late to do anything about it. Instead she grabbed the vodka bottle and waved it at him. 'Join me?'

'No, I'm driving.' Brilliantly blue eyes raked her from top to toe. 'Are you OK?'

'Perfectly fine. Why do you ask? Don't I look OK?' Aware of the belligerent tone in her voice, she picked up the glass she'd been drinking from earlier, took a swig and hiccupped. 'Why are you here?'

'I heard about the break-in, Rachel.'

Was no one apart from her capable of keeping anything to themselves? She squinted at him. 'Who told you?'

'Word gets around.' Of course it did. The legal world was a small one. He glanced around the room. 'I was expecting chaos.'

'I had help tidying up.' Then she thought about what he'd said.

'You came all the way from Edinburgh to see I was OK?' She was touched. Angus's feelings for her – if he had any – had always been an unknown. Their friendship had revolved around climbing, mostly in silence, always competitive. Until they'd had sex. Never repeated. To her lingering disappointment. Something he could never know.

'Is that so crazy?'

'Why does everyone insist on treating me as if I need protecting?' she grumbled, aware she was blushing. 'I'm perfectly able to look after myself.' Only she knew exactly how much.

'Touché. Anyone who knows you would realise that the best thing they can do is to keep their distance from you,' he said, his eyes creasing at the corners. 'A Bully XL needs more protecting than you. Why are you always so damn prickly?'

Rachel took another slug of vodka, knowing she was in danger of losing control. 'Don't fucking patronise me.' She glared at him and he glared back. They'd had fights before, usually on the mountain when they'd argued about what routes to take, or when he'd insisted she wasn't ready for a particular climb and she'd disagreed.

Suddenly, a grin spread across his face as if he too had been transported back in time. He gave a shout of laughter. 'God, I never thought I'd say this, but I miss hanging out with you.'

What a load of bullshit. If he'd missed hanging out with her, he'd had plenty of opportunities to rectify that. She took another slug of vodka. That was a mistake. Her head started to spin again. Did he have to look so bloody good? Memories pushed their unwelcome way into her head. The climb up Braeriach in the middle of winter. The scrape of their boots, climbing in sync as they'd done so often there was no need to talk. The freezing mist coming down. Enveloping them, wiping out visibility. Knowing it wouldn't lift before dark, the decision to pitch a tent. The pair of them squeezed in together. Lying side by side in their respective sleeping bags, touching along one side. The palpable tension between them. She couldn't remember who had turned to face whom first, or who had made the first move. But she remembered in minute detail what had followed. Peeling the clothes off each other while unzipping their sleeping bags. The feel of skin on skin, the hardness of muscle under her fingertips, the feel of his hands running over her. Now, she had an uncontrollable desire to wrap her arms around his neck. She'd done that before. Years ago. During her father's trial. She'd been drunk then too. He'd knocked her back and he hadn't even had a girlfriend then. But jeez, it had been a while since she'd had sex. She swayed towards him.

'How's Miss Do Good, or whatever she's called,' she said. 'Still saving the world, one person at a time?' She winced inside. That was particularly catty by anyone's standards. Clearly she was even more pissed than she'd realised. She put her glass down with a clunk.

'Amanda and I have split up. I discovered something about her I couldn't get past.'

'What was that then? She snores? Farts in company?' The sober part of her was appalled by the words coming out of her mouth. But the drunken part was delighted at her wit. Why couldn't she be more like this without the help of booze? Her woozy brain spiralled back to what he'd said. He'd broken up with the latest squeeze. That meant he was available.

Nothing ventured, nothing gained.

She took a step towards him. Now there was only an inch of air between them and when she swayed, there was less than that. The room was spinning, making it difficult to focus. If he'd hang onto her, tether her to the shifting floor, that would help.

As the room tilted again, she reached for him, missing his neck and landing against him, her arms around his waist. It felt good, particularly when he wrapped his arms around her. She tilted her face in his direction. It was too far above her to reach easily, so she stood on tiptoes, which was a big mistake as she swayed again and was forced to hook her arm around his neck to remain upright. He was smiling down at her and she pursed her lips and looked up at him, waiting for his kiss. 'Shall we go through to my room,' she slurred with what she hoped was a wicked twinkle in her eye.

Instead he reached up and removed her arm from around his neck. 'As much as I'd like to sleep with you, I'm going to give it a miss.'

Rachel wasn't so drunk that she didn't flush with embarrassment.

'S'OK,' she slurred. 'I'm not looking for rings – I mean strings.' Oh crap. And as if it could have got any worse, she realised she was going to be sick.

.   .   .

The next thing Rachel knew she was waking up in her bed. If her mouth had been dry before, it was nothing like it was now. She imagined this was what a fish felt after it had been plucked from the water. She checked her phone: 06:00. She was expected at the office by nine and had a full schedule of work in front of her, including a meeting with Greg Berkeley, the genealogist Alison had put her in touch with. Thank God she had a few hours to get her head together.

She groaned as bits of the evening came back in spurts and flashes. Angus had come over, that much she remembered. He'd broken up with his girlfriend – she remembered that too. After that it was all a series of stomach-clenching images. Literally. Her folded over the toilet bowl. Angus holding her hair back as she vomited.

Oh God, at one point, hopefully before she'd been sick, she'd decided to seduce him.

She opened one eye. She was still wearing what she had been the evening before, so it was unlikely they'd had sex. Did that mean he'd turned her down? Not that she could blame him. She moaned again. How the hell was she ever going to look him in the eyes after this?

There was a glass of water beside her bed and she drank it greedily, spilling it when she jumped as the door opened and a dark head appeared.

Angus smiled at her. As if last night had never happened.

'Coffee?' he asked.

Rachel resisted the impulse to pull the duvet over her head and stay there for the rest of her sorry life. Instead she sat up and smiled as if they were guests at the same dinner party.

'You stayed?' she croaked, after a sip of strong, hot coffee.

'I didn't think I should leave you alone. After you were sick, you passed out. I had to carry you to bed. If your intruder had returned, you'd have been defenceless.'

'Oh please! Are you telling me you stayed to fight them off.'

His smile widened. 'Of course.'

Rachel couldn't bear to ask what he'd done when she'd come on to him.

'I was very flattered, Rachel,' he continued, apparently reading her mind. 'But I've never slept with a woman who wasn't fully able to give consent. I kipped on the sofa. I could have done with it being a bit longer but, as you know, I've slept in tighter spots.'

Oh, for God's sake. Strike two. He'd rejected her advances for the second time. She was never, ever going to drink in his company again. She was never going to drink again. Alcohol solved nothing. On the contrary, it made matters worse. It felt as if she were blushing from the tips of her toes to the roots of her hair.

'Thanks for looking after me,' she mumbled, acutely aware she sounded less than gracious.

'Do you think you can eat?' Angus said. 'I've been to the shops – you really need to keep your fridge better stocked, by the way – and bought rolls and bacon. I find that does it for me when I have a hangover.'

She wasn't sure she could eat anything. She sat up, relieved the action didn't make her nauseous. 'Let me get in the shower and we can take it from there.'

As it turned out, rolls, stuffed with crispy bacon and washed down with several mugs of strong, black coffee were exactly what Rachel needed. She and Angus sat outside at her table in the garden, looking out to sea, watching the sun dance on the flat calm water and talking about climbs they had taken together and apart. It was one of those perfectly clear mornings where they could see Braeriach in the distance, ironically the same mountain they'd had sex on. Rachel wondered if Angus had clocked it too and was thinking the same thing.

If he was, he gave no sign of it. They moved on to trials where he'd been senior counsel for the defence in a number of high-profile cases – most of them covered by the press – which had meant Angus had become a minor celebrity. He had a reputation for being ruthless in court and was expected to be appointed as a King's Counsel in the next couple of years.

'I like being in court,' she told him. Like climbing, talking about work was safe ground. 'I wasn't sure I would enjoy being the centre of everyone's attention. Particularly when the press keeps going over my history every chance they get. How do you cope with it? You're always in the papers.' She slanted a glance at him. 'And not just because of work.'

He shrugged. 'I'm used to it. The firm likes it. It's good for business. The criminals know where to come.'

'I imagine it helps that you haven't any skeletons in your closet.' Whereas she had so many there was no room for more. Yet they kept appearing.

'I don't know why you think that. It's true I've mostly been a good boy, the dutiful son. But it was easy for me. I had two loving parents who were always around to guide me. Then at uni I was too focused on getting the best degree possible to get into serious trouble. I've had my moments, though. No one gets through life without them. I've sailed close to the wind more than once. I've had to, in order to win.' He picked up a small, flat stone and flung it over the wall and into the sea. It skipped three times before sinking. 'You should give yourself more credit. You're making a name for yourself, although I have to admit opinion in law circles is somewhat divided as to whether that's in a good way.'

Rachel picked up a stone of her own and, drawing her arm back, sent it spinning across the water. To her delight it skipped five times. She shot Angus a look of triumph.

'What are they saying?' Rachel asked, although she could imagine.

'That you cross lines that shouldn't be crossed. That you get results. That you're fearless. That you're reckless. Other stuff too.'

This wasn't what she wanted to hear. It was important Du Toit and her law colleagues didn't view her as a loose cannon.

'What other stuff?'

'I'm not sure you want to know.'

Rachel wasn't sure either. At least not today. Her head ached. It was as if a small army of ants armed with hammers were pounding her skull from the inside.

After they'd finished their rolls, Angus turned to Rachel. 'I came here last night, partly to check you were OK, but also because I thought you needed to know that your father was attacked in prison yesterday. I didn't want to tell you last night, when you were pissed and clearly still reeling from the break-in.'

'Is Dad OK?' She said, startled. As always mention of her father, brought mixed feelings, mostly negative, although she had to acknowledge – painful though it was to admit – that buried deep inside, a kernel of love remained. Her stomach churned.

'So I understand. He was slashed across the face. Luckily a guard was in the vicinity and found your father moments after the attack. He had to have stitches, was observed overnight, but didn't require hospitalisation. He's asked to see you.'

'Last time I visited, he told me not to come back.'

Angus shrugged. 'I'm only the messenger.'

'Don't you think that's quite a coincidence? Dad's attacked, my house broken into, my neighbour left unconscious on my floor. I also got this text the night it happened.' She found the message and passed her phone to Angus so he could read it. She wasn't going to tell him about the record though.

He frowned. 'I hope you're going to tell me you reported it to the police.'

'I was with a police officer when I got it. She's going to try and trace the number it came from. I received a similar threatening text a few weeks ago. I assumed back then it was from the murderer I was after at the time, but what if it wasn't? What if both that text and this one came from the same person?'

She eased the tension from her shoulders. 'I think someone wants me to stop looking into the sex-trafficking case. Maybe even a police officer.'

She explained her thinking.

'Christ! I wouldn't have given you the transcripts if I'd thought there was any chance it would put you in danger. Maybe you should move into a hotel for a bit,' Angus said.

Rachel shook her head. 'No one is going to make me leave my home. 'Besides, a friend put up some CCTV cameras for me yesterday morning.'

Angus still looked dubious. 'I don't like it, Rachel. Up until now, you've got away with confronting the bad guys by the skin of your teeth. You won't always be so lucky. I'm deadly serious. Let this go.'

'Do you really think I'm going to do nothing while someone tries to shut me up?' She gave an exasperated sigh. She was fed up with people telling her to back off. It was the equivalent of running away. 'Instead of telling me what to do, I want you to look into my father's defence. I know there will be stuff that didn't come out at trial, and I want to know what it is.'

'I'm not sure I should.'

'If you don't, I'll find someone who will. Maybe someone I don't trust as much as I trust you.'

He glanced at his watch. 'Hell is that the time. I have court this afternoon and prep to do beforehand. 'Anything else I can do?' He'd conceded more easily than she thought he would.

'Yes, as a matter of fact. DI Bright discovered I had a knife on me when I was in Uist. If he manages to persuade his pal in the force to charge me, I'll be in deep trouble. I might even need you to defend me.' To her embarrassment – as if she wasn't mortified enough – her voice shook a little.

Angus gave a bemused shake of his head. 'Why do you have to make life so difficult for yourself?'

'It was my gutting knife – I forgot it was in my pocket from the last time I went fishing.'

'What did the police report say?'

'I don't know exactly. I think Du Toit tried to fudge things to help me out.'

'If you retain me as your lawyer, I'll ask for it to be quashed. Anything else?'

Not that she wanted to admit. At least not at this point. 'That's it for the time being.'

He raised his eyebrows, a smile hovering on his lips. 'So I work for you now?'

'If you want to see it that way. As long as you don't expect to get paid.' She returned his smile with one of her own. 'And while you're setting about the tasks I've assigned you, I'm going to get in touch with the prison to arrange a visit with my father.'

TWENTY-TWO

With the help of breakfast and a couple of paracetamol, her headache was receding by the time Rachel reached the office. Her first meeting of the day was with Greg Berkeley, the genealogist Alison had put her in touch with.

Greg was a small, neat man who could have easily been a professor in his gold rimmed glasses. He was wearing light-coloured chinos and an open-necked shirt.

He'd been happy to meet Rachel at the Ministry of Justice and she'd come down to the foyer to greet him once he passed through the metal detector.

'Can I buy you a coffee?' she asked. Fortunately the ministry's café, barely a café – a few long, rectangle white plastic tables and benches, but serving coffees and toasties for staff who didn't have the time nor inclination to pop out for coffee or lunch – was quiet. Rachel bought a black coffee for herself and a black tea for him. He refused her offer of a scone with cream or a muffin to go with it.

'I hope I haven't dragged you away from work,' Greg said, 'but I thought it was better to explain what we do in person, not just in this case but for any cases you might have in the future.

We are making strides both with the identification of criminals as well as the identification of missing persons.'

'I'm delighted to have an excuse to leave my desk for a while.' Rachel said truthfully.

The case she was currently working on was a simple assault she didn't expect would make its way to court because the witnesses kept withdrawing their statements. It had been cancelled several times already and she had the sinking feeling that the chief witness, the man who had been assaulted, would change his mind about appearing, leaving his attackers free to continue their thuggish attacks, possibly going on to commit a more serious assault. Never mind the countless wasted hours of police time, as well as her own.

She pushed the depressing thought away and concentrated on what Greg had to say.

'What do you know about GEDmatch?' he asked.

'Nothing,' Rachel admitted.

'I'm assuming you know about the commercial sites. Maybe used them yourself?'

'I've heard about Ancestry.com, although I've never used it. I'm not particularly interested in tracing my ancestors,' she added with a smile.

'It's the biggest of the commercial sites. There's around six at the moment and the numbers are increasing. They all operate in much the same way. Someone buys a kit from any of the sites, takes a swab from inside their cheek, posts if off and, lo and behold, a few weeks later they will have their DNA profile, their ethnicity estimate, relationships with anyone they share DNA with and how close that relationship is. To put it simply, how many genes they have in common determines the closeness of their relationship. Of course, finding a match is only possible if their relative is using the same site. Are you following me so far?'

Rachel nodded.

'People who want to improve their chances of finding family links can upload their DNA profile to the GEDmatch database. It's free, so lots of people sign up to use the service. But whereas the commercial sites don't share information, GED match allows the police to access users' DNA profiles.' He took a sip of his tea before continuing. 'It does this via GEDmatch PRO, a database which is currently accessible only to law enforcement. It makes it possible to look up the DNA of anyone arrested, DNA found at crime scenes, DNA from missing persons or, as in your case, DNA from unidentified bodies or body parts, as well as DNA profiles from individuals registered with commercial genealogy sites who've given permission for their information to be shared. This way we can link an exponentially large number of DNA profiles.

'As you can imagine, it's an extremely useful tool for law enforcement.' He gave Rachel a brief smile. 'This is how the Golden State killer was found. You may be aware, this was the American serial killer who'd escaped capture for decades until he was caught via a DNA match.

'I've also had some success linking unidentified bodies and body parts – of which there are a surprising number – to family members. Of course, as you'll appreciate, actually tracking down close relatives isn't always possible and is very time consuming.' He gave a little cough. 'However, I must admit it's the part of the job I enjoy the most. I find it a bit like finishing a *Times* crossword or a fiendish sudoku, and if it helps bring criminals to justice or gives closure to families whose loved one has disappeared, that is particularly rewarding.'

Rachel's hangover headache was getting worse again.

'Do you know there is new technology called Massively Parallel Sequencing, MPS for short, that can provide visual traits of criminals from the DNA they leave at a crime scene, allowing investigators to predict gender, biogeographical ancestry, eye colour and, in the near future, hair colour. Of course, at the moment it's very expensive, but it will get cheaper and more precise. Eventually there will be nowhere for criminals to hide.' He gave her a warm smile.

Rachel drifted a little as he went through a number of complicated scenarios and examples. She had a ton of work to catch up with.

'Unfortunately, I didn't find a link for your John Doe on GEDmatch. So I've uploaded his DNA results to the two biggest sites, Ancestry and 23andme. I'm still hopeful we might get a hit there.'

'Any idea how long that might take?' asked Rachel.

He gave a cheerful smile. 'None. But as soon as I hear, I'll be in touch.'

TWENTY-THREE

That evening Selena and Rachel were in Rachel's garden with cold Cokes and a bag of crisps and dips. Selena's feet were propped up on a wicker garden chair. She'd popped in to check how Rachel was doing. Rachel was touched. She'd spent the day at work, slogging through her backlog while coping with the hangover from hell. In some ways both had been a welcome distraction from her worry about Eric and her embarrassment about the night before. She'd used her position with the COPFS to arrange a short notice visit to her father the next afternoon. The thought of coming face to face with him repelled her, but if he knew anything about what was going on – who was behind the assault on him and the break in at her place and if it was linked to Eric's disappearance, she needed to know.

She turned her face to the sun. 'Have you heard from your PC?' she asked Selena.

'Joe?' Selena replied, a dreamy expression in her eyes. 'He rang me yesterday. We went to the pub. We have a lot in common: Country and Western music, *Line of Duty*, reading thrillers, walking on the beach... I really like him.'

Mags popped her head over the fence. 'I thought I heard

voices out here.' Rachel winced. Mags' face was a bruised and battered mess.

She'd been discharged early that morning. Her daughter had offered to stay over a couple of nights, but Mags had insisted she'd be fine on her own. 'It'd drive me mad, having her underfoot,' she'd told Rachel when she rang at lunchtime to see how she was doing. At least mother and daughter were talking once more.

Mags peered at Rachel, a big grin on her face. 'Your man gone then? I have to say, ah wouldn't mind being humped by him.'

'I wasn't humped by him,' Rachel said with an inward groan. 'He turned me down, actually. Not that it's any of your business.'

Selena widened her eyes at Rachel. 'Who?' she mouthed. Rachel gave a shake of her head in return.

'I've telt you often enough that you need to make an effort,' Mags continued. 'Put some make-up oan. Get a low-cut top. Show off your breasts – little pancakes that they are.'

'Thanks for the advice, Mags. I'll bear that in mind,' Rachel said. She wore make-up to the office – mascara and nude lipstick, a bit more on a night out– but didn't bother when she was at home.

'Are you going to let me in?' Mags continued. 'Hey, maybe we should put a gate in the wall. That would make life easier. Save me banging on your door and you not replying.'

That was not going to happen.

'How are you, Mags?' Selena asked. 'Feeling OK?'

'Never better. Getting bashed in the heid by some arsehole isnae going to change what I do. It just makes me mair determined.'

'Maybe you should have called the police instead of going after him,' Selena ventured.

'Ahm going to remind you it wasnae me that went looking

for a fight.' Mags jerked her thumb in Rachel's direction. 'I was looking after her, wasn't I? God only knows what would have happened to her if she'd come home and found him in her hoose. She and trouble are best mates, if you ask me.'

Rachel wished people would stop saying that about her. She resisted the impulse to remind Mags that she was at least half her age, as well as half her weight – definitely more muscle than fat these days – and, as she'd proved more often than she would have liked, able to hold her own in a fight.

'I'm assuming you've got no plans the night, Rachel,' Mags said.

'I don't,' Rachel replied, trying not to feel miffed that her neighbour guessed she hadn't.

'In that case, I need you to come somewhere with me.' She made a strange jerking movement with her head in the direction of town and winked, implying not very convincingly that it was somewhere hush-hush. 'No need to get dressed up, although you might want to put on some make-up. For crying out loud, how do either of you hope to get a man if you don't make an effort?'

Perhaps Mags had a point, Rachel thought, eyeing her bare feet that hadn't had a pedi in at least a year. Climbing left her with bruised toes and blackened nails. She hadn't been to the hairdresser for months either, now she thought about it. Although there was little anyone could do to tame her curly hair.

'As a matter of fact, I do have a man,' Selena said to Mags, her eyes sparkling with amusement. She looked at her phone. 'He's going to meet me when I leave here.'

She was in the best mood Rachel had seen her in for a while. How much PC Adamson had to do with it, Rachel didn't know. Quite a bit, she suspected. Hopefully the teasing at work would stop soon.

'Where are you taking me?' Rachel asked Mags.

'You'll find out when you get there.' Mags smiled, exposing the gap where her missing tooth had yet to be replaced. 'Will an hour be enough for you to get ready?'

'Give me five minutes,' Rachel replied.

Fifteen minutes later, the three of them were walking along the canal, Selena and Rachel on either side of Mags. To keep Mags happy, Rachel had put on some lipstick and mascara and exchanged her leggings for a pair of jeans.

It had clouded over but the afternoon's warmth lingered in the air. They cut through the park, turning left before they reached the harbour, and walked in the direction of the town centre.

'Have you caught the bugger who did this to me yet?' Mags asked Selena, pointing to her temple.

'Give us a chance! But we will get him. Don't worry.'

Mags nudged Rachel in the side with her elbow. 'Are you no worried he'll come back?'

'That's why I installed cameras,' Rachel replied. 'Besides, I know there's another pair of eyes watching out for me. Yours.'

'Have you heard from Gentleman Tim?' Selena asked Mags. 'I'm sorry about what happened. I would have left him in peace where he was, but my boss reminded me it wasn't legal.'

'He couldn't really stay in what might have turned out to be a crime scene,' Rachel said. 'Did he manage to find another place, Mags?'

Mags harrumphed. 'It's not as if there's a choice of weather-proof buildings out there. And he's no as young as he was. I telt him he could bide with me while social found a place for him. He stayed the night and was gone the next morning. I wasnae surprised, to be honest. Tim likes living the way he does.'

Rachel noticed a familiar figure coming towards them. 'Isn't that your Joe?' she asked Selena.

Selena smiled, looking puzzled. 'Sure is. I wonder where he's heading?'

Mags had paled. 'Have you met him before?' Rachel asked sotto voce as Selena moved forward to meet Joe.

'Aye. Once or twice. The last time was aboot five years ago. Bugger arrested me.' She tugged on Rachel's arm. 'Let's leave them to it. I don't want either of them to see where we're going.'

They said their goodbyes and left Selena and Joe on the towpath.

'Where *are* we going?' Rachel asked as they approached the town centre. Mags had been unusually quiet since they'd parted ways with Selena and Joe.

'Back to the pub I took you to before. I was in for a bevvy the night I got bashed. I found a woman who thinks she knows your dead man. She's going to meet us there. It's someone I used to work with.'

'On the streets?'

'Aye. A long while back. You said the man you were asking aboot was around thirty, didn't you?'

'As far as we can guess.'

'If it's the same lad – and I'm thinking it is – Nicky thought she saw him in Inverness the day afore the body turned up. And she hadn't seen him in years.'

Rachel's pulse skipped a beat. 'Was she sure? Did this Nicky speak to him?'

'She tried to. But he seemed in a rush. Upset. He brushed her off.'

'Do you have a name?'

'Look, you can ask Nicky yerself.'

They'd come to the door of the pub Mags had brought Rachel to before. The same heavyset man was standing guard. He nodded and opened the door for them to enter. 'I told her I was bringing you.'

It was busier than it had been the last time Mags had

brought her here, with more of a night-time crowd, and the fuggy atmosphere was even thicker tonight. Mags led the way to where a woman with long, grey hair tied in a ponytail was sitting with two other women. When Mags approached, the other women got up and sat at another table.

'This is Nicky.' Mags introduced the woman. 'Nicky, this is Rachel. Now, what can I get you both to drink?' Nicky asked for a whisky and Rachel asked for Diet Coke. This wasn't the sort of establishment that served lattes.

Mags reached out. 'If you give me a tenner, that should cover it.'

Rachel handed over the cash and sat down opposite Nicky.

'Thank you for agreeing to talk to me,' Rachel said.

'I wouldn't normally talk to the law, but Mags convinced me.'

'Tell me about the man you saw.'

'Wee John?'

'Was that his name?'

'It was when I knew him. Mind you, this was about thirteen, maybe fourteen years ago. They called him Wee John back then. Because he was so young – a kid really, and not very tall.'

Their John Doe was around five eleven. That didn't necessarily rule him out. Didn't men have a growth spurt around fifteen or sixteen?

'What about a surname?'

Nicky shook her head. 'No one knows anyone's surnames. Hardly known by their Christian name either, for that matter. Especially if they were a runaway like John and didn't want anyone snitch on them to the police, who would have tried to take them back to their family.'

So John had a troubled past.

'He used to hang out the streets. Pimp himself,' Nicky went on.

Just like Louis – Rachel's friend from the streets – then. For a second, Rachel was catapulted back to the times she and Louis had huddled under the bridge, Louis doing his best to make time pass with his jokes. Leaving her alone while he went in search of punters. He'd left home because his step-father didn't want him around. His mother hadn't cared enough to try and stop him. When Rachel had run away, she'd thought her father would move heaven and earth to find her and beg her to come home. He hadn't. They'd never spoken about that time. She would have searched night and day had she been the parent.

'What else do you know about him?' she asked Nicky, dragging her thoughts away from the painful memories. It was the present that mattered. At least she was a step closer to finding who their John Doe was.

'Not a lot. He was only on the street for a few weeks. Then apparently he found someone to look after him. A punter who took a real shine to him and wanted exclusive access, if you know what I mean?'

'You mean this punter set John up in a place of his own?'

'That's what he said when I last saw him. The last time before last week, I mean. The punter was much older than Wee John. And married.'

If John had moved into high-end escorting it might explain why he was so well groomed and expensively dressed.

'Did John tell you his name?'

'He said he had to keep it to himself. Otherwise he could get the punter into real trouble. I got the impression he was in the polis. Or the law. Or a politician. He came here once with John. Only stayed a minute. I'd seen him before, maybe on telly or in the paper. Whoever he was, he definitely had money to splash. After John met him he started dressing all fancy.'

The possibility he was in a relationship with a member of law enforcement was another dimension. A whole new can of worms.

'Did John say where this flat was that the man moved him into?'

'Not in Inverness. He might have mentioned Edinburgh, but I can't be sure. All I know is that John moved away and I didn't see him again until last week.'

Was Edinburgh where his home was? Rachel made a mental note to follow up the purchase of the shoes with Selena.

'Tell me about that. Are you sure it was him?'

'Almost sure. He was taller than I remembered. He was in the town, crossing the Muirtown Swing Bridge when I saw him. I called out to him and he turned around. I got a good look at his face and I was even more sure it was him. But he turned around and practically ran away. I thought it was because he had gone up in the world and didn't want to be seen with me. Then Mags was asking everyone about the body that was found in the grave-yard. The way she described him made me think of Wee John straight away. Now, when I think on it, I reckon he was scared, but I might only be thinking that because he ended up dead.'

'When was this?'

'A week last Wednesday. I was on my way home from the bingo.'

So two days before his body was found. The night he'd spent as an uninvited guest of Gentleman Tim's.

'Did the John you know have any distinguishing marks?'

'A tattoo on his upper arm. Of Scotland. Including the islands. I always thought it was an odd thing to put on your arm, but young folk have their ways.'

It was highly likely that Wee John and their John Doe were one and the same.

Had he remained with his punter, or moved on? Judging by the way he'd been dressed, he had money to spend. Perhaps he'd got a well-paying job.

But in that case, Rachel would have expected colleagues to have reported him missing.

And if their John Doe had been important to someone, why hadn't that person reported him missing? Unless, of course, they had something to do with his death.

It was frustrating. They needed John's full name. Every day that passed was another day his loved ones didn't know he was dead. While they waited for GEDmatch to come back to them or Alison to track down the manufacturer of the plate in his arm, there had to be other ways of finding out.

She needed Alison to chase up toxicology. They didn't know yet if John had been killed or died by accident or design.

'Did you ever meet a woman called Monika Troka? She was from Albania,' Rachel asked.

'Let me think.' Nicky took a sip of her drink before shaking her head. 'Nope, soz.'

Although Rachel continued to quiz Nicky, she had nothing else to add. Eventually Rachel decided it was time to leave. Mags walked her to the door.

'Well then, did ony of that help?'

Rachel smiled at her next-door neighbour. 'It was very helpful. Great intel. Worth a pay rise, if I paid you in the first place, that is.'

A blush stole up Mags's cheeks and she scowled. 'I telt you you needed me, didn't I?'

TWENTY-FOUR

After Mags had gone back inside the pub, Rachel texted Selena to ask if she was at home. When she got a reply in the affirmative, she sent another saying she was on her way over.

When she got there she found Joe on Selena's sofa, swigging a can of beer.

'I'll leave you two alone, shall I?' he said, to Rachel's relief. She didn't want to tell Selena what she'd learned with him within earshot. He looked down at Selena with a smile. 'I'll bring a takeaway with me when I come over later? Chicken Jaipuri, you said.'

'And a peshwari nan while you're at it,' Selena grinned back, definitely more like her old self. Joe was clearly having a positive effect on her mood. Rachel hoped she wouldn't fall too fast and too hard but, given her own track record, she was hardly in a position to dish out romantic advice.

Selena slumped back in her chair and gave a happy sigh. 'I wonder what Mam will think of him?'

'You're thinking of introducing him to your mother? Like taking him to Uist?' That was fast.

'Obviously not tomorrow or any time soon. But maybe one day.'

'I know you have somewhere to go, so I'll get to the reason I wanted to meet.'

'I'm all ears.'

'That place Mags wanted me to go to with her is a pub, although you'd never know from the exterior. It doesn't exactly advertise itself. From what I can gather, it's where Mags and other sex workers, as well as a select number of small-time crooks, hang out when they want to avoid the police or the more serious criminals.'

'Sounds intriguing.'

'Mags introduced me to a woman there called Nicky, who thinks our John Doe might be a man she knew as Wee John. She first met him around about thirteen or fourteen years ago. He was a runaway then and a sex worker. Apparently John initially worked the streets but found someone, an older man, who moved him into a flat. Nicky saw them together once.' She leaned towards Selena. 'She thought he was someone important – a police officer, or a politician. Someone whose face she might have seen on telly or in the paper.'

Selena sat up straight. 'Maybe he was still a sex worker at the time of his death, although clearly not working the street. Possibly a high-class escort. That would be one explanation for the expensive clothes and shoes. In which case, was his death connected to his lifestyle?'

'More importantly, Nicky saw John recently,' Rachel continued. 'The Wednesday before his body was found, he was near Muirtown Swing Bridge.'

Rachel saw her own excitement reflected in Selena's eyes.

'With a bit of luck we might get him on CCTV, now we know roughly where he was and when he'd been there,' she said. What about John's protector? Rachel wondered when Selena nipped to the loo. Did he know Rachel was investigating his lover's death? Could that be the real reason behind the break-in? Had she made a mistake thinking DI Bright was behind it and the threats to her? Did she need to rethink everything she thought she knew? No. She still believed everything was linked. She just couldn't see how.

Rachel came back down to earth with a thump. She was getting ahead of herself. They still didn't know for certain John been murdered. They needed a cause of death first. Once they had that, along with his full name they'd be a giant step forward. They'd be able to get an address for him, possibly a phone number.

'I'll need to get a statement from Nicky,' Selena said, when she returned from the loo. 'In the meantime, I'll pass what you've told me on to Audrey.' She lifted her glass and clinked Rachel's. 'Well done. We're getting close to finding out who John was and what happened to him.'

TWENTY-FIVE

The next morning, before leaving for Peterhead prison, Rachel called Alison Halliday. 'I have a possible first name for our John Doe – John, ironically – but that's not much use without a surname. If he's who I think he might be, then he was a male prostitute at one time.'

'I was about to phone you,' Alison said. 'His toxicology came back. I knew you'd want to know.'

'And?'

'John had a significant dose of xylazine – or tranq, as it's better known to its users – in his system.'

'What's tranq?'

'It's a powerful sedative that's been flooding the market in the US and is becoming more common in the UK. It can be injected, inhaled, snorted or swallowed.'

'So he could have overdosed by accident?'

'It can't be ruled out. When the tox results came in I went back to look at his body and noticed what appears to be faint bruising around his mouth.'

'You didn't notice before?'

'Sometimes in cases involving smothering, bruising only appears a couple of days after death.'

'No signs of a struggle?'

'None I could see. His assailant might have been someone he trusted to get close enough to him to render him incapable of defending himself. But before you get wedded to the notion he was murdered, there is another explanation for the bruising. Rough sex. Sometimes people like to get high when having sex and either cut off their own air supply or their partner's. Apparently it heightens sensations.'

'Perhaps that's what happened and whoever he was with panicked and dumped the body,' Rachel mused. 'Might also explain why they removed John's ID.' Her mind went to the man John had met when he'd been on the street. Was it possible they were still together? If he was well known, he might have a vested interest in ensuring his name wasn't linked to John or his death.

'I've also tracked the plate in our John Doe's arm to Inverness General,' Alison continued. 'It was supplied to the hospital around fifteen years ago.'

'That fits,' Rachel said, feeling the familiar buzz of getting close to solving a problem. 'He was in Inverness then.'

'I still don't have a full name. But I gather the police are on it. Having a first name should help.'

After Rachel disconnected she leaned back in her chair and considered what this latest information might mean.

Had John died from a drug overdose after all? In which case where had the drugs come from? Had he been hiding from his dealer? Maybe not paid his debt? They needed to know more about John. Starting with a full name.

In the meantime she was expected at Peterhead prison.

TWENTY-SIX

Peterhead prison put Rachel through the same rigmarole as the last time she'd visited her father. There was nothing pleasant about the experience. First, the endless wait, as if time in prison didn't exist or matter. Then going through security, being searched, putting her phone and other valuables in a locker. Women – Rachel wondered if that included the female prison officers – were forbidden to wear under-wired bras – so a number went without, their nipples visible under their T-shirts. Then more waiting with other resigned or frustrated visitors.

As far as Rachel could tell, visitors were divided into three camps. The first was made up of wives, partners and family who looked exhausted and dispirited from having visited on too many occasions. The second group were the women for whom it was still a novelty; they thought that having a partner in prison was exciting and somehow gave them kudos in the outside world.

The third group all of their own were the bored and petulant children.

After waiting over an hour, the door at the far end opened

and Rachel's father shuffled in accompanied by a guard on either side.

Rachel caught her breath. She should have been prepared for what she saw, but she wasn't. Not at all. He'd aged in the weeks since she'd seen him. The knife wound had left a gash that ran from just below his eye and disappeared under his jawline, a ladder of thick black stiches knitting the edges together. It was clear no plastic surgeon had been involved. Quite the opposite, it looked like the work of an apprentice butcher. Pity curled behind her ribs. No one deserved to be hurt like that, no matter what they'd done.

'Rachel,' her father said by way of a greeting. 'Thank you for coming.' She searched his face, unable to work out what he was feeling. She'd always found him difficult to read.

'What the hell happened to your face? Angus told me you'd been attacked.'

He touched his cheek with a tentative fingertip and gave her a rueful smile. 'Someone decided they didn't like the look of me.'

Rachel knew there had to be more to it than that.

'When did it happen?'

'Sunday. When most people were at church.'

So the day after Rachel's house had been broken into. And the same day she'd received the text telling her she'd be next.

No way was it a coincidence.

'Someone broke into my house the night before you were knifed. My neighbour interrupted them and they attacked her. She ended up in hospital. That night I got a text. From my uninvited visitor, I suspect. Warning me off. I don't suppose you know anything about it?'

Her father's face grew even paler. But in seconds the urbane mask she knew so well was back in place. 'Do what the text says, Rachel. Keep your nose out. Stop looking. That's why I asked to see you – to tell you.'

Rachel's stomach churned. 'That's not an option.'

He sighed. 'You always were stubborn. I used to love that about you.'

His choice of words didn't escape her. Was he deliberately trying to increase the distance between them? 'When I first took you up a hill, you were three,' he continued. 'You insisted on climbing the whole way by yourself. You got to the top of Ben Macdui when you were six – without help from me. It took twelve hours to get up and down, but you never complained once.'

Rachel brushed his attempt at nostalgia aside. 'Do you know Eric Hunter? The journalist?'

'No. Should I?'

'He's missing. Has been for over a week.'

Her father looked puzzled. 'I'm afraid you're going to have to tell me why you're asking me this.'

'He was chasing a story. And from what he told me, it had to do with the trial Mum was due to testify in before she went missing. I've been looking into it too. Now Eric's missing. My home's been broken into and I get a clear warning to stop look-ing. You get attacked. It can't be co-incidence. You clearly know something. You have to tell me what is going on. What does it have to do with Mum? Or Eric?'

He jerked back as if she'd kicked him in the balls. 'I told you before, there are things it's better for you not to know. If I explain I'd be putting you directly in the path of some very dangerous people.'

'It's too late for that. I'm already in their path. Who attacked you? Why? And why are they after me?'

'I can't tell you,' he said, stony-faced.

'You have to'

He glanced over to the guard and lowered his voice 'Listen to me, Rachel. I'm not exaggerating when I tell you how ruthless these people can be. People you and I can't afford to irritate. If I had my way, you wouldn't even be on their radar. For fuck's sake! You have to stop poking around in their business.'

'I need more than that to convince me. The best way of protecting me is to tell me what's going on.' She drew a steadying breath. 'Did you come across a DI Jason Bright while you were working as a solicitor?'

He shook his head. 'If I did, I don't remember.'

'That's odd. Because there were only two DIs back then. Are you seriously telling me in your long career defending criminals you never met him? Moreover he remembers you. And not too fondly.'

Her father shrugged. 'On the whole, police don't care for criminal defence lawyers.'

'What about DC Eilidh Souter? Did you ever come across her?'

'I have no idea who that is.' He leaned forward until his face was inches away from Rachel's. She looked into eyes the colour of her own. He pointed to the wound on his cheek. 'The message – if I have to spell it out yet again – is that you and I have to leave well alone or we'll both get hurt.' His gaze darted between the guards. He lowered his voice. 'I was lucky to get off so lightly. We both were. You mustn't trust anyone. These people have contacts everywhere. Even in prison – especially in prison. Even among the staff. They know I can't protect myself, let alone you, while I'm in here.'

Rachel's heart hammered in her chest. Was he telling her someone else was responsible for her mother's death and that he knew who it was? Had she spent years hating a man who had sacrificed his freedom to protect her? Did she have her father to thank that she hadn't vanished of the face of the earth like Eric?

And was her search for the truth putting her father's life in danger?

It was a crazy thought. But if it *were* true, she had to get him out of prison. That would take months, even years – supposing there was any truth in what he was insinuating. And supposing the gang hadn't killed them both in the meantime.

She'd have to accept that for the time being her father would have to stay in prison. Where he was clearly vulnerable – easy to get at.

Her father looked directly into her eyes as if he were trying to communicate something to her by the intensity of his gaze.

Thoughts whirled around her head. She should get his lawyer – Angus's firm – to request he was put in solitary confinement. He'd be safe there.

When she suggested that to him, an expression of horror crossed his face.

'No, Rachel. Don't do that. I couldn't bear it. I might as well be dead.' He grasped her wrist, letting go when the guard stepped forward. 'Please, I beg you, Rachel, stop searching. For my sake if not yours. If anything happens to you, I don't think I can go on. Don't come again. I won't agree to see you. Stay well away from me. Stay well away from anything your mother was involved in.'

He turned to the guard standing by the door. 'I'd like to go back to my cell now.'

Rachel stumbled to her feet. She didn't know what to think. Was her father's life at risk because he was protecting her? Or was he playing her, just as he'd done in the past? How was she to know?

Back outside, she sat in her car tapping the steering wheel with her fingertips, turning everything over in her head, before she came to a decision.

She needed to know if her father was innocent. And if he was, she needed to appeal on his behalf.

Only new evidence was grounds for an appeal.

So that's where she had to start. She needed to find evidence linking her mother's murder with the OCG ring. That was the only way she could be sure. She needed to find it fast and with as few people as possible knowing what she was up to. Only the people she would trust with her life – and her father's. Du Toit had essentially ruled himself out. That left Selena – and Angus. She wasn't ready to face Angus, so it had to be Selena.

Despite what Du Toit had said.

TWENTY-SEVEN

Selena had walked past the house Skinny Ian lived in several times since Rachel had told her about the cuckoos taking over his home. Until now, she hadn't seen anything out of the usual.

But this time was different, maybe because it was later than usual. Although it was after nine, it was still daylight. She was on the other side of the road, her beanie pulled down over her hair.

She was just approaching the house when the door opened and a smartly dressed man in a blue suit and white shirt emerged, accompanied by another man much more casually dressed in a hoodie and loose jogging trousers.

The well-dressed man said something to someone standing behind him. Selena couldn't see who. Ian, perhaps?

As she passed the house, she risked a glance behind her. Both men were getting into the driver's seat of a SUV further down the street. Selena wished she'd taken note of the vehicle registration but, if she was right about the man, he'd be back and she'd get it then.

She knew full well that she shouldn't be surveilling the house by herself and without permission. But when she'd passed on the information about the cuckoo situation to Audrey, instead of her sergeant being overcome with admiration, she had been anything but. Apparently they'd been told this before, had raided the house and found nothing. Du Toit had found the funds to provide twenty-four-hour surveillance, but nothing had come of it. No one suspicious had gone in or out over the weeks they'd watched.

Audrey said she'd pass it on to the team responsible for serious organised crime but Selena wasn't sure she believed her. When Selena had finally admitted that the information had come from Rachel via Mags, Audrey's eye-roll had been so exaggerated Selena could almost feel it.

And so she'd taken to making a detour past the house on her way to and from work. As long as no one noticed her, what harm was there?

Besides, she needed to do this. She hated the way her colleagues talked down to her, trivialising her views and opinions as if she were on work experience instead of a fully productive member of a team. The way they were treating her was starting to keep her awake at night. But if she could deliver these cuckoos to the team, they'd have to revise their opinion of her. Du Toit was kind, but Selena was too junior to have much to do with him. The person she had to impress was Audrey, and this was the only way she knew how.

TWENTY-EIGHT

Rachel pulled into the Tesco's superstore car park. Mags was in the passenger seat beside her. Rachel took her neighbour to the store every couple of weeks so she could do a 'big shop' and not have to carry it home on the bus.

Before they got out of the car, Rachel turned to Mags. 'I'll be keeping my eye on you. Anything goes into the bag without being paid for – I'll arrest you myself.'

Mags looked hurt. 'I telt you I wasnae going to do any of that anymore. And it's me who is going to be keeping my eye on you, remember?' Unable to think of a pithy reply, Rachel let the comment pass.

They were retrieving their Bags for Life from the car boot when Rachel was prodded in the shoulder.

She whirled around to find a woman in her late twenties, blond hair scraped back in a ponytail, wearing a sweatshirt frayed at the neck, jeggings, and a tormented expression, standing behind her.

'Were you having an affair with him?' the woman demanded.

Rachel glanced around, assuming the woman had mistaken

her for someone else. She jabbed Rachel again with the tip of her finger. 'I'm talking to you.'

Mags looked on, arms folded across her chest, watchful but not interfering.

'I don't believe we've met,' Rachel said stiffly.

'I know exactly who you are. Rachel bloody McKenzie, I've seen your photo in the papers. You went climbing with my husband. He had all your details on his phone. He was always talking about you. He was obsessed with you.'

'I still don't...' Rachel said. Then realisation dawned. 'Are you Ella?'

Eric was still missing. The search and rescue teams helping the police scour the area around Fort William had found no sign of him. The search was continuing, but hope of finding him alive was evaporating. Rachel desperately wanted him to be hiding out – re-appearing like a genie just when they'd given up.

'He was always sneaking out to take phone calls. Going off for days at a time, not telling me or the kids where he was going, who he was meeting, or who he was with.' She leaned towards Rachel. 'Tell me where he is!'

'I wasn't having an affair with Eric. It wouldn't have even crossed his mind. He loves you. And I don't know where he is. I wish I did!' People entering and leaving the store had stopped to stare.

'Look,' Rachel said. 'Let's go somewhere more private. Will the café in Tesco's do? Mags, you can get on with your shopping. Come and find me when you're done.'

Mags shuffled her feet, looked at Ella, looked at Rachel. 'If you're sure?'

Rachel nodded, exasperated. Despite the assault, Mags was still taking her bodyguard role to heart.

The café was busy, but Rachel managed to find a table in the corner with no one at the table next to it.

Ella asked for a coffee and Rachel bought one for each of them and brought them over to the table.

Ella emptied a packet of sugar into her mug and stirred it, looking as if she didn't quite know where she was.

'It's weird how your life feels like it's come to a stop, but the world keeps turning.' She gestured at the shoppers in the store. 'I still have to care for the kids, which means I still have to go shopping, cook, clean, get them ready for school. It all seems so banal. So pointless.'

Ella took a sip of coffee and grimaced. She looked at Rachel, suspicion back in her eyes.

'Why did you say Eric loved me? I mean, it's not the kind of thing people say to a person if they hardly know them.'

'He told me when we saw each other on Ben Macdui.' Rachel knew well enough not to mention to Ella that Eric had followed her up there.

Almost immediately the suspicion was back in Ella's hazel eyes. 'So you have been seeing him.'

'No. Not like that. I've seen him twice, maybe three times, recently. We were members of the climbing club when we were at uni, but I hadn't seen him for years – until recently, that is.'

'Why should I believe you?'

'Because it's the truth. He told me he adored you and that you and the boys were the best thing to have happened to him. So you can put any thought of him having an affair with anyone, let alone me, out of your head.'

Tears welled in Ella's eyes and spilled down her face. 'I'm just so worried about him. I know there can't be a good explanation for him being still missing.'

'I gather his phone last pinged off a mast near Fort William,' Rachel said gently. There was no way of telling whether he'd been heading north or south. 'Was he heading to Glencoe to climb there?'

'I don't think so. He has a bothy in Glencoe. He took his

camping gear with him and he only does that when he's not
planning to stay there. Anyway, it was thoroughly searched. No
one saw him, and Eric was well known in the area.' She stared
out of the window, as she struggled to regain her composure.

When she looked back at Rachel her eyes were filled with
pain, her expression bleak.

Rachel hesitated. Eric had made it clear that he was
following a story and that he hadn't wanted Ella to be involved.
But things had changed since then. And he'd charged Rachel
with finding out what it was.

'Are you sure it wasn't to do with a story?'

'The police asked me the same thing. He did mention a
story. Then again, it's always a story with Eric. All he said was
that he was meeting someone, but didn't say who. When he
went missing, I thought it might be you. Or at least something to
do with you.' She stared out of the window again and was silent
for a few minutes. 'Come to think of it, he'd been behaving
oddly the last few weeks. All secretive and jumpy. Excited too.
That's why I thought he was having an affair.'

'Can you remember anything Eric said about the person he
planned to meet? It could be important.'

Had to be important.

Ella's ponytail swung as she shook her head. 'No. That's
why I thought it might be you.'

'What did he tell you about the story he was chasing?'

'Not a lot. He just said it would be the story that would
make his career. No more *Inverness Courier*, it would be the big
boys for him. A story he could syndicate globally.'

Rachel already knew all this. She needed to know more –
find the trail Eric had promised to leave her.

'Do you have access to his computer?'

'No. I don't have his password.'

'What about a cloud account?'

'I don't know!' Ella reached over and grabbed Rachel's

wrist. 'I'm terrified he's lying dead in some gully. That he's been there days and days. Alone.' Her voice caught and she looked at Rachel with pleading eyes. 'What do you think?'

How to answer? 'I think if anyone can get himself out of a sticky situation it's Eric,' Rachel said, 'so it's too early to give up hope.'

TWENTY-NINE

Rachel returned to find a washing machine on her doorstep. She groaned. With everything that had been going on, she'd forgotten it was due to be delivered today. Her old one had broken down the week before. She'd been too busy to go to the laundromat and her laundry had been piling up.

Mags had left her shopping in the boot of Rachel's car to be collected later and had gone to the pub so Rachel couldn't ask her to help. She couldn't leave it outside. It wouldn't fit through her front door, so she'd have to manhandle it round to the patio doors at the rear.

She'd managed to walk it about ten foot when she heard a soft laugh. 'Thighearna's a Dhia, what's going on here?' Rachel turned to find Selena behind her. Joe, a grin on his face, was standing next to her.

'Oh hello. I forgot it was being delivered today.'

Joe rushed forward. 'Let me help.'

It was much easier with three of them.

'Thanks,' Rachel said, once they'd manoeuvred it into the kitchen. 'I'll take it from here.'

'I'll plumb it in,' Joe said.

'I can manage,' Rachel protested.

'Let him do it,' Selena said, with a wink. 'While we talk.'

'I've got a last name for our John Doe: Duggan,' Selena said. They'd moved to the sitting room, leaving Joe in the kitchen. 'He attended A&E at Inverness General in 2010 with a broken arm. He was admitted to the orthopaedic ward and taken to theatre to have his fracture plated the next day. We tried to call the number he gave the hospital but it was no longer in use. Either it was written down incorrectly, or wasn't the right one in the first place.'

Rachel gave a sigh of relief. At last they had a name! As long as he'd given the correct one.

'What about an address?'

'The one he gave the hospital was in Inverness. Doesn't exist either. Maybe because he didn't have a permanent address. But just in case the house number was written down incorrectly, a couple of uniforms went out to check the street. They knocked on a few doors, but no one knew anything about him.'

'That's disappointing.' The earlier buzz of elation was rapidly disappearing.

'We didn't give up there!' Selena said scathingly. 'We checked for bank accounts, GP registration, driver's licence in that name, the register of death and marriages – all the usual. Nothing. Not a dicky bird on social media either. Google returned several results across the social media platforms, but none of them were our John.'

That was weird. It was impossible not to leave a trail these days. Moreover, everyone under the age of thirty, herself excepted, had some sort of social media presence. Maybe not on Facebook, but Instagram or TikTok – it was practically oblig-atory. Unless he'd given the wrong name along with the false number and address. It was the most likely scenario.

'It appears the John Duggan who went to the hospital

doesn't exist,' Selena continued, clearly having come to the same conclusion. 'But when he was admitted to hospital he gave his grandmother as next of kin. Shona McLean. Her address back then was Waternish in Skye.'

Skye? Eilidh Souter lived on Skye. A coincidence? Had to be. Nevertheless, a prickle ran up Rachel's spine. Her gut was telling her otherwise. Another thought struck her. Was it possible Eric had got hold of Eilidh's address too and gone to see her?

'The plate was fitted fourteen years ago so we weren't confident that she was still alive, or even existed,' Selena continued. 'But when I checked the electoral register, there was a Shona McLean registered at that address. I checked with the local police. They went to see her. She confirmed she had a grandson living in Edinburgh. She also said his surname was McLean, not Duggan.

'They only spoke a couple of times a year, so she'd no reason to think he was missing. But when the police showed her the photo I sent them, of his face and tattoo, she confirmed it was him.'

The buzz was back. They had a name and someone to claim John.

'What else could the grandmother tell us? What about friends? Partners? Place of work?'

'She was in shock, as you can imagine, and wasn't really able to tell the uniforms very much. Says John went missing when he was sixteen, and she didn't hear from him again until a phone call five years ago. He phoned on her birthday every year after that. He always asked about her but never said very much about what was going on in his own life.'

That fitted with what Nicky had told Rachel in the bar. Finally they were getting somewhere. She just needed to put the pieces together.

'Anything on the DNA under Mags's nail?' A name for the

person who had broken into Rachel's house and attacked Mags was another piece in the puzzle they needed.

'I checked this morning. The lab did find DNA under the fingernail. But there wasn't a hit on the police database. Sorry. I know that sucks.'

To say that Rachel was disappointed was an understatement. Rachel thought of Greg Berkeley, the genealogist. Perhaps he could do the same thing with the DNA as he'd offered to do for John's?

'Can you have it uploaded to GEDmatch?' she asked Selena.

'Already done.'

'I'm going to call the genealogist to see if he can work some magic. I need to know who attacked Mags.'

'So do we, Rachel,' Selena said tersely. 'In the meantime we're chasing down the CCTV around the date and time Nicky thought she saw John McLean. DS Liversage puts me on it when she feels I need something to do.'

So things were still tense at work then. Before Rachel could probe, Joe returned from the kitchen. 'All done,' he said. He glanced at Selena. 'Ready to go?'

'We're going for a hike, if you'd like to come?' Selena said to Rachel.

'What? And play the spare wheel! No thanks. Another time, perhaps.'

That evening Rachel ran towards Tomnahurich Cemetery. As she pounded the streets she turned Eric's disappearance over in her head. What could she do to help find him? He'd said if anything happened to him he'd be depending on her to get to the truth. But getting to the truth relied on her knowing what story he was chasing and who his source was. He'd said she would know. But she didn't.

The police were currently looking for any internet accounts Eric might have in the hope that would lead them to him. In the meantime, Rachel intended to go to Skye.

Plover hadn't been thrilled when Rachel had told her she wanted to go Skye to speak to John McLean's grandmother in person. Said there was too much to do for staff to go off on a jolly, only relenting when Rachel had said she'd take the day as annual leave . Naturally, she didn't tell Plover she planned to speak to DC Souter while she was at it.

She left the canal path and cut through Ballifeary, towards the cemetery.

She hadn't run through it since they'd found John there. It hadn't felt right until she had discovered who he was and had given him back his name.

She entered the graveyard and stopped beside the grave where he'd been found. Someone had left a bunch of flowers, still wrapped in cellophane in front of the gravestone. Rachel checked the card. They were from the woman who'd found his body. Apart from that there was no sign John had ever been there. She took the rucksack from her back and, after a quick look around, removed the bulbs she'd bought from the garden centre. Louis had once told her that crocuses had been his favourite flower because they reminded him that spring was coming. Over the last couple of weeks she'd thought of him more than she had done for years. Almost certainly because John had reminded her of him. Louis would even have been the same age had he lived. Perhaps that was why the two had become entangled in her mind.

She'd been little more than a kid when Louis had died. Back then she'd thought they'd both live for ever.

She dug holes for the bulbs, a dozen in all, and planted them with an ache in her heart. She'd never found out what had happened to Louis's body, or even if there had been a funeral.

The best she could do was to remember him here, where John had died,

The grave had once belonged to a Simon Sturgeon. He'd died in 1821, so she didn't think he'd mind that she'd disturbed the earth above him.

'Sleep easy, Louis,' she whispered. 'And you too, John. I'm going to see your gran and I'm going to find out what happened to you. And I'll do the same for you, Eric, although I could use a little help here.'

A man with a terrier had come around the corner and was walking in her direction. She stood, slipped the rucksack on her back and headed home.

THIRTY

Selena gave a sigh of pleasure, trying to ignore the whisper of guilt that threatened to spoil her mood.

She didn't normally have sex quite so soon – hadn't, to be honest, had much sex at all, especially recently – but it had felt completely right with Joe.

She sneaked a glance at him. He was still sleeping, long lashes closed over his hazel eyes, the rising of his chest slow and steady. It – he – was the best thing that had happened to her since she'd come to Inverness. She'd been so excited when she'd been offered the detective constable post. It had always been her dream. In her head, in no time at all she was going to be the next DS Kate Fleming, her favourite TV character from *Line of Duty*. People at home, Mammy and her brothers, were going to be so proud when she casually mentioned she'd helped solve this crime or another murder. A job, possibly in Scotland Yard or the National Crime Agency, would follow pretty soon after. Or so she'd imagined.

But that didn't look likely now. As she'd told Rachel in the ladies of the Tomlin Bar that night, her fellow officers treated her like a bit of a numpty. Actually called her Baby Cop. There

were even hints Du Toit had brought her on to the team
because they'd had an affair. She knew a bit of teasing was par
for the course, but that was too much. It made her feel stiff and
unnatural around the inspector.

And so far, her under-the-radar surveillance of Skinny Ian
had been a waste of time.

But Joe made everything bearable. From their first meeting,
he'd been impressed she was in CID. Some men might have
been envious – especially if, like Joe, they'd been a police
constable for years. But he said having close contact with the
public, getting to know them and them getting to know him, was
what he loved most about his job.

He asked loads of questions about what her job entailed and
appeared genuinely interested in her answers. As yet she had
little to tell him. He already knew everything about the case
involving the serial killer, so she told him about the case in Uist,
how she'd met Rachel there, how she'd helped her, played her
part in solving a murder and busting a crime ring. Even
admitted how much she admired Rachel. Joe remembered
Rachel from school, knew about her past, and had filled Selena
in on the bits she didn't know. He seemed as interested in
Rachel as the case in Uist.

She'd considered telling him about Skinny Ian but had
decided against it. Something held her back. A natural disclina-
tion to share non-essential information, bolstered by the fear
he'd disapprove. She'd not told Rachel either, having decided to
wait until she had something tangible for her.

She suppressed a sigh. Work, work, work. She needed to
learn to forget about it sometimes. She rolled onto her side the
better to see Joe.

He was very cute if a little dull, although that could be
down to shyness. He'd lived in Inverness all his life, went to
school here and, apart from the interests they shared, he liked

Marvel movies and gaming. There was bound to be more she hadn't discovered yet.

After their hike they'd gone for dinner, followed by drinks. Lots more drinks, judging by the state of her head. Somehow they'd ended up at her place, and eventually in her bed.

Careful not to wake him, she crept out of bed and went to her kitchen.

Should she make him coffee, or do what they did in the movies, dash across the road to Starbucks for real coffee and pastries? All she had was instant and some slightly mouldy bread. She could cut the crusts off, she supposed. But if she got dressed now it would be more difficult to sneak back under the covers...

Her dilemma was solved when arms wrapped around her waist and pulled her close.

'You're up early,' he said, nuzzling her neck.

'I thought you might be hungry,' she replied, suddenly shy, but leaning into him.

'Not so much,' he said. 'At least not so hungry it can't wait.'

THIRTY-ONE

Early on Friday morning Rachel and Selena set off for Skye. Rachel had phoned John's grandmother and arranged to see her that evening.

When Rachel told Selena she was planning a trip to Skye, Selena insisted on coming too. 'Monday is a public holiday,' Selena said. 'And I just happen to have both Friday and Monday off. Joe is going to see his folks in Aberdeen.'

They'd agreed to take Rachel's car as Selena had decreed, despite its tiny boot, it was more fun to drive than her Fiat 500. They were sharing the driving. Selena had found a self-catering unit with a couple of bedrooms in a place in Waternish that had three nights available. It was close to where John's grandmother lived and coincidentally not too far away from Eilidh Souter either. The last time Rachel had gone to the islands she'd flown. But she'd driven to Skye on several occasions to climb the Cuillin, a range of jagged mountains on the island.

Selena took first stint at the wheel. She was a fast but skilful driver, having driven the road many times. Instead of chatting they took turns at streaming their music through the car media player. They'd agreed on Bruce Springsteen as the soundtrack to their journey, belting out favourite tracks along the way.

Two hours after setting off they'd crossed the Skye Bridge and were sweeping through valleys, past waterfalls and imposing mountains, breezing along valleys and glens. The mostly empty roads would change soon as the tourist hordes headed to Skye.

Eventually they pulled up outside the accommodation Selena had booked for them in Waternish – a glass-fronted wooden cube on the croft of the main house. It had two small bedrooms, a tiny kitchen, a wood burner and a sofa looking out to sea. In the field below ears of corn, swayed in unison as if dancing to soundless music.

'That's Uist you can see,' their hostess, a dark-haired woman with warm brown eyes told them, pointing across the peninsula to the other side of the Minch – the expanse of water – between Skye and the Outer Hebrides. It was clear enough for them to just about make out a low-lying lump of land on the other side of the Minch. 'But of course you'll know that,' she added, turning to Selena.

'Mhairi's husband is a friend of my older brother Kenneth,' Selena told Rachel.

That explained how she'd managed to secure this gorgeous little stopover on short notice and at a rate that had Rachel thinking they were headed to a dorm in a bunk house.

After ensuring that she couldn't do anything else to make their stay more comfortable, and warning them they might have difficulty getting a signal on their phones on Skye, Mhairi left them alone to settle in.

Selena propped her feet on the pouffe in front of the sofa. 'Can't we put on a fire, pour a glass of wine and spend the rest of the day relaxing? It's the start of the weekend, after all.'

They'd arranged to see Johnny's grandmother at six, when she 'was bound to be back from checking on the sheep'.

'You go ahead,' Rachel said. 'I might stretch my legs while you do.' The truth was she wanted to take the chance to talk to Eilidh. When she'd learned that Johnny's gran lived on the same island, it had felt like serendipity. She suspected Selena would insist on coming with her if Rachel revealed her plans. Selena had done enough personal stuff on Rachel's behalf. Rachel couldn't risk getting her in trouble – especially when Selena was feeling insecure vis-à-vis her position in her team.

After Selena disappeared off to her room, Rachel picked up her keys and headed out the door.

THIRTY-TWO

Former DC Eilidh Souter lived in Borreraig, a hamlet of five or six houses around twelve kilometres from Dunvegan and down a single-track road.

The short journey took about twice as long as Rachel had anticipated. It was impossible, never mind dangerous, to drive fast on the windy, narrow road. Before she'd set out, Rachel had looked up the exact location of Eilidh's house on Google Earth and as she crested the hill into the village, she scoured the houses on her left looking for a single-storey bungalow directly across from the piper monument on the other side of the road. Given the number of houses in the village, it wasn't hard to find.

Rachel parked the car in a lay-by. The former DC's cottage had no immediate neighbours and an empty fenced-off field opposite. Eilidh Souter clearly didn't require the convenience of one of the towns with access to shops, bars and restaurants.

Rachel was perfectly aware by coming here she was sailing close to the wind again.

A red-headed woman, her hair tinged with grey opened the door to Rachel's knock. She was wearing a jumper with jeans tucked into walking boots. She was either about to go out or had just returned from somewhere.

'Eilidh Souter?' Rachel asked.

The woman narrowed her eyes. 'Who wants to know?'

Rachel introduced herself as a fiscal based in Inverness.

'What can I do for you?' Eilidh asked, sounding wary. 'I don't know if you're aware, but I left the force ten years ago.'

'It's to do with a case that happened over ten years ago. When you were a DC.'

'What case?'

'Could I come in?'

'I'd like to know what this is about first.'

'Do the names Kevin Solomon, Toby Storr and Murray Wild ring a bell? They were found guilty in a human-trafficking case you were involved in.'

There was a long pause as several emotions Rachel couldn't identify flashed across Eilidh's face. 'I suppose you'd better come in.'

The interior of the house was small with low ceilings making it appear cramped or cosy, depending on a person's point of view. There was a solid fuel pot-bellied stove, above which was a wooden mantelpiece with framed photographs on it. A small TV with an armchair in front of it, a bookshelf to its left, completed the furnishings in the room. There was a basket of knitting beside the chair. It seemed Eilidh liked to lead a simple life.

Eilidh offered tea and when Rachel accepted, she disappeared into the kitchen. Rachel took the time to study the books on her shelf: Ian Rankin, Helen Fielding and a few biographies, including *SPARE*. There were only two photographs on the mantelpiece. One was of Eilidh with an arm around an older man and woman. Judging by the likeness to Eilidh they were her parents. The other photo was the same one Rachel had found on Facebook. The one taken outside Marischal Hall at

Aberdeen University. Rachel squinted at the face of the fair-haired woman with Eilidh. The photo had been taken from a distance so wasn't very clear, but a close-up of the same woman was tucked into the frame. She glanced through the open door of the kitchen. Eilidh had her back towards Rachel as she waited, hands planted on the kitchen worktop, for the kettle to boil. Rachel bent to study the photo of the other woman. She had a slight overbite and a wide, confident smile. She clearly meant something to Eilidh. A friend? A partner? Difficult to say, and none of Rachel's business.

Rachel had returned to the sofa and was pretending to be scrolling on her phone when Eilidh returned holding two mugs of tea. She placed them down on a coffee table that had been fashioned from oak.

'You have a lovely home,' Rachel said. Although she was part of the group who would find it more claustrophobic than cosy.

'Thank you. My grandmother left me some money when she died a few years ago. It was enough to buy this place and make some simple improvements. It's small and basic but it suits me. Since I left the force, I find that I appreciate the simple things in life more every day.'

'When did you leave Inverness?' Rachel asked.

'About six months after I quit.'

'You were very young to retire. Why did you?'

'I'm sure you've met plenty of police officers in your time.' Eilidh gave Rachel a questioning look. 'In which case you'll know about burnout.'

Rachel nodded. As Eilidh raised her cup to take a sip, her hands trembled. Only slightly, but noticeably.

'I was fed up at work,' Eilidh said. 'I love Skye. I'd been here on holiday a number of times.' A shadow crossed her face and she looked off to the middle distance. 'When I was twenty-eight my father died suddenly. A couple of years after that a friend was diagnosed with terminal cancer. She was only thirty-five, for God's sake. It struck me then that life was too short to spend hating what you did. So I resigned and came to live here. I never thought I'd still be here almost a decade down the line. I kind of thought I'd give it a couple of years, figure out what I really wanted to do and go do it.' She shrugged. 'That's not happened. At least not yet.'

'I know a bit about living on an island,' Rachel said. 'I imagine it gets lonely sometimes.'

Eilidh shrugged. 'I knit, walk, help out in one of the restaurants in Dunvegan in season. I'm thinking of putting a pod on the croft and getting some extra income that way. There's no shortage of tourists looking for places to stay.' She fidgeted with the beaded bracelet on her wrist.

All of that made sense. On the face of it she was very open, chatty even. Yet Rachel had the distinct impression Eilidh was holding out on her. To be fair, the woman didn't know Rachel from Adam. In which case, she was being more open than Rachel would have been in her shoes.

'So what do you want to know about the sex-trafficking case?' Eilidh asked, leaning forward. 'It was a long time ago, so I'm not sure I remember it all that well.'

'I gather DI Bright was the senior investigating officer, and you were his DC? Did you know him well?'

Eilidh pinned Rachel with a stare. 'Well enough. As a colleague. I worked a few cases with him.'

'What was he like to work with?' Rachel asked.

Eilidh took her time answering. 'Old-fashioned. A bit of a misogynist, if you ask me.' She smiled sourly. 'Par for the course in the police at that time.'

'Was he a good detective?'

'Good enough. Look, I'm not comfortable answering your questions. I want you to tell me what this is about before I answer any more.'

'Apparently the police were tipped off there was an OCG operating brothels in Inverness, and your team was tasked with catching them.'

Her gaze sharpened. 'What about it?'

'Did you ever think someone within the team – or known to the team – might have been leaking information to the gang?' Rachel asked bluntly. Sometimes the only way to proceed was head on.

Eilidh flinched. 'Why would you say that?'

'Didn't you find it strange that just before each raid happened – except for the last one, of course, when there had been no planning meeting – the brothels had been cleared out and moved on?'

'No. These people move their brothels on a regular basis. It was only a matter of time before we caught them,' Eilidh replied, a definite edge to her tone.

'Do you recognise this man?' Rachel showed her the photo of John, taken in the mortuary.

An expression of distaste crossed Eilidh's face. 'No. Should I?'

'His grandmother lives on Skye.'

Eilidh shrugged. 'So? Lots of people live here.' She picked at the cuticle of a nail-bitten finger.

Rachel decided to move along. 'What about the witness in the case, Monika Troka? Why wasn't her death investigated properly?'

'It was. She drowned. She'd been drinking.' Eilidh narrowed her eyes. 'Where are you going with this?'

'You were one of the officers in charge of investigating her death. Didn't you think it odd that she died so soon after testifying in a trial?'

'On whose authority are you here?' Eilidh snapped, getting to her feet.

'I'm a fiscal. It's my job to investigate deaths.' That was

stretching things a little. This death had been investigated and apparently signed off by Rachel's boss.

'I'd like you to leave,' Eilidh said. And they'd been getting on so well. Aware she had no option but to do as asked, Rachel stood.

As she got back in the car, Rachel was keenly aware of Eilidh at the window, staring out at her, mobile pressed to her ear. She wondered who she was phoning. She hoped to God it wasn't Du Toit or Plover.

Selena was pacing the road outside their accommodation when Rachel pulled up.

'Where did you go?' Selena demanded.

'To see Eilidh Souter.'

'Are you serious, Rachel? What the hell were you thinking, going without me?'

'My visit to DI Bright didn't go down well with Du Toit. In fact, he was furious. Accused me of exploiting my friendship with you. I didn't want you to be accused of aiding and abetting me with something that's essentially a private manner.'

'Thighearna's a Dhia! That's up to me. Don't you dare presume to know what's best for me.' Selena sucked in a breath. 'I've gone out on a limb for you time and time again. Because you and I believe in the same thing: bringing the bad guys to justice.' She gave a despondent shake of her head. 'Despite everything I've done for you, you still treat me like a numpty. You're no better than some of my colleagues!' Her hands were balled into fists. 'You know, Rachel, some people might think you have no compunction about using them. I'm not one of them. I'm one of those who come into your orbit and want to stay there. I don't understand why. You're not exactly warm and fuzzy. Maybe it's because when you think people aren't watching, you look like a wounded beast. People are driven to try and fix you. At the very least you could return some of the respect given to you.'

Rachel winced internally. Maybe she did need fixing. But the world needed fixing more.

Rachel didn't say that. Instead she smiled at Selena. 'Do you know what I like most about you, Selena? It's that you don't put up with my shit. After we've seen Johnny's gran, let me buy you dinner to make up.'

Selena gave Rachel a long, hard look before replying. 'OK. But only if you promise not to freeze me out again.'

Rachel couldn't promise her that. She owed it to her colleague – and yes, like it or not her friend – to do what she could to protect her from the evil that seemed to trail in Rachel's wake.

'Right then,' Selena said, apparently taking Rachel's agreement for granted. 'Let's go and see Johnny's gran. You can tell me what DC Souter had to say on the way.'

THIRTY-THREE

Shona McLean lived in a modern bungalow on the road to Ramasaig. She met them at the door with a collie at her side. She was a small wiry woman with snow white hair captured in a long plait and an anxious look in her eyes.

She ushered them in to her sitting room.

'I've prepared a tray of tea,' she said. 'If you'll just excuse me for a couple of minutes, I'll fetch it.'

The sitting room was furnished with a three-piece suite in a paisley pattern. A nest of side tables stood beside a well-used armchair facing a TV. On top of it was a photo of young John with an older man in oilskins.

Shona returned with a tray laden with a pot of tea, cups and saucers and a plate of homemade scones. They waited until she'd poured and offered the scones. Rachel and Selena knew better than to refuse. Rachel flashed back to when she'd been on the islands as a child. Even then she'd been aware that the islanders took offence if you didn't eat every scrap of everything you were offered. She and Selena exchanged a knowing smile.

'I recognise John in that photo.' Selena pointed to it. 'Who is that he's with?'

'His grandfather. They used to go fishing for lobster together.' Tears welled in her eyes. 'Those were such happy times.'

'I am so sorry about John,' Rachel said. 'Tell me about him. What was he like?'

Shona closed her eyes and a small smile crossed her face. 'Just lovely. He came to live with us when he was a baby. His mother had him when she was very young. Ann wanted to go to university so we said we'd take him. She met someone at university. They were together for ten years before they got married. John was eleven and settled here so when Ann's husband was offered a job in America, she went with him. She's in bits about John as you can imagine.'

'Did John have brothers and sisters?'

'Yes. They are in high school over there.'

'How did he break his arm?' Selena asked.

Shona's eyebrows shot up. 'I didn't know he had. When was this?'

'It was an old injury, long healed,' Selena replied. 'When did he leave Skye?'

'When he was fifteen. He wanted a more exciting life than he could get here. He went away to naval college in Glasgow. I didn't think it was for him. We should have visited him more often, or maybe not let him go until he was older, but he was a stubborn lad and determined to go. He left college without telling us and disappeared into the ether. His grandfather never saw him again.'

Tears streamed down her cheeks. Rachel crossed the room and crouched by her side. She took Shona's hand and gave it a squeeze.

'Did John know his grandfather had died?' she asked.

'Not straight away.' Shona gave Rachel a beseeching look. 'He would have come home for the funeral if he'd known. But as soon as he heard, he got back in touch. We'd all but given up hope that he would.'

'When was that?' Selena asked.

'Five years ago.'

'When was the last time you saw him?' Rachel said, getting to her feet and returning to the sofa.

Shona gave a wistful smile. 'A couple of weeks ago, as it happens. He didn't warn me he was coming, just arrived at my door. I barely recognised him. He was much skinnier than the last time I saw him. I told him he needed a good feed.'

'Did he say why he'd come?' Selena asked.

'To see his gran, of course.'

'Did he come to visit often?'

Some of the pleasure left Shona's face. 'He only came back the once before – after his grandfather died. But he'd phone once or twice a year to check I was doing all right,' she added, sounding defensive. 'His job kept him busy, he said.'

'What job was that?' Rachel asked.

'I don't really know,' Shona replied. 'He said he was self-employed. Something to do with the internet. He said I wouldn't understand if he tried to explain.'

That could mean anything, including working as an escort. In any case it was odd he hadn't been on social media. They'd checked all the platforms for both John Duggan and John McLean.

Shona's face was flushed. 'He was clearly doing well for himself. He was driving a sports car. Now, I don't know much about fashion but I could tell that what he was wearing was expensive. He even had a Rolex. And it wasn't a pretend one either. He showed it to me and told me that a person can tell it's not fake by the way the second hand goes around. Like one smooth arc.'

He hadn't been wearing a Rolex when he was found. Did that mean they were looking at robbery as a motive after all? In which case how did that fit in with the bruising around his mouth? Unless he'd met someone for sex, and died during some sort of sex game, his partner bolting taking John's ID and watch with him? But how did that fit with John hiding out in Inverness?

'Anything else about that visit that stuck in your mind?' Selena asked. 'How did he seem in himself?'

Maggie thought for a moment. It looked as if she was trying to decide whether to tell them what was on her mind.

'When he arrived he told me he was planning to stay at least a week. Maybe even longer.' Shona couldn't hide her hurt. 'We didn't go out that first night, we spent the time catching up over a cup of tea around the fire. It was such a lovely evening. The next day he took me to Greshornish House for afternoon tea. I felt very fancy. John was in such a good mood. He was so happy to be treating me. But then, I don't know why, suddenly he looked shocked. As if he had got unexpected bad news. I don't know if he got a message on his phone, or if it was something else, but after that he was preoccupied. He tried to shake it off and carry on as if nothing had happened but his mood had definitely changed.'

'Did you ask him about it?' Rachel asked.

'I did, but he insisted it was nothing. He said everything was just fine. But later he said he had to cut his trip short and go back to Edinburgh. He left the next morning.' Her eyes filled with tears. 'I never imagined it would be the last time I saw him.' She took a crumpled tissue from her pocket and dabbed the tears from her face.

'Did you hear from him after that?'

Shona blew her nose. 'Yes, I did. As a matter of fact, he phoned me a few days after he left.'

'Could you be more precise?'

'About two, maybe three weeks ago?'

'Do you have a mobile, Mrs McLean?' Selena asked.

'Yes. I do.'

'Could you have a look at it? The date of the call should be logged there.' Even better, they would have a phone number for John. Finally, they were getting somewhere.

Rachel could tell from the expression on Selena's face that she felt the same way.

Shona got up and, taking her time, walked over to the sideboard and picked up her phone. She spent a few minutes scrolling through it until she found what she was looking for. 'The seventh of May. And before you ask, it was about a week after he came to see me.'

That was only a few days before his body was found.

'What about friends? Did he mention anyone in particular? Someone he might have confided in?'

'He always mentioned a Chris. They were good friends, I gather. Sometimes went on city breaks together.'

A tingle ran up Rachel's spine. 'Did Chris have a surname?'

'I can't remember John mentioning it.'

'Did John tell you about anything going on in his life that he was worried about?'

'Not specifically. Although the last time we spoke – it's always difficult to tell over the phone – he sounded excited and anxious at the same time, if you know what I mean?'

'Oh?' Rachel prompted, with an encouraging smile.

'He said he was hoping to come into some money.'

'Did he tell you what the source of the money was?'

'Only that he'd discovered something I wouldn't believe. That people were never what they seemed.'

No one knew that better than Rachel. She wondered if John had been planning to blackmail someone. His well-known lover perhaps? But why now. Of course it was entirely possible he had met someone else in the meantime. Another person who didn't want his connection to John to come out.

'Are you sure he didn't say anything more?' Selena asked.

'I'm old, not senile,' Shona snapped. 'Sorry,' she immediately apologised. 'I know you're only doing your job, but it's been a dreadfully upsetting time.'

'How did John get here, Mrs McLean,' Selena asked.

'He drove. He had a lovely car. Very fast.'

'Do you happen to know its registration?'

'Oh, dear, no!'

'What about the make?'

'I couldn't tell you that either. But it was blue. A deep royal blue.'

So where was his car now? The police had checked DVLA for one registered to a John McLean but had come up blank. Rachel racked her brain for something else to ask as Selena wrote down John's telephone number. Fingers crossed, it would be the treasure trove of information they hoped for. There was bound to be names of contacts, texts and messages on it. And the number would be linked to his current address. Discovering the truth behind John, why he'd ended up dead in the cemetery, was inching nearer.

'Would you mind, Shona, if I take a photo of the picture on your side table?' Rachel asked.

'Go ahead.'

Rachel took several with her mobile. She'd crop it when she got back to their accommodation.

'How did John die?' Shona asked, as they prepared to leave. 'The local police could only tell me he'd been found in a graveyard. He was a young man. Far too young to die. I need something to tell his mother.'

'We don't know yet,' Rachel said gently. 'As soon as we do, you'll be the first to know.'

THIRTY-FOUR

Rachel changed into her running gear and went for a run along the road, leaving Selena to catch up with Joe on the phone. They'd agreed to go to the nearby inn for something to eat later.

Selena had forwarded John's number to Audrey, who had promised to get on it as soon as she had a moment.

After Rachel had returned from her run and showered, she and Selena walked down the road into the village. It was a beautiful, still evening. The sea was as flat as glass, the reflection of small boats, a mix of fishing vessels and yachts, perfectly mirrored in the water, Uist in the distance tantalisingly close.

The bar was already beginning to fill with people. A waitress dressed in a red-and-black tartan skirt and a crisp white blouse came to take their order. Her name, according to her tag, was Flora Campbell.

'Now, ladies. What can I get you?'

'A glass of Chenin and a glass of Merlot, please,' Selena asked, after giving Rachel an enquiring look and receiving a nod in return.

Flora was back with their order before they had chance to look at the menu. 'Now then. Who's having the white?'

Rachel lifted her forefinger. Her pledge to never drink again hadn't lasted long.

Flora placed the red wine in front of Selena and straightened. 'Where are you ladies from? I know you're not from here. Have you come far?' She turned to Selena and added, 'I'm detecting an island accent.'

Selena and Rachel exchanged amused glances. Small towns were the same across Scotland.

'I'm from Inverness,' Rachel said. 'My friend here is from Uist.'

'Your first time in this pub, I'm guessing. I've not seen you before and I've an excellent memory for faces.'

On impulse Rachel showed her the picture she'd taken of John's photo at his gran's house. 'What about him? Did he come in here?'

The waitress took the photograph from Rachel and studied it. 'Oh Shonny Beag, Wee John. That's Tommy, his grandfather with him.'

She smiled wistfully. 'He was brought up by his gran. He was a lovely lad with a smile for everyone. Clever, everyone said. But he was restless. Had big dreams.' She looked out across the sea as she remembered. 'John always looked so lost and lonely. It was obvious to most of us that he was gay from early on. No one cared about these things back then, but I don't think he wanted his gran or granddad to find out. His granddad died without ever knowing, although I don't think he would have cared. And if he had, he would have got over it.'

'John was on Skye recently. You didn't happen to see him?'

'Was he? Well, he didn't come in here. I haven't seen him for years.'

Going with her gut again, Rachel showed her the photo Eric had taken of the two of them on top of Ben Macdui and sent to her.

'What about him?'

The recognition was instant. 'Now *he* was here recently.' She gave Rachel a questioning look.

'Are you sure?' Rachel asked, feeling a kick of adrenaline. Why had no one discovered this? To be fair, they hadn't been looking for Eric in Skye. Yet it fitted. He must have been headed here when his phone had last pinged. The further north a person drove the fewer masts there were. In addition, as Mhairi had pointed out, reception was patchy across Skye – probably due to lack of said masts.

'As I said, I never forget a face. And he was nice. Left a big tip. I don't forget the good tippers, in case they come back.' She looked at Rachel and winked. 'Keep that in mind.'

The door swung open, admitting an elderly couple. They took a seat on the other side of the room.

'Now, getting back to your man – what did you say his name was?'

'Eric Hunter,' Selena replied.

'He stopped here for a pint. He had his laptop with him and worked on it for a while. After he was done, he took out a map, a proper paper one, and opened it on the table in front of him. It looked like he was planning a walk.'

'When was this?' Rachel asked.

Flora thought for a moment. 'A week last Sunday.' The day his phone had last pinged. When her stomach plummeted, Rachel realised she'd hoped it had been more recent.

'You didn't happen to see what he was looking at?' Selena asked.

'I did, as a matter of fact. It was of Skye, this peninsula in particular. I don't know why he needed a map. There's a decent path to the point as long as you stay to the right and come back the way you came. The one on the left is rubbish, positively dangerous after all the rain we've had. The cliff has been crumbling for years. I don't know why the council don't close it. If you slip, you can easily fall into the sea.'

Was that what had happened to Eric? Were they looking at an accident after all? It didn't seem possible, given how sure-footed Eric was, but accidents could happen to anyone, even people with Eric's experience – particularly in poor conditions. But what was he doing in this corner of Skye? If he'd intended to go climbing, wouldn't he have headed straight for the Cuillin – the spine of mountains on Skye?

'I asked him if he was going to visit the lighthouse there,' Flora continued. 'Just to be friendly like. But my question seemed to annoy him. Don't know why. He folded his map up and left. Luckily, he'd tipped already.'

'Did you see him after that?'

'No. I assume he did his walk and went home.'

'So you didn't hear that he had gone missing?'

'No! I'm terribly sorry to hear that.'

'Could you ask some of your regular customers if they saw Eric?'

'Sure.' She glanced over to where the elderly couple were looking around, hoping for service. 'Now what can I get you ladies to eat?'

Rachel ordered a Caesar salad, Selena fish and chips.

They took their drinks outside to a wooden table looking out to sea. Seagulls squalled overhead, hoping for scraps. Rachel smiled as she remembered Selena telling her about her mother's method of stopping the seagulls dive-bombing her by waving a broom over her head. It seemed it was a similar situation in Skye with the gannets. Maybe they should borrow a walking stick left next to the door of their wee house just in case.

Making sure they couldn't be overheard, Selena leaned across the table.

'Eric was here! Does that mean his disappearance and

John's death are linked? Or have some connection to the story he was chasing? Or both.'

It was the same thought that had sprung to Rachel's mind.

'Shona said Johnny visited a couple of weeks before his last phone call and left after two nights. That would make it sometime towards the end of April. The last time anyone heard from Eric was the twelfth of May – the same evening he was here.'

So they weren't here at the same time. Yet it couldn't be a coincidence that he and John had both recently been on Skye.

'Maybe he's still here,' Rachel said, with more hope than conviction. 'Hiding out in his camper van.'

'In which case, it's well hidden. A burnt orange camper van doesn't exactly blend into the landscape,' Selena said. 'I'll get on to Du Toit and the local coppers, ask them to let search and rescue know. I'll also tell them to look out for the camper van. I have the licence plate number saved on my phone.' As she spoke, her thumbs were jabbing out texts. 'I'll ask them to check ANPR on the island too. If there are any number plate recognition cameras on Skye that is. Bugger! No signal. Hopefully, they'll send as soon as I get a connection.'

If they found Eric's van that would be a step closer to finding him.

Even if there was only a slender chance he was still alive, Rachel wasn't going to give up on him until she knew one way or another.

Flora came out with their food and put the plates on the table. 'No luck, I'm afraid. None of the other staff or the locals in the bar remember seeing Johnny Beag. Or Eric.'

Selena put the chips that had accompanied her fish on the table between them. 'Help yourself, Rachel,' she said, dabbing grease from her lips, 'otherwise I'll eat the lot – and I really, really don't want to.'

Flora returned with a bottle of tomato ketchup and another

of mayonnaise. She hesitated. 'Why are you asking me all this? Is Johnny in trouble?'

'I'm afraid he's dead,' Rachel said gently.

'Oh no. I hadn't heard. What happened?' Flora asked, clearly shocked.

'That's what we intend to find out.'

It was just about light enough to see their way as they walked up the road towards their accommodation. A bird of prey circled overhead. The lights of Uist twinkled in the distance.

'It feels like we could swim across,' Rachel said, experiencing an unexpectedly powerful yearning to be there. 'I promised my grandfather I'd go back to see him. .'

'Do you keep in touch with him?'

'We speak on the phone most weeks. We keep the calls short. We're still feeling our way with each other.' Rachel and her grandfather had been estranged until recently.

'Why don't we go?' Selena suggested. 'There's not much more we can do here. Monday's a public holiday for you and I'm not scheduled to work either. There's a ferry mid-morning from Uig tomorrow and one back from Lochmaddy on Sunday morning. Go on. What do you say? It will be a surprise for Mam. She misses me. To be honest, I miss her too. I even miss Kenneth and Donald, my two scallywag brothers. And I never thought I'd say that.'

It was a tempting idea. Uig was only a short drive from where they were, the ferry crossing under two hours and she could check up on her grandfather, make sure he was OK. But she wasn't finished with Skye. 'I want to take a walk out to the tip of the peninsula in the morning. See it for myself.'

'We could go before the ferry.' Selena was not to be dissuaded. 'It's not until two thirty.'

'I'll need to find a hotel for the night,' Rachel said, tempted.

'I don't feel my relationship with my grandfather is at the point where either of us would feel comfortable spending a night under the same roof.'

'You can stay with me! There's plenty spare beds now we're all out of the house.'

Rachel couldn't think of a single reason why not.

'I'll give my grandfather a call. If he's up for a visit, let's do it.'

THIRTY-FIVE

The Waternish peninsula was an expanse of moor bordered by steep cliffs. There was a lighthouse on its northernmost tip and a circular path going the whole way around. Before setting out the next morning, Rachel and Selena had studied the map in their unit. Rachel recalled what Flora, the waitress, had said about the narrowness of the path on the west side. If Eric had slipped and fallen it would be there.

They parked at Trumpan Church and took the path on the right, the narrow track as worn as Flora had warned. In some places they had to cling to the cliffside to get past. Nevertheless, Rachel couldn't imagine the sure-footed Eric finding it so difficult that he slipped and fell to his death. Knowing it couldn't be ruled out, she kept an eye out for signs that someone had fallen there recently – skid marks from boots, dislodged rocks or flattened bushes. She couldn't find any. The treacherous stretch was short and soon widened.

As the path opened up on the headland, a woman appeared from a farmhouse, the only building on the peninsula apart from the lighthouse, and marched purposefully towards them.

'Here you two,' she said crossly. 'Will you make sure to give my house a wide berth. I'm fed up with people peering in the windows as if it wasn't somebody's home.'

'Gaelic achad?' Selena asked. *Do you speak Gaelic?*

'Tha,' the woman replied, her demeanour softening.

Selena introduced herself and Rachel. The woman gave her name in return; Seonag Wilson.

Selena removed the photograph of Eric from the pocket of her jacket and showed it to Seonag. 'Have you seen this man?'

Seonag took the photograph from her and studied it, before shaking her head. 'He doesn't look familiar.'

'Were you at home on your croft on the twelfth or thirteenth of May?' That was the day Eric was seen with the map and the day after.

Seonag thought for a moment. 'The thirteenth was a Monday, wasn't it? Yes I was. I never go anywhere on a Monday. I do my shopping in the Co-op in Portree on Wednesdays. Wait you. Come to think of it, that was the day that damn four-by-four drove through my gate and across my croft. The cheek of it! I have signs posted telling people that this is a working croft and to leave their cars at the gate. Most folk do that. Unfortunately these days there are more and more folk who think they can do what they like.' She was getting increasingly annoyed with every sentence.

'Did you speak to the driver?' Rachel asked.

'I was going to, but he got out of the car, him and his pal, and headed to the lighthouse. I shouted at them but they pretended they couldn't hear me.'

'Did you see when they came back?' Rachel asked.

Seonag shook her head. 'I kept an eye out when I went to feed the cows. But they must have returned to their car while my back was turned. They left deep tyre gouges on my croft. The hooligans!'

'Did you happen to get the registration of the car?' Selena asked.

'No. All I know it was a big black four-by-four. I didn't recognise it. Probably tourists.'

'What about the men? Can you describe them?' Selena asked.

'I only saw them from the back.'

'Are you sure they were both men?' Rachel asked.

'Aye. At least, I think so. The smaller one was in a hoodie, so I can't be one hundred per cent sure.'

Could either of them have had anything to do with Eric's disappearance? He had told his wife he was meeting someone. It was worth bearing in mind.

Selena took a note of Seonag's contact details and gave her one of her business cards in return.

'If you remember anything, if you see the man in the photo or the men in the four-by-four, could you call me?' she said.

Sheena took the card reluctantly and studied it. When she realised Selena was a police officer, her body language changed. 'Yes. Of course.'

Rachel and Selena took the other path back to Rachel's car.

'Hopefully the local police will find Eric's camper van soon,' Selena said.

Rachel prayed they wouldn't also find a body. She was increasingly, crushingly certain when they found Eric he wouldn't be alive. But she wouldn't give up on him until she knew for certain he was dead. And if he was, she'd make it her business to bring the people responsible to justice.

'Could you ask them to look for black Range Rovers on the ANPR too?' Rachel asked Selena.

'I planned to. I suspect there are dozens of them on the island, but hopefully not too many heading in this direction.' She glanced at Rachel. 'Don't look so despondent, Rachel Luach. We will find him.'

THIRTY-SIX

Rachel remained on deck during the ferry crossing to Uist, letting the wind blow away the cobwebs and stresses of the last week. There had been no further news about Eric, but police were concentrating their search on Skye, focusing on the coastline around Waternish peninsula. The local police were looking for Eric's camper van, but given there were only two patrol cars covering the whole of Skye, Rachel wasn't holding her breath. As the ferry approached Lochmaddy, the port on North Uist, memories rushed back. Of her mother, the grief, guilt and sadness of her death. Of the case that had nearly got Rachel killed. But there were good memories associated with the island too. Happy days spent with her mother and grandmother when she was a child. Running wild on the sands, the wind in her hair, searching for crabs under stones. Uist was the place where she most felt her mother's presence, had her best memories of her. Now her maternal grandfather was her only living relative – apart from her father. Her grandfather had sounded pleasantly surprised when she'd phoned and asked if she could come and see him. He'd been planning to call her anyway, apparently an old friend of her mother had been to see him, and he had something to tell Rachel.

Selena's mother, a portly woman with a smile as wide as her daughter's, was waiting to greet them on the dockside. Rachel parked her car and she and Selena got out to greet her.

After hugging her daughter, Donalda grasped Rachel's hand. 'I am very pleased to meet you, Rachel. Selena has told me so much about you. Now then, I have some lentil soup waiting. I'm sure you'll be hungry.' She turned to Selena. 'Your brothers will be along later.' She squeezed Selena's arm. 'We've missed you.'

Selena's home, a short walk from the ferry terminal, was a chaotic mix of ornaments and mismatched furniture. A well-used armchair, with a basket stuffed with knitting in progress, was positioned next to an open peat fire that, although unlit, scented the air. Two collies greeted Selena in a frenzy of delight before flopping on the carpet tails still wagging. A tabby cat watched the new arrivals from the windowsill.

Rachel's chest tightened with a longing she couldn't articulate. All she knew was that this was the kind of family she would have loved to be part of, and she envied Selena.

After a bowl of lentil soup Rachel left Selena and her mother to catch up and set off to see her grandfather.

When Rachel reached his house in Daliburgh, she knocked on the door and, in the Highland way, called out a greeting as she let herself in.

Her grandfather, Ailean Dubh, creaked towards her, a broad smile on his face.

'Mo ghraigh, I am so happy to see you again. I didn't dare hope it would be so soon.'

Rachel was relieved to find that he appeared no different to when she'd seen him last. On that occasion, he'd told her death was beckoning.

Once they'd caught up over tea, her grandfather leaned towards her. 'It's very handy that you are here.'

'Why?'

'As I said, I planned to phone you, but it is better that we talk about this face to face.' He seemed bemused.

'Is this to do with Mum's friend coming to see you?' Rachel asked, concerned.

Her grandfather seemed lost in thought as the liquid song of blackbirds came from outside. It was a few minutes before he spoke again.

'Your mother and Jean were friends all through school. Jean went to live on Vancouver Island in Canada shortly after she got married, but she and Mary Ann kept in touch, mainly by letter. Jean came to see me last week. It was the first time she'd been back to Uist in fifteen years. Naturally we talked about your mother and what happened. She told me something that worried me. I wasn't sure if I should tell you at first, but then I thought, Rachel is a bright girl. She'll know what to do.'

'Why don't you just tell me?' Rachel suggested.

He hesitated, still uncertain. 'Very well. The last time Jean came to Scotland she stopped off to see Mary Ann in Inverness. This was only a few months before Mary Ann disappeared. Jean knew Mary Ann and I weren't speaking back then.' He looked down and gave a sad shake of his head. 'Naturally, Mary Ann confided in Jean. She told her that she and David were having problems, although she didn't say how serious they were. But here's the thing I thought you'd want to know. Your mother told Jean she'd found a suitcase filled with fifty-pound notes in the attic. She asked your father about it. He said some clients insisted on paying him in cash. Mary Ann didn't buy it. She was worried and didn't know who to talk to about it. When Jean suggested she went to the police, Mary Ann's mood changed.

She tried to laugh it off. She said she couldn't possibly. There was bound to be a simple explanation. Looking back, Jean thought Mary Ann might have been scared what David would do to her if she went to the police.'

Rachel's heart felt as if it had been pricked with a thousand needles. She hated thinking of all the possible scenarios leading up to her mother's murder. In many ways it was like reliving her death over and over again. The only reason she could think he might have cash in his attic was if he were money laundering for his criminal clients. Maybe her mother had confronted him and he'd lashed out. Was that why he'd killed her? Had Rachel been barking up the wrong tree, looking at the sex-trafficking OCG?

'Did Jean tell this to the police?'

'She was back on Vancouver Island when your mother went missing. When Mary Ann didn't respond to emails, she let it slide. She assumed Mary Ann had changed her email address, or had lost interest in keeping in touch, the way people often do when they don't see each other much because they live in different continents. It was only when Jean came home for a cousin's funeral that she heard what had happened to Mary Ann and that your father was the one convicted for her murder. She was horrified, as you can imagine.'

'Is she still here? I'd like to speak to her.'

'I'm afraid not. It was just a short trip home, and she only came to visit me on her last day. She left her card with her email address and telephone number. Wait you now and I'll get it for you.'

When he lumbered to his feet, using furniture for support as he crossed the room, Rachel had to stop herself from going to help him. She knew her grandfather valued his independence. He passed Rachel a small card with Jean's details on. She slipped it into her pocket.

'Now then. Would you like to look at some photos?'

'Yes, I would. Definitely.'

He picked up a photograph album he'd clearly set aside when he knew she was coming to visit.

She moved her chair next to his, exclaiming over each photograph: long-dead relatives, her mother in school uniform, in a suit, in a summer dress, with Rachel on her hip, tucked into her side. He pressed them into Rachel's greedy arms. She asked questions about her mother until he began to flag.

'Next time I'll come for a longer visit,' she said as she prepared to go.

His eyes lit up – the sadness looking at the photos had brought, banished. 'Perhaps we could visit Harris together? It's where your grandmother and I took our last holiday. We always planned to go back but' – his expression dimmed – 'she became ill and we never did.'

Rachel's heart ached for him. 'I would like that very much.'

This was what family meant, Rachel realised suddenly. A shared past. Shared interests. But also responsibility and commitment. And just maybe she was up to it.

The sun was still in the sky, bathing the moors in a golden glow when she left her grandfather. She sat in her car with the ignition off, thinking what her mother's old school friend had said. There was no good reason for her father to be hiding a stash of cash. Her heart sank again. When would she learn? Her father was a bad man. Why did she keep persisting with the pathetic fantasy he might be innocent, only pleading guilty because he wanted to protect her.

No more. Enough. Let him rot in prison.

Another thought occurred to her. Was the money still in the house? If not, what had happened to it? The last time she'd been there, she'd gone through every room in her childhood home including the attic, but had she looked in every suitcase? Under every bed? She should go back and check on the house.

Her home had been searched, maybe her father's had too? Was it money her intruder had been looking for?

She opened the window but didn't put any music on. Instead she let the wind ruffle her hair and let the sounds of birds undulate through the car. She looked through the photographs her grandfather had given her, brushing her thumb over her mother's face, thinking of her, letting the good memories come to the fore. After a while she placed them carefully in her rucksack.

She drove off, feeling something approaching happiness.

Selena and her family had finished their evening meal by the time Rachel went inside. Both brothers were there with their musical instruments. While the table was cleared and pushed back, Rachel went outside to give the family some space. There was a magical quality to the light in Uist at this time of year.

Laughter rippled through the still air only to be drowned out by the sound of an accordion and fiddle.

Rachel felt a pang, feeling more apart from 'normal' people than ever.

She stayed where she was, listening to the music and breathing in the sea salt air. She felt a presence and Roddy, Selena's oldest brother, came to stand next to her. He grinned at her – the same open, uncomplicated smile that Selena had.

'Are we a bit much for you?' He nodded his head in the direction of the house behind him.

'Not at all. You've been very welcoming.'

He offered Rachel a cigarette and, when she refused, lit one for himself. 'Terrible habit,' he said. 'I try to limit myself to this one in the evening.'

At that moment the one of the purest voices Rachel had ever heard soared above the musical instruments. The words were in Gaelic but Rachel knew enough of them to recognise it was a song about leaving home and the longing to return. It was a few minutes longer before she realised she recognised the voice.

'Is that Selena singing?' she asked.

Roddy smiled. 'My sister has many talents, right enough.' He gave Rachel a pensive look. 'But she's not as confident as she likes to make out. I think something is bothering her and Mam thinks so too. She means the world to all of us. We'd do anything to protect her.' He took a final draw on his cigarette before grounding it out with the toe of his shoe. He turned to Rachel his expression serious now. 'She looks up to you. She'd be furious if she knew I told you that. She thinks you're some kind of fearless warrior that she has to follow into battle. Like she did when you worked that case here together.'

Right now Rachel felt too emotionally bruised and battered to have this conversation. Furthermore, Roddy was underestimating his sister. Selena had made it clear she wanted to make her own choices.

'I think you'd be surprised how tough your sister is. She rescued the girl from the well. Saved my life. She's young to be a detective, I grant you that, but she would never have been appointed to the team in Inverness if the DI didn't rate her.'

Roddy contemplated Rachel for another long minute. 'I hope you're right.' His expression hardened. 'If I find that you have led my little sis into trouble again...' He didn't finish his sentence.

Rachel didn't reply. She slipped back inside and, after waiting for Selena to finish singing, said her goodnights, pleading tiredness, and went upstairs to bed.

THIRTY-SEVEN

Rachel drove straight to her old family home in Moy after dropping Selena back at her flat on Monday. Before leaving Uist she'd phoned her godfather, who was also Angus's father, and arranged to meet him later. Selena had promised to let Rachel know the minute she had news about Eric.

She let herself in, holding her breath, not sure what she'd find. The house, however, was as she'd left it. She did a quick recce to make sure. Satisfied no one had broken in, she opened windows to dispense the musty smell. Then she searched the house from top to bottom. She didn't even find one fifty-pound note, let alone a suitcase stashed full of them. The last time she'd been here, Lorna Ferguson, her father's neighbour and friend, had said that she'd used the spare key her father had left with her to clean the house after her father had been sentenced. Rachel had thought it odd then. Not least because she'd been unable to imagine prim Lorna Ferguson down on her hands and knees. Had she used a professional cleaning company? Was there any point asking if either they or Lorna had found money? If they had, Lorna would have said. Surely?

Rachel turned to the wodge of letters from behind the door.

There hadn't been any last time Rachel had come. Lorna must have dealt with the mail in the years she'd held the key. Most of it was junk and could go straight in the bin. Before she disposed of them she needed to check there wasn't anything urgent amongst them.

Her father had wanted to give her Power of Attorney when he went to jail, but by the time he'd tried to set it up, Rachel had wanted nothing to do with him. Before then, they'd agreed to set up standing orders for all the utilities.

The remaining envelopes were bank statements. She ripped them open. How weird. Up until recently, every month since her father had been in prison there had been a debit of around three hundred pounds taken from his account for electricity. That was a huge amount. Almost £4,000 for each year. And that was before events in Ukraine had caused electricity prices to leap.

Far from the utility charges draining her father's account though, it had continued to grow by around £2,000 a month over the same time period. The credits had no helpful identifying name attached but they were always from the same account. Was this from stocks and shares her father had, or interest on a savings account? Or proof he'd been laundering money?

How could she find out? Ask him, she supposed. But he'd expressly forbidden her to come to see him again and she had no doubt he would refuse her request to visit. Would the advocate who had defended him or the solicitor who'd instructed him know? More importantly, would they tell her? As far as the electricity was concerned, had someone been squatting in the house, running up huge bills? Lorna would have known if that had been the case.

Rachel had noticed at least two cars through the bars of her neighbours' gated driveway when she'd arrived. Someone was home. She would go and ask.

She locked up and walked the long way round to the Ferguson home, as the shortcut along the burn was overgrown, and pressed the buzzer on her neighbour's gate. Sunshine and a light breeze filtered through the leaves of the impressive oak tree between the Ferguson's house and Rachel's.

If the neighbours wanted privacy, they'd certainly got it.

After Rachel identified herself to the disembodied voice who answered her ring, the gates swung open to let her in.

As she walked up the driveway, she noted that, apart from the two she'd seen, there were two other cars parked in the driveway. They hadn't been there the last time she'd visited. She recognised one as a Lamborghini, the other a Ferrari. The Fergusons – or their visitors – had a taste for expensive cars.

Lorna Ferguson met her at the door, looking flustered.

'Rachel,' she said. 'What a surprise. I didn't expect to see you again so soon. Andrew and Georgie are here. They were about to leave, but when you rang the bell and we saw it was you, they thought they'd wait to see you. They're dying to catch up with you.'

Unlikely. They'd shown no interest in Rachel before now – nor she in them. Andrew was five years older than Rachel, Georgie three, and when Rachel had met them last, when she was a teenager, age gaps like that mattered. They'd been more interested in looking good. The flash cars most likely belonged to them. In which case, they must be doing well.

Lorna took Rachel through to the enormous state-of-the-art kitchen they'd chatted in before. Flame-haired Georgie was sitting straight-backed, legs crossed at the ankles on the sofa, while Andrew lounged against the kitchen wall, his dark hair slicked back. He was wearing dark trousers and a pink shirt. In some ways he reminded her of Alastair.

'Rachel, it's lovely to see you again,' Georgie said in a throaty voice. She unwound her legs and stood. 'Mother tells us you are a lawyer now. Who would have thought.' Georgie's red hair was short on one side, longer on the other. Under a soft leather jacket she was wearing a short, white crop top that revealed bronzed, taut abdominal muscles. On her left hand she wore a ring with a diamond the size of a cashew nut. Her lips had been enhanced with filler, her hair thickened with extensions, her lashes elongated with false ones.

Andrew stayed where he was and sketched a wave in her direction.

'What do you guys do?' Rachel asked.

Brother and sister exchanged a glance. And a smile.

'I'm a chartered accountant in London,' Georgie said, somewhat smugly, Rachel thought. She looked more like a reality star from *Real Housewives* or *Love Island* than an accountant. 'And Andrew sells real estate in Dubai.'

'Unfortunately that means we don't get together as often as we would like,' Lorna said. 'I try to get to London for a few days every few weeks and Andrew comes over when he can.'

'That must be lovely for you all,' Rachel said. It felt surreal, as if she was a participant on one of the reality shows.

'I'm afraid Andrew and I have somewhere we need to be,' Georgie said, 'So we're going to have to love you and leave you. Do give our regards to your father when you see him next. Tell him we were asking after him.'

Bitch.

When they'd left, Lorna offered Rachel a drink. She accepted a glass of iced water. Lorna suggested they sit on the sofa – still warm from the heat of Georgie's body.

'Now what can I do for you, dear?' Lorna said. 'I imagine you are here for a reason.'

'It was really Bill I wanted to speak to.'

'I'm afraid he's out. Maybe I can help?'

'I wanted to ask if he knew any of my father's other clients.'

'My goodness, I can't imagine he does, but I'll ask him when he gets back. Is there a particular reason you're asking?'

'I am thinking of selling the house,' she said – which was true. 'I was gathering information for prospective buyers when I came across some substantial bills for electricity. Almost all after my father had been sent to prison. About three hundred pounds a month. I know it's a large house and electricity prices have skyrocketed recently, but that seems excessive. Can you think of any reason that might be? You told me the last time we met that you kept an eye on the house over the years – and thanks again for doing that – so were you aware of anything that could have drained the electricity to those sort of levels? I mean, it wasn't occupied by anyone during that time, was it?'

Lorna blinked. 'What are you suggesting? That we sublet it without permission?'

'No, of course not.' Although it had crossed her mind, she'd immediately dismissed it. The Fergusons couldn't take the chance Rachel wouldn't return to her childhood home unexpectedly. Besides, they clearly didn't need the money.

'Could there have been squatters?' Rachel asked. 'I know you said you kept an eye on the house, but did you ever go inside?'

'Well, yes. Once or twice. When we arranged for it to be cleaned, certainly.'

'Apart from you and me, did anyone else have a set of keys?'

'You'd have to ask your father that!' she snapped. Not the meek and mild Lorna that Rachel remembered from her previous visit. Lorna looked at her watch and stood.

'Did you ever come across a large amount of cash in the house? You said you used a cleaning company, perhaps one of the cleaners did?'

'Are you suggesting I would have kept it if I had?' Lorna said frostily.

'The thing is,' Rachel said, realising the meeting was coming to an end. 'I was curious how the bills didn't bankrupt Dad. So I took a look at his bank accounts. I found regular transfers into his current account. Two thousand a month. I'm trying to track down the account the money came from. That's why I wanted to speak to Bill. See if he had any idea. Dad might have told him. They were friends as well as clients. You told me last time I was here, Bill visited him in prison.'

But it seemed Lorna had had enough of speaking to Rachel about her father.

'I really haven't a clue. I'll ask Bill but I can't imagine he would know either. Now, I'm afraid you are going to have to excuse me. Like my children, I have somewhere I need to be.'

THIRTY-EIGHT

After leaving the Fergusons, Rachel drove to North Kessock where she'd arranged to meet her godfather.

It was another blustery day although sunny. There were a number of dogs on the beach with their owners throwing sticks for them. Children were splashing happily, parents watching over them, many of the men with their shirts off, their Scottish skin already turning pink. It was the same every year in Scotland. At the first hint of sunshine people stripped off, regardless of the temperature.

Peter, her godfather and her father's best friend, was waiting for her on a bench near the bus stop, his white hair fluttering in the breeze. He had something that looked like a walking stick next to him. He gave a broad smile when he noticed her. 'Rachel, how good to see you!' He stood, using his stick to lean on.

Rachel kissed him on the cheek. 'And you. I'm sorry to hear about the hip.' When she'd phoned to arrange to see him, she'd suggested they go fishing. He'd demurred. His hip had been causing trouble. 'As I said, it's a pain, but I'm not going to let it stop me making the most of my retirement.' Peter had been a consultant pathologist until he retired a year earlier. 'I'm planning a cruise up the coast of Norway on the Hurtigruten with some friends later in the summer.

'And let me tell you about my new hobby. See this contraption here? It's a metal detector.' He waved the thing that had looked like a walking stick. 'I wave it over the ground, and if it pings that means I've found something.'

'Does that happen often?'

Peter grinned at her. 'Not once in the three weeks since I got it.'

They walked in companionable silence for a while. 'I went to visit Dad,' she said finally, getting to the reason she'd asked for the meeting.

Peter's eyes crinkled with concern. 'Oh. How was he?'

'Didn't Angus tell you?'

'Tell me what?'

'Dad's been attacked, his face sliced from the corner of his eye to below his chin.'

Peter blanched. 'That must have been a shock for him – and you. Who did it?'

'He wouldn't say. Just that it was a warning. To him. To me. It was Angus who told me Dad had been attacked, otherwise I wouldn't have known.'

'Whoa, hold up. A warning about what?'

'To stop me looking into matters that I shouldn't, apparently.'

Peter gave a dazed shake of his head. 'I'm going to need a drink while you explain.'

They found a table outside a small café and Peter ordered a whisky while Rachel settled for black coffee. Seagulls wheeled around over their head squawking, ready to swoop down should the slightest morsel drop on the ground.

'I'd forgotten I hadn't seen you since I went to visit Father in the spring,' Rachel said, after they'd ordered.

'I thought you were finished with him.'

'I was, until my grandfather told me what my mother had told my grandmother – remember?'

The waitress arrived with their drinks and Peter took a satisfied slug of his whisky. 'One of the small pleasures of retirement – that and the free bus service. The latter meaning I can enjoy the former, every now and again. Now, about your mother. You said she was concerned about something or someone connected to her work. Is that correct? That would have been looked into thoroughly, surely?'

'According to Angus, it was. But before Mum disappeared she was due to testify in a trial – an organised gang of sex traffickers. They'd been caught partly – maybe even largely – because of her. Mum went missing – was killed, as we now know – before she could testify. And now I'm even more worried that what Mum was anxious about led indirectly to her death.'

There it was, out. The thing that had been churning her up inside.

Peter's brow knotted as she repeated what her mother's friend had told her grandfather.

'Angus brought me a copy of the trial transcripts,' Rachel said. 'The trial continued without Mum's testimony. They had more than enough proof to convict three of the gang members on trial without her, but it's clear that the police believed the men sent down were not at the top of the tree. Not even remotely. That's why I went to see Dad. I had to know what he knew about it.' She took a sip of her scalding coffee before continuing. 'He implied that he took the blame for Mum's death to protect me from some dangerous people – although he didn't say who.'

Peter looked dismayed.

'Someone broke into my cottage,' Rachel continued. 'Shortly after that I got a message telling me to stop looking –

although they weren't precise as to what they meant by that. The next day Angus pitches up at my door to tell me Dad had been attacked.'

As images of that evening flashed through her mind, she became acutely aware that a blush was stealing up from her neck to her cheeks. Thank God Peter couldn't see inside her head. 'That's why I went to visit my father,' she said. 'He implied the attack on him and the break-in at my house were orchestrated by the same people – to warn us off. He said I was stepping on some very sensitive toes by looking into the trial.'

She drew a shaky breath. 'What if Dad's been telling the truth all along? What if he didn't kill Mum.' It was the question that had been tormenting her. It felt like vomiting up a worm.

It was only when Peter handed her a clean cotton handkerchief that she realised tears were running down her cheeks. Embarrassed, she buried her face in Peter's hanky. She wasn't sure where the tears had come from. Only that the last weeks had been stressful and her godfather always brought out the little girl in her.

Peter covered her hand with his and she felt instantly comforted. He'd been more of a father than her own ever had. She blew her nose. 'I'll return the hanky once I've given it a wash.'

'Keep it. I assume you spoke to Angus about this? What did he have to say?'

'I think he's as flummoxed as I am. He's going to see what he can find out. Look into whether there was anything Dad's defence team knew but didn't disclose. In the meantime, he's going to speak to Dad's lawyers about getting him put into protective custody.'

'What are you thinking, Rachel?'

'I'm thinking if there is any truth in what Dad told me, I have to find out who attacked him and who broke into my house. I have to know the truth. If Dad's innocent, I need to get him out of jail before he gets killed.'

'From what you told me, your mother was scared of him and planning to leave him,' Peter said gently.

'But why would he kill her for that? Why not just let her leave?'

'I don't know, Rachel. I can't pretend to understand why some men do what they do. Most abused women are killed when they decide to leave. You must know that.'

Of course she did. 'On the other hand, not every abused woman is murdered by her partner,' she countered.

'All this must be very tough on you,' Peter said, the sympathy in his voice making her feel like bubbling all over again.

They sat in silence for a while before Peter spoke again. 'He was really worried when you ran away,' he said.

'Dad?' she asked, incredulous. He couldn't have been that worried. When Rachel had run away, she'd taken care to make sure she couldn't be found. She knew now these precautions shouldn't – wouldn't – have deterred any loving parent determined to trace their child. As far as she was aware, her father's attempts to find her had been perfunctory.

'No, not your father. Angus,' Peter said. 'He knew you'd be annoyed, so he made me promise not to tell you. But I think you should know. He hired a private detective to find you.'

'What?'

'When you went,' Peter continued. 'I rang Angus to let him know.'

This was the first Rachel had heard about this. 'Angus hired someone to find me?' Rachel said, still trying to process what Peter had said.

'Yes. He's not that different to you. Doesn't say much. And no one can accuse him of wearing his heart on his sleeve either. But when he wants something, he goes all out to get it.'

That was the bit that didn't surprise her.

She thought for a few minutes, images kaleidoscoping through her head. The weeks spent on the street. The fear, the loneliness, the anger. The sick panic that her life was out of control and she didn't know what to do about it. How she'd teetered on the brink of giving in to the darkness inside her.

'What did he find out?'

'You'll have to ask him. I took a decision not to. I didn't think it was fair.'

Rachel felt nauseous.

'I shouldn't have said anything,' Peter continued, distress in his eyes. 'But I want you to know you are not as alone as you like to think. People care about you. I care. Angus cares. No doubt many others.' So people kept telling her – usually when they wanted her to stop doing something. 'That's why I don't think it's a good idea for you to carry on pursuing your father's innocence or guilt.' Peter continued. 'I worry about what will happen if you do. Not just physically, but mentally.'

Rachel was barely listening to Peter as she ran what he'd just said through her head again. Angus had employed a private detective to look for her! Several emotions vied for ascendency – humiliation, surprise, pain and fury. Unable to bear the heartache, she let embarrassment and anger win. How dare Angus violate her privacy like this! What else did he know? Had he found out about the nights in the open, the stealing, the dossing down with drug addicts, her friendship with sixteen-year-old Louis who had died. Whose overdose had brought Rachel into the orbit of Gillian Robertson, the nurse whose murder Rachel had helped solve. It was as if he'd spied on her – peeped through the curtains at her when she'd been unaware anyone was looking. How could she trust him again? Feel comfortable in his company? And – it left the biggest question of all: if he'd known where she was, why hadn't he come to see her? That was the most painful thing about Peter's revelation. She refused to ask Peter and would never ask Angus.

'Look, while we are being honest, you asked me the last time we met if I thought your father was guilty,' Peter continued. 'I was evasive. I didn't want to hurt you more than you'd already been hurt. The truth is, your father and I were never best friends. We were friends, yes, when you were little. At university your father was the kind of person whose orbit people wanted to be in; charismatic, charming, great fun. But as I got to know him over the years, I began to realise he didn't care about other people. Especially if they challenged him. They didn't have a label for it then, but these days they'd call it narcissistic personality disorder.'

Every word was like a punch to Rachel's solar plexus. It dawned on her that she'd allowed herself to begin hoping her father wasn't the man she knew he was.

'By the time your mother went missing,' Peter went on, 'David and I hardly saw each other. When we did, there were things that didn't make sense. Sometimes he seemed short of cash, at others he'd be flinging it around as if he'd won the lottery. And, no, it wasn't evidence of a bipolar disorder. Remember I told you the last time we went fishing together that I thought he liked representing criminals in court? That I thought it gave him a buzz?' Rachel nodded, still too stunned to speak. 'Again, I was being economical with the truth. I think he saw himself as being on their side. And I think he revelled in it.'

'You think he killed my mother, then?'

Peter's grey eyes were filled with pity. 'Not just think, Rachel; I'm convinced.'

THIRTY-NINE

When Rachel got into the office the next day, she asked Ginny Plover, Alastair, and Du Toit if she could meet with them. She was doing what she'd promised – being inclusive. Du Toit was busy so sent Selena in his place.

The four of them were squashed into Mainwaring's office, Alastair's knees practically up to his ears, Selena and Alastair's chairs uncomfortably close together. She could see it in Selena's face. Rachel stayed standing – there was nowhere left to sit any way.

'I've called this meeting because I believe the disappearance of Eric Hunter and the death of John McLean might be linked,' she said.

In full view of everyone, Alastair rolled his eyes. Rachel ignored him.

Rachel told them about the waitress and the map. She repeated what John's grandmother had to say about him, and that he had been to see her, the first visit in a number of years and only a couple of weeks before his body was discovered in the graveyard. She went on to tell them what John had said to his grandmother the last time he phoned. About coming into some money.

She'd decided to keep her visit to Eilidh to herself for the time being.

'I don't believe in coincidences,' she said. 'Eric and John being there at the same time can't be chance.'

'One of your feelings again,' Alastair sneered.

'Can we find out who Eric might have been meeting?' Rachel continued.

'*We?*' Alastair replied. 'You mean the police. And how would they do that? They don't know who he was meeting or where this meeting was taking place. I keep telling you, we are not investigators, we are lawyers. We are there to get the facts, decide whether we have a case, and whether said facts can prove our case. The police are the people in charge of finding evidence.' He spoke slowly, enunciating each word as if she were a child and a not very bright one at that. 'Would you like me to write it down for you?'

Although Rachel seethed inside, she fought not to show it. She was trying to build bridges. Why the hell was she bothering?

Alastair turned to Ginny. 'She did this when Douglas was in charge. He was always having to rein her in.'

'Did what?' their temporary boss asked, clearly bewildered.

'Going off on her own, acting like she's a member of the police force instead of a lawyer.'

'That's not fair, nor strictly true,' Rachel protested. Why was Alastair so determined to confront her at every turn? 'I have every right to investigate sudden deaths. Indeed, that's my clear responsibility.'

'My DI asked me to come to this meeting,' Selena said. 'He would have come himself if he wasn't immersed in other matters. He trusts Rachel's judgement. Surely you want to know what Rachel and I found out on Skye? Why we think the two men's fate might be connected.'

'If either man turns out to have been murdered,' Rachel said, 'it will be over to you, Alastair. I imagined you'd want to be involved sooner rather than later.'

'Eric Hunter is missing.' Alastair was not to be denied. 'We have no evidence he is dead. Nor that John was murdered, for that matter.'

'Then why did he go to such lengths to obscure his identity?' Rachel challenged him. 'Why was he hiding in a disused building? What was he doing in Inverness? Where's his car? None of it makes sense.'

'I've asked his mobile provider for his phone records,' Selena said. 'But it will take time. We'll be able to speak to friends and contacts then.'

'Speaking of friends, it would be useful if the police could track down the man who John met when he was on the street,' Rachel said. 'Maybe they were still in touch. He could be the Chris his gran mentioned. Maybe John had come to Inverness to see him. If this man is a public figure, perhaps John was tapping him for money – even blackmailing him.'

'We're still trying to trace the store where shoes were bought,' Selena said. 'We're hopeful that will lead us to who paid for them. If it was John and he used a credit card, that would give us a load of helpful information, including financial information.'

'In the meantime, I am increasingly concerned about Eric Hunter,' Rachel continued. 'As I said earlier, I think we should assume John's death and Eric's disappearance are linked. If Eric isn't dead already, I'm convinced he is in danger.'

'This is just fantasy,' Alastair said. He stood. 'Involve me when you have evidence of murder.'

'I have to agree with Alastair,' Plover simpered, living up to the nickname Suruthi had given her – Ginny Pushover.

'Let the police investigate, Rachel, while you concentrate on the core business of the department. We're short-staffed as it is.'

The meeting broke up and Rachel returned to her desk. Bugger Plover. Bugger Alastair Fuckwit Turnbull. If it was the last thing she did, she'd find out what happened to Eric, starting with the story he was following. That day on the mountain, he'd said he was counting on her to do exactly that. And she'd no intention of letting him down.

She pondered her next move. She'd thought getting a name would put the case of John McLean to rest. It hadn't. It wasn't enough. She needed to know for certain what had happened to him – if he and Eric had ever crossed paths. A recent address for John might help.

The plate had been inserted in Inverness General. He'd attended A&E there. Rachel now knew, from bitter experience, that hospital records held a whole bunch of information. Not just the name and addresses and contact numbers of next of kin, but also the patient's GP. Dr Kirsty Burns might be able to find out more. If Rachel could persuade her.

An hour later Rachel sat across from Kirsty Burns in one of the doctors' room. Happily, they had it to themselves. She and the doctor had got to know each other when Kirsty had been targeted by a serial killer.

They had developed a bond over the course of the investigation.

'Rachel. It's good to see you,' Kirsty's tone was warm.

'And you. How's the hand?'

The murderer had sliced a nerve in Kirsty's wrist in his final attack on her.

Kirsty wriggled her fingers. 'I'm getting more movement every day. I'm hopeful I'll get back to operating soon.'

Kirsty Burns was an obstetrician/gynaecologist, soon to be appointed as a consultant.

'There's something you want from me?' she continued.

'How did you know?'

Kirsty smiled. 'Because you asked to see me. Usually I do the asking when it comes to us meeting.'

'You're right,' Rachel said with a familiar pang of guilt. 'I do need to ask for a favour. Can you access A&E records for a John McLean or Duggan, date of birth 17 March 1995?' She'd got his date of birth from Shona. 'I promise this request is completely legit this time.' Unlike the other requests for information Rachel had practically coerced Kirsty into revealing. But that had been a matter of life or death, she told herself. Again. Guilt curled in her stomach. Fair, fully and fiercely. As long as anything she did followed that mantra, she thought she could defend her actions to herself.

Kirsty gave Rachel a long appraising stare before turning to the computer on her desk, logging in and entering the details Rachel had given her.

'OK, I've found him,' she said after a few minutes. 'He attended A&E fourteen years ago with a compound fracture of his radius – the bone in his forearm.'

'Did he say what happened?'

'The notes aren't very detailed, but it looks like he gave a vague story about tripping over a wall when he was drunk. The A&E staff weren't convinced. They suspected he'd been in a fight. But he insisted on sticking to his story.'

Rachel sat back in her seat. 'I need his current address. The one he gave when he came to A&E was false. Any idea how I might find it?'

'Do you have a warrant?'

Rachel smiled. She totally got Kirsty's reticence. She knew better than most that Rachel didn't shy from bending – if not breaking – the rules if it got her what she wanted.

'It's a legitimate part of my enquiries into his death.'

Kirsty looked as if she was unsure whether to believe Rachel or not. 'Let me go into his GP record. That'll have a note of his most recent address.'

Rachel waited impatiently while Kirsty tapped at her keyboard.

'Got it! Flat 1/3 Logan Close, Stockbridge. Whether it's real or not is another matter.'

That fitted with what Rachel had learned so far. Stockbridge was one of Edinburgh's most affluent areas. She'd get the info to Selena who would make sure it got to the right people.

John was coming alive in her mind. What she still needed to know was whether he'd taken the tranq willingly, if the marks around his mouth been inflicted with his agreement and, if so, who had been his partner? And what, if anything was his connection to Eric?

FORTY

The ringing of Rachel's mobile dragged her kicking and screaming from a deep and dreamless sleep. She fumbled for her phone noting the time as she pressed the green answer button. 5 am. Her heart lodged in her throat, was it the prison? Calling to tell her father was dead? Murdered?

'You know our missing man – Eric the journalist,' Selena's voice came over the line. Rachel could hear the sound of tyres on tarmac in the background.

Rachel sat up, her heart still thudding painfully even as she accepted the call was nothing to do with her father. 'What about him? Has he been found?'

'A passing motorist came across him a couple of hours ago in a ditch by the side of the A9 just outside Perth.' The A9 was the main road between Falkirk in the East of Scotland and the Thurso in the north.

'Is he OK?' Rachel asked, her brain too befuddled to grasp what Selena was saying.

'No, mo ghraigh. I'm sorry to have to tell you, Eric Hunter is dead. I'm at the scene now.'

The words were a kick to Rachel's gut. Her thoughts flew to

his wife and children. This would be devastating news for them. Devastating news for everyone who loved him. Wide awake now, she tossed aside her duvet, shoved her feet into flip-flops and went into the kitchen.

'Do you know what happened?' Rachel switched on the kettle

'It looks like it might have been a hit-and-run.'

Rachel rejected the hypothesis straight away. She knew with utter certainty Eric had been murdered. She didn't need to wait for a post-mortem. She'd known for a while. 'The driver of the car that came across him had pulled up to have a piss,' Selena continued. 'Freaked out when he saw there was a body a couple of feet to his left.'

'How did he get there?'

'Unfortunately there were no witnesses, and no onehas any idea what he was doing there on foot. Nor any idea how he got there.

'Ironically, the police in Skye found his camper van down at the end of the road in Stein yesterday afternoon. They might never have found it had a lobster fisherman not noticed it had been there at the beginning of the week and was still there a week later when he passed that way again.'

Stein was the village on Waternish, where he'd last been seen by Fiona. Where Rachel and Selena had had supper. 'It had been ransacked,' Selena continued. 'Almost completely torn apart. The seat leather ripped to pieces. Bits of the chassis pulled off. The local police secured it and sent for the DC stationed in Portree. She's the only detective on the island. She called in the SOCOs and let Du Toit know.'

'So whoever did it was looking for something.'

'Seems so. His laptop wasn't there. Maybe they took it.' Selena paused to say something to someone 'You know how his wife said he'd taken his climbing gear with him?'

Rachel nodded.

'It was all there. His ropes, his harness, his climbing shoes. The rucksack he always climbed with.'

'I never thought he'd died climbing.' Rachel felt awash with sadness – and failure. 'Where are you exactly? I should come. See the scene for myself.'

'Du Toit is here. As are the traffic investigators. The road will be closed for another few hours. Alison is here too. They're about to take Eric's body away. Alastair arrived a short while ago. I'll bring you up to speed in when I get in later.'

Rachel went outside. Dawn was breaking and, in the distance, the outline of Braeriach was emerging from the darkness.

What had happened to Eric in the interval between the last time he used his phone, and him being found at the side of the A9?

Had Eric and John been murdered by the same people?

Rachel's gut told her yes.

And it hadn't let her down so far.

She made a promise to Eric, his family and herself. She'd failed to find him alive. She wouldn't fail in her hunt for his killer or killers.

FORTY-ONE

Rachel had no sooner arrived at work than she got a call for Du Toit asking if she could come to his office. Thinking it would be about Eric she told him she'd be there in five minutes.

When she got to his office she found Plover there already. And a police superintendent. It was good that they were taking Eric's death seriously.

Du Toit stood. Something in his expression unnerved her. 'Thank you for coming. Superintendent Matthews would like to speak to you. I asked Ms Plover to join us too.'

Matthews stood and shook her hand. He was tall. Imposing. No need for the stripes to convey his seniority.

'I'm assuming this is about Eric's death,' Rachel said.

'In a way.'

The superintendent waited until everyone was seated, then spoke. 'Miss McKenzie, I'm Superintendent Adam Matthews, head of constabulary for the region.'

Rachel gave him a quizzical smile and waited for him to continue.

'You've made quite a name for yourself in the last few months, Miss McKenzie, so it is good to meet you at last.

Recently I've become aware of matters arising, deeply concerning matters, and I need to be sure that your involvement in these matters is professional rather than personal. Do you understand?'

Not really, Rachel thought, but she nodded.

'What do you know about Eric Hunter's death?'

'Only what Inspector Du Toit and his team knows.' She glanced at the other faces in the room. Du Toit looked uneasy, Plover intrigued. 'He was chasing a story. Was in Skye presumably to meet someone connected with it. And appears to have been murdered. That's about it.'

'Are you aware that his wife thought the story he was chasing was something to do with you?'

'It wasn't. At least not directly.'

'His wife said he'd discovered something about you that no one else knew.'

The superintendent slid a sheet of paper across the desk. It was a printout of the article Eric had written about her. The last lines had been underscored.

Her stomach dropped to her boots. They were the same ones that had alarmed her when she'd read the article.

'I'm not sure where you are going with this,' Rachel said, relieved to hear her voice sounded steady. 'I'm afraid you are going to have to elaborate.'

She slid another glance at Du Toit. He gave her an almost imperceptible nod.

Matthews smiled. It would have been less disconcerting had he put a set of handcuffs on the table. 'Unusual career choice for someone with your background, law. And to take it up while keeping your own name. Courageous, in many ways. And a gift to a blackmailer.'

Finally the penny dropped. 'For God's sake, you can't be suggesting I played any part in Eric's death. I'm the one who told just about everyone in this room he'd been following a story when he went missing and that they needed to find him urgently. I even asked them to provide protection for his family. You find the real story he was chasing, then you'll find his killer.'

The superintendent continued as if she'd hadn't spoken. 'Hunter was asking about your mother's murder, about the case she was due to testify in. He asked for the trial records under the Freedom of Information Act. And for copies of your father's trial records while he was at it. Any idea why he was so interested?'

'No. Only that looking into my history had rekindled his interest in OCGs.'

Matthews and Du Toit exchanged a glance.

'How did you feel about Hunter digging into your past?' Matthews continued.

Rachel's heart jumped to her throat. She did her best to keep her expression neutral.

'Appalled. Frustrated. As I'm sure you're aware, my name has been in the paper more than once. Anyone who wants to know anything about me would just have to look online. It's all there. Regrettably,' she replied. *Not quite all of it. Not yet.* 'Furthermore, the piece' – she indicated the article with a nod of her head – 'was more to do with the two recent cases I've been involved in. You'll note he took a dig at the police. I assume you're not going after Inspector Du Toit here for Eric's murder?'

Now that she'd regained her composure, Matthews looked smaller. Less intimidating.

'So you have read it. Weren't you interested in what he found out about you?' Matthews asked, tapping the underlined words.

'I have a good idea what he found out about me. Most of my life was raked over when my father was arrested for my mother's murder. I might not have agreed with him snooping into my private life, but I accepted he was only doing his job.'

Matthews looked as if he'd sucked on a lemon. 'His wife – widow now – came to the police about you when Eric couldn't be found. It was she who told us Eric had been looking into your past and had found something that surprised him. Can you tell us what that was?'

If they didn't know then Eric couldn't have told Ella what he'd learned about Rachel. Thank God. 'I can't imagine.'

'She also said she thought you were having an affair.'

'We weren't. I thought I made it very clear to her that wasn't true. Eric loved his wife. So help me out here. What point are you trying to make? That I wanted Eric dead because I thought he knew something about me and was blackmailing me? Or I wanted him dead because we were having an affair? You know that's ridiculous from start to finish. How the hell would I kill someone who was fit and strong.'

'You'd met with him just before he went missing. Perhaps he told you what he planned to write about you and you didn't like it.'

'So I drove him and his camper van to Skye? Then went back there to cover my tracks.'

'You're no stranger to violence. You have used a knife against someone before,' Matthews continued calmly. 'Recently. As a lawyer, you of all people must be aware that carrying a weapon is against the law. Might get you disbarred or worse.'

Fuck. Her heart pounded against her ribs.

Ginny Plover stared at Rachel wide-eyed. 'What's this?' she demanded. 'You were carrying a knife? Which you went on to use?' She couldn't have sounded more horror-struck if Rachel had admitted to mass murder.

'It was a gutting knife I used when fishing. I'd forgotten it was in my jacket pocket. It was a stupid mistake. And the man was about to kill me.'

It wasn't much of a defence and Rachel knew it. She'd still

been carrying a concealed weapon. Furthermore, it wasn't the only time she'd threatened someone with it.

'We've had a complaint from a retired police officer, DI Jason Bright. He said you were snooping around in past cases and insinuated that he might have worked for an OCG,' Superintendent Matthews continued.

Rachel's stomach churned. 'That's not exactly true. I simply asked him a couple of questions.'

'DIs, even retired ones, do not welcome lawyers coming to their home to ask them questions about previous cases, or to cast aspersions on their professionalism.'

'That wasn't my intention. I was following – what I now suspect – was Eric's tracks. Given Eric had requested the trial transcripts, I couldn't imagine Eric hadn't gone to see Bright too, although the inspector denied it. I visited Bright's DC too. Eilidh Souter who just happens to live on Skye. Where John McLean had been recently. And Eric too. Why is no one following this up instead of wasting time?'

Was that the real reason they were here? To make her professional life difficult? Because Bright had complained to his friend the superintendent? A thought struck her. DC Souter hadn't complained about Rachel's visit to *her*.

Matthews stood. 'Thank you, Miss McKenzie, for clarifying the situation for me, for us,' he said. 'Now I imagine we all have a great deal of work to be getting on with.'

Plover rose from her chair. 'Thank you, Superintendent. I shall look into the allegation you have made regarding Miss McKenzie.' She looked at Du Toit. 'May I get a copy of the police report from Uist?'

Rachel gathered her notepad and was about to leave when Plover addressed her. 'Rachel. A moment. If you don't mind?'

Ginny waited until the two police officers had left the room.

'You are aware that carrying a knife is against the Criminal Justice and Licensing Act 2010?'

'Yes, but I explained it was unintentional.'

'I'm going to have to ask you to go home while I look into what is, I'm sure you appreciate, a very serious matter.'

'There's too much to do here.'

'You can work remotely. I'll look at the report as soon as I get it and make a decision.'

Rachel shook her head. 'Do your enquiries and let me know what you decide. But I'm staying on the case until you do.'

FORTY-TWO

Rachel sat across from Alison Halliday in her office at Inverness General. She called Rachel to ask if she were free to come over. Rachel had been about to leave for home when she'd called.

Although Rachel and Alison had spoken on the phone on a number of occasions, this was the first time they had met in person. Alison was tall and willowy with short blond hair cut in a bob at the front, very short at the back. She was older than Rachel. In her early forties perhaps.

'I thought you might want to get the results of Eric's PM in person,' Alison said, 'and it seemed an opportunity to meet you. To be honest, you're younger than I expected.'

'And you're younger than I expected,' Rachel replied, returning her smile.

'I finished Eric's PM this morning. I came in early to do it.' Alison's expression turned grim. 'It was a tough one to do. My younger sister went to school with him. That's the problem working where you grew up, especially when you're a pathologist.'

'I totally get it.' An image of her mother's body on a steel trolley flashed through Rachel's mind. She pushed it away.

'I've passed my findings on to the police,' Alison said. 'There's no doubt Eric was murdered. He had several broken ribs and a ruptured spleen, which might be consistent in a hit and run, but I also found two bullet wounds, one in his thigh, the other in the back of his head. It left no exit wound, so wasn't obvious at first sight, especially given he was covered in blood.'

So Rachel's worst fears had been true. Her chest felt hollow.

'He had zip-tie marks on his ankles and wrists. He'd been bound. We found scrapings of rock and grass, under his finger-nails – I've sent those off to a forensic colleague who specialises in soil science. She promised to get back to me as soon as she can,' Alison continued.

'Is there any way she can tell if they were from the cliffs at Waternish in Skye?' Rachel asked. Could he have been killed on Skye, tortured somewhere else, before his killers had dumped his body on the A9? This would be important informa-tion when it came to bringing his killer or killers to justice.

'I'll ask. Eric was a local lad and, if he was murdered, we are going to do everything we can to find his killers.'

That was good to hear even if Rachel had never doubted it.

'The worst thing is, Rachel,' Alison continued, 'when I examined his injuries, some of the bruises and slashes on his body were older than others.' She swallowed. 'I believe Eric was tortured, possibly over days, before whoever shot him put him out of what must have been a special kind of hell.'

FORTY-THREE

Rachel stared up at her bedroom ceiling, unable to sleep, her stomach churning. There wasn't a fucking thing in her life that was going right.

She'd come on to Angus and been spurned. That was nothing compared to the rest.

She could lose her job – a job that meant everything to her. And she'd likely landed Du Toit in it along with herself.

Her father was at the very least involved in money laundering.

Eric's death might be indirectly down to her. His interest in OCGs had been sparked by Rachel. And so far she'd been unable to find anything that might lead to his murderer or murderers. He'd depended on her and it felt as if she'd let him down.

She took a deep, calming breath. Giving up wasn't an option. She had to stiffen her spine, pick herself up and carry on, hold fast to the motto she tried to live by, to investigate fairly, fully and fearlessly.

Eric, John, brothels, organised crime, her mother. They were all connected somehow. And she needed to find the link.

Skye had to be one. Eilidh Souter possibly another. Eric and John had been on Skye at almost exactly the same time. Both had turned up dead shortly after. The other link had to be OCGs – in particular the one running the sex trafficking ring eleven years ago. Before she'd gone to bed last night she'd texted Angus, asking him if she could meet him when he was done with court. The only benefit of being barred from the office was that she was free to meet him. She needed to know what information – if anything – he'd discovered that had not been presented either by the prosecution or defence in her father's trial. Had her father ever explicitly mentioned OCGs? Or claimed to have been blackmailed? Had he named the person he claimed planted Mum's cards and passport in his safe? In addition she wanted to know who had her father's power of attorney. Other bills apart from electricity must be paid by someone, rates for example and work for the upkeep of the house.

Although not yet five it was daylight outside. Rachel flung back her duvet, pulled on her running gear and, grabbing a banana, went outside. The only way she could think of easing the churning in her stomach, the rising acid in her chest was to go fishing, climb a mountain, or run until she was breathless. Given she'd arranged to meet Angus in Edinburgh later a run it would have to be.

FORTY-FOUR

It had been a long time since Rachel had visited Edinburgh, even longer since she'd been to the High Court in Lawnmarket. The last time, her father had been sentenced to life for the murder of her mother. The only reason she'd attended on that day was to see her father sent down.

Now, Angus was defence counsel in a murder case that was expected to continue for a number of weeks and had suggested she meet him after court had adjourned for the day. Rachel arrived early for their meeting and slipped into the back row of the public gallery . She'd never attended a trial where Angus was the lead counsel for the defence and was intrigued to see him in action.

He was a striking figure in his wig and gown. Most advocates looked ridiculous in their wigs, but Angus managed to carry it off. He didn't fiddle with it like his opposition was doing. Although she might be biased. At any rate, it was difficult to reconcile the teenager she'd known with the man in front of her. Presumably he found it equally difficult to adjust to the woman Rachel had become.

Watching Angus perform, because that was surely what it

was, was like watching an actor command a stage. He didn't look at his notes, didn't fumble for words. He was brutal with the witness for the prosecution, gentle with the witness for the defence.

At his side a nervous-looking junior scribbled notes on a yellow legal pad. Rachel leaned forward in her seat. This was what she wanted to do. Argue murder cases in front of a judge and a jury in the High Court, although as a prosecutor, rising one day to the heady rank of advocate depute. First, though, she had to work her way up through summary and solemn sheriff courts until she was able to argue murder cases in front of a judge and a jury in the High Court. And find a way not to get fired in the meantime.

After the court was adjourned for the day, Rachel made her way outside to wait for Angus. She found a bench and turned her face to the sun and closed her eyes.

She opened them when a shadow fell over her. Without his wig and robe Angus was more familiar. She felt absurdly shy. It was difficult to look at him without remembering the last time they'd met.

'A drink? Or an early dinner?' he asked.

She stood. 'Both.'

'In that case let's go to the Witchery. It's nearby and they always manage to find a table for me.'

As they walked along the High Street, Rachel matched her strides to his. 'Are you going to win your case?' she asked, as they dodged tourists.

'Undoubtedly.'

Yup. That was Angus. So damn sure of himself.

The Witchery was situated near Edinburgh castle and luckily had a table free. They were led to their table by a smartly dressed waiter in a white shirt, dark trousers and a tartan waistcoat.

Subdued light from candles and wall lamps, tables with

starched white table clothes, laid with crystal and china and
vases of flowers, together with the carved wood ceilings and
walls gave the room a cosy, romantic ambiance. She wondered if
that had been Angus's intention and immediately dismissed the
thought. She doubted he'd even noticed. Rachel took a seat on
the red leather banquette against the wall while Angus took the
chair opposite. She waited until the waiter had taken their
drinks order – a pint of ale for Angus and a titchy glass of pinot
gris for her – before speaking.

'Eric Hunter is dead,' she said baldly.

'I'd heard. It was a shock. I'd climbed with him a few times.
I liked him. Do the police know who did it?'

'Not yet, but I'm convinced there's a link to organised
crime.'

Angus frowned. 'In what way?'

'He was tortured before he was killed. His murder looks like
it was a professional job.'

Rachel explained about the story the journalist was chasing.
'He only started investigating organised crime in Scotland
because he was looking into my background and came across
the trial my mother was due to testify in. What if it led him to
the people who murdered him? What if everything is tied to my
father in some way?'

Kenneth, their waiter arrived with their drinks and asked if
they were ready to order. Angus ordered a steak, medium rare,
Rachel carbonara. Neither wanted a starter.

'Explain what you mean about your father,' Angus said
when Kenneth had retreated again.

Her words fell over each other as she told him about her
visit to her father in prison, how he suggested he'd gone to
prison to protect her, what Angus's father had said about David,
the report by her mother's friend that her father had been
hiding cash and her suspicion he'd been money laundering for

criminals. She finished with what Angus's father, Peter had said about being convinced her father was guilty.

Angus listened without saying anything until she came to a faltering halt.

'I don't know what to think anymore,' Rachel continued. 'One minute I'm certain he's guilty, the next I'm riddled with doubt. Do you think it's possible he had links to an OCG? That he was set up?'

Still Angus said nothing. She knew he'd be running through his mind what he could disclose. At the time of her father's trial he'd been devilling for the advocate who had represented her father. Client confidentiality was critical to the client-lawyer relationship.

'You know that isn't a question I can answer, Rachel. My firm might never have asked him. Perhaps because they didn't want to know the answer.'

He waited until a returning Kenneth had placed their plates in front of them.

'Why don't you request the records of your father's trial? You'd see what information both sides gathered prior to the case going to court.'

'That will take time. Anyway, it's what *isn't* in the transcripts that interests me. I sat through most of the trial and can't remember anything being said about organised crime. Anyway, you promised you'd help me.'

Angus speared a chunk of steak and chewed for a moment. 'Okay. Here's what I found out. Lorna Ferguson had power of attorney for your father. There was no mention of OCGs in anything submitted to us by the prosecution, or in the defence notes. Your father did tell his defence team that he'd made enemies while he was working as a criminal solicitor, that there were a number of people who had good reason to want him in jail – people with rival interests to his clients in particular. But enquiries never got off the ground as your father wasn't able – or willing – to provide a single name. That's everything I can tell you.'

In that case it would have to do. She took a couple of mouthfuls of pasta and thought about what Angus had told her. She would go and see Lorna. She must be able to tell her something although it was odd that she hadn't mentioned that she held power of attorney for Rachel's father.

'I gather your father has taken up a new hobby because his hip has been bothering him.'

Angus smiled. 'The metal detecting? He told me.' He leaned across the table and brushed the corner of her mouth with his thumb. 'Sauce,' he said.

She should have known choosing pasta would be a mistake. She put down her fork and took a gulp of wine, before broaching the other reason she wanted to speak to him. 'He also told me you paid a private detective to look for me when I left home.' She sounded more accusatory than she liked.

A myriad of emotions passed across Angus's face until his expression settled into the non-committal one she knew so well.

'Did you think I would just let you disappear? Don't you know me better than that? You were like the sister I never had. I was worried. I knew you were tough – at least on the outside. But you were only fifteen.'

'You weren't much older.'

'Nineteen. Old enough to know the world could be a dangerous place. I was halfway through my law degree by then, reading everything I could get hold of about crime. I was scared stiff you'd be trafficked or prostituted...' He paused and something that looked like pain flashed in his eyes. '... murdered.'

In all the time they'd known each other, this was the most personal conversation they'd ever had. Rachel laughed because she didn't know what else to do to hide the panic she felt inside.

'You just said I was tough. Didn't you realise I could see off anyone?'

Her attempt at passing his comments off with humour didn't work. He turned to face her, looking directly into her eyes.

'You were tough physically, I'll give you that. But I knew you were hurting on the inside. Christ, I was a nineteen-year-old guy, my emotions all over the place, my hormones going rampant. Your eyes and smile churned me up inside, rendered me speechless. You have always rendered me speechless, even as a teenager. You were so alive, so feisty, people were always drawn to you. You've always had the sort of beauty that can't be achieved by make-up or art. But, after your mother disappeared, in the year before I left for uni, I saw something else: fear and vulnerability. You tried to hide it, but I knew you. You'd never been afraid of anybody or anything before then. My father told me your behaviour had been getting out of control, that you had been bunking off school, creeping out at night to go and hang with the cool guys, and that your grades had plummeted. Dad was worried. Your father was either unable to control you or just not interested. He'd changed too. Dad hadn't seen him much in the two years prior to your mother leaving, but reached out again when she left. Your father said you were morose and angry. Hardly surprising, given the circumstances. Back then you believed your mother had left you without even saying goodbye. That would screw anyone up.' His eyes hadn't strayed from her face. 'Dad suggested I take you climbing, try to talk some sense into you.

'Before I had the chance, you disappeared. I was terrified some monster had you.'

Rachel held her breath. Her heart – and hormones – were going crazy.

'I felt like the big brother who had failed to protect you.'

'You didn't behave like a big brother that night in Braeriach.'

He smiled. 'I didn't feel like one. The big brother pretence I'd try to sell myself passed the day I turned up at your halls of residence. You were so beautiful you took my breath away, but I saw immediately something in you had changed again. You were suspicious of everyone and everything, wounded, vulnerable.' He paused. 'But also more determined, tougher.'

To Rachel's disappointment, Kenneth bustled over again and the spell was broken.

'Everything all right with your meals?' he asked, looking pointedly at Rachel's half eaten plate. Angus hadn't eaten much more of his.

'Everything was lovely, Rachel said, wishing Kenneth would bugger off.

'What did your detective find out?' Rachel asked, when they were alone once more.

'That you were in Glasgow. Living under a bridge with a dozen other homeless people, some of them addicts, some prostitutes. He saw you defend yourself against a drunk, was about to go to your aid when you floored the guy.'

'I remember him, he was very pissed.' Once again Rachel tried to keep her voice light, but she was mortified and ashamed Angus knew all this about her. Until Peter's revelation, she'd had no idea about his involvement.

'For the record. I never sold myself. I came close, when my money ran out and I didn't have enough to buy food.' She took a breath. 'But I stole – shoplifted. Only food – a loaf of bread, cheese, that sort of thing.'

He looked at her, his expression unreadable. Was it pity she saw there? Admiration? Disgust?

'Weren't you terrified?' he asked.

'Not at first, weirdly. I was so angry with the world, with myself, my mother, my father, I almost wanted something to happen to me.' Telling him this was like ripping herself in two, but also cathartic. 'But when the anger passed, yes, I was scared for a while.' Her mind drifted back to those gut-wrenching weeks. 'I felt less alone when I met Louis. He was sixteen. A runaway from London. We had each other's backs. He'd been on the streets for a year before we met. He did sell himself. He'd started to take drugs and needed to feed his habit. I was so scared for him. But he'd make light of it, make me laugh, promise me he knew how to take care of himself. I was so young back then, I believed him.' Her voice caught.

As images of that last, desperate journey to hospital spooled through her mind, she was quiet for a moment, fighting to get her emotions under control.

'One day he overdosed on heroin that had been laced with fentanyl. I took him to hospital. Remember the nurse who was murdered? Gillian Robertson. Well, she was the nurse in charge of A&E that evening.' Rachel took a shaky breath. 'They couldn't save Louis. They tried everything. Naloxone, bagging him, shocking his heart. But it was no use.' Her voice broke as tears filled her eyes. Kenneth drifted over again but Angus waved him away. She used the moment to regain her composure.

'Gillian sat with me. She remembered me from school, but even if she hadn't, I don't think it would have made any difference to her kindness towards me. She told me Louis had died. That they'd done everything they could but hadn't been able to save him.

'She let me cry for a bit. Then she told me that she'd remembered how bright I'd been at school, that she knew my mother had left the family home. She asked if Dad was abusing me. He wasn't,' she added hastily. 'So Gillian said, and I remember every word, that I had only one chance of a wild and wonderful life – she was paraphrasing I know now from a poem – that she knew that I *could* have a wild and wonderful life – but I needed to go back home – go back to school, finish my education – and live the life that was meant to be mine to live.' Rachel's throat was tight. 'It struck a chord. I think I'd been wanting to go back home for a while – would have if Dad had ever tried to find me. He didn't.' She sniffed loudly. 'But I did what Gillian suggested. I went back home, caught up at school – no easy task – got accepted to study law at university.'

Angus placed his fingers on top of hers. Her skin tingled.

She'd told him this much, there was no reason to stop now.

'I want to become an advocate depute – prosecute the most serious crimes in the High Court, but I know if I get that far, my past will come up over and over again. If your detective found all that out about me, so can anyone else if they want. How do you deal with the media attention?' She smiled wryly. 'I appreciate in your case it's different, being seen at social events with smart, high-profile women, can only enhance your reputation.'

He shrugged. 'To be honest, it does, but I don't date these women to be seen, but because I enjoy spending time in their company. I like intelligent women. Always have. That's why I like you.'

Rachel was aware the atmosphere between them had shifted. Every nerve ending felt on full alert.

Kenneth returned with dessert menus. Functioning on automatic pilot, Rachel took one and stared at it as if she'd forgotten how to read.

'I admire you because of your brain, but also because of your courage.' Angus continued. He'd refused a menu. 'You have a big heart – even if you try to hide it. You might have spent time on the street, but you didn't let it damage you – quite the opposite. That's where your compassion comes from. Never lose that. Use it when you become an advocate depute, as I have no doubt you will, regardless of any obstacles thrown your way. And you'll be a fierce and deadly adversary.

'Your past is bound to come up, but my advice is to brush it off or use it in your favour. Lean into your reputation as a maverick. If what you've done impresses me, it will impress others. You did the right thing, keeping your name, not hiding your past. The bad guys will never be able to use it against you.'

'Maybe they already have,' she pondered, her mind going back to the texts and the break-in.

Rachel was still reeling when Angus called for the bill. It was the longest personal speech she'd ever heard from him. The most open and direct he'd been with her. She'd no idea he felt that way about her.

She appreciated his admiration but wanted him to lust after her too. First there was something he should know.

Since they were baring their souls maybe it was time to get over her yearning to keep as much of her private life as private as possible, given that particular barn door been opened, ripped off its hinges and flung into the abyss anyway.

She sucked in a breath. 'You're still my lawyer, right?'

'Guess so.'

'When I was in Glasgow, I was arrested.'

Angus's eyebrows shot up.

'For affray. Louis and I were walking. It broke the monotony. It was late at night. Some guys approached us. Louis was carrying a cheap bottle of wine. The guys took it off him. Smashed it on the ground. Then they started kicking Louis. I thought they were going to kill him.' She plunged on, scared she would lose her nerve before he knew it all. 'I threatened them with a shard of the bottle to try and get them to back off. The ringleader tried to grab it and ripped his palm open in the process. I don't know what would have happened if someone hadn't called the police. The men ran off, except the one with the blood running down his arm. He blamed the whole thing on me. Louis told them what had happened, even had the bruises to show for it. It didn't make a difference. They were university students, Louis and I lived on the streets. I was arrested. Had to appear in the juvenile court the next day. I was given a choice – plead guilty and get a suspended sentence or go to juvenile detention until I appeared in the children's court.'

Anger flashed across Angus's face. The pressure of his hand on hers increased.

'I took the plea deal. My record was sealed. I didn't declare it when I applied to do law. I think someone knows. And if the Law Society learns about that, along with my carrying a knife on Uist – they could disbar me.'

Angus swore under his breath, then looked Rachel in the eyes. Her heart was beating like a pneumatic drill. 'I'll make it disappear. In the meantime, ditch using knives as weapons. Stop accusing retired police officers.' He shook his head, but Rachel could tell he was amused. 'And just generally stay on the side of the law you're supposed to be on.' As Kenneth drifted towards them again, Angus leaned towards Rachel, 'Fuck this. Let's get out of here,' he whispered in her ear.

'Now then, what are we having for dessert,' Kenneth said, addressing Rachel.

'Just the bill, please,' Angus said.

Normally Rachel would argue for going Dutch, but something told her it would be a waste of time – on this occasion anyway – and suddenly not wasting time took precedence over everything.

Kenneth re-appeared like the ghost at MacBeth's funeral. 'Anything nice planned for the rest of your evening,' he asked as Angus tapped his card to pay.

When Rachel caught Angus eyes, and his mouth twitched, she suspected he was thinking the same thing as her.

They spilled outside and Angus took her arm, pulled her into the doorway and kissed her until they were both breathless and had to come up for air. His mouth had tasted of hops.

Even in the dim light she could see the desire in his eyes. She could only imagine what he saw in hers.

'Will you come home with me?' he asked.

That answered her unspoken question then.

. . .

Much later Rachel lay next to Angus listening to the regular sound of his breathing as he fell asleep. She turned on her side and ran a light finger along his jawline. 'Why didn't you come and get me?' she whispered.

The next thing she knew it was daylight and Angus was standing over her, carrying a mug, a smile on his face. Disappointingly he was dressed.

'What time is it?' she asked sleepily. He put a mug of black coffee on the table next to her and sat down on the bed.

'Just after seven. I have to go to work. Unfortunately. I would rather have stayed with you.' He brushed Rachel's hair from her face and kissed her. She would much rather he hadn't been working either. 'When can I see you again? I'm busy over the next few weeks, but let's go for a climb and have dinner soon?'

What did that mean? Friends with benefits? They'd had sex before, in a bothy when they'd been trapped by snow, but that had been almost ten years before. Rachel didn't think she could go another ten years.

After he'd left, telling her she just needed to close the door when she was ready to leave, she showered and dressed in the change of clothes she'd brought with her.

She'd not taken in much of Angus's flat last night except that it was in the old Royal Infirmary, now converted into luxury flats adjacent to the Meadows. The other flats were new builds with a number of bars and restaurants and coffee shops as well as a gym. Right in the middle of the old town, it was near the university, the National Library and museum as well as the Advocates Library.

His flat was immaculately tidy. As if he didn't spend much time in it or had a cleaner. Maybe both.

The sitting room had three large sash windows overlooking

the Meadows. It had a white sofa, two matching armchairs, a glass-topped coffee table. Several paintings hung on each wall. Rachel recognised one, a figure painting by Stephenie Rew and another a large sweeping Scottish landscape by Beth Robertson Fiddes, a Bob Dylan sketch, and a Peter Robson.

The kitchen was on the other end of the main room. Miele appliances, marble worktops, a double oven, a sink on an island that separated the kitchen from the living room.

He had money to spend, that was obvious. She'd never doubted it. She wondered if he'd furnished the flat himself or had a previous girlfriend done it, picking the paintings too. But it was undeniably masculine. There were no cushions, no frills.

Unable to resist, she opened the kitchen cupboards and was unsurprised to find only a jar of coffee, a bottle of olive oil, an open pack of water biscuits. The fridge was similarly unencumbered. It contained two bottles of wine, an opened bottle of vodka and some blue cheese. Another wine rack, built into one of the units, was filled with bottles of red wine.

Once she'd thought she knew Angus, but now she realised she could tick what she knew off on the fingers of one hand: he was driven, a workaholic even, could climb as well as anyone she knew with the possible exception of Eric or professional climbers, he liked to wear expensive suits, had expensive tastes in general, liked to go to openings of art shows, to the theatre and the opera – that much she'd gleaned from the papers.

And she thought she might be in love with him.

And that terrified her more than coming face to face with any murderer.

FORTY-FIVE

She found it lodged under the mat inside her front door. On her return from Edinburgh she'd set about cleaning her house with an intensity brought on by nervous energy. She had no idea how long it had been there. It had been weeks since she'd vacuumed, sloth that she was. It had come through the post, like an ordinary letter. Not that she got many of these. Or any at all. She didn't recognise the handwriting. Intrigued, she flicked on the kettle and as she waited for it to boil, opened the envelope. There was nothing inside. Or so she thought at first. She could feel something small and hard. She up ended the envelope and a small key fell into her palm. It was smaller than a yale key but larger than a padlock key. There was no identifying tag with a name or an address or even a number.

She finished making her coffee and took it outside to drink. Who would be sending her a key? What did they expect her to do with it?

She checked the name and address on the envelope. Definitely her name, her address, but not handwriting she recognised. Then again, most people she knew texted or emailed when they wanted to get in touch. She studied the postmark. It was stamped Skye and dated over two weeks ago.

Electrified she knew immediately who had sent it. Eric. He'd promised he'd find a way to lead her to the story he was investigating.

Was this key the clue? Would finding it earlier have saved Eric's life? The thought made her nauseous. But she couldn't think about that now. She needed to find the lock the key fitted.

She put her half-drunk cup of coffee on the counter and picked up her jacket.

First things first. She needed to confirm that the writing on the envelope was Eric's, and if it was, whether his widow knew what lock the key opened.

FORTY-SIX

Ella opened the door to Rachel's knock, clearly surprised to see her.

'Why are you here? Is it about Eric? Have you found the person who killed him?' Her eyes were anxious, her fine features drawn. She'd lost weight in the days since Rachel had last seen her.

'No. Not yet. Or at least, not as far as I know. Look, can I come in? There's something I want to ask you. It won't take long.'

Ella stepped back, reluctantly allowing Rachel to enter. The porch was filled with wellington boots of various sizes, clearly belonging to the children. Next to them were a pair of ladies Hunter boots and, heartbreakingly, next to those, an even bigger pair that must have belonged to Eric. The hall displayed similar evidence of a life lived outdoors: walking boots, waterproof jackets, cycle helmets.

Ella showed Rachel into a toy-strewn sitting room and invited her to sit. 'I'm sorry about the mess,' she said dully. 'I can't find the energy to tidy up. It's all I can do to get the children's packed lunches ready, to send them off to school in clean clothes.'

'That's understandable. It's not been very long.' Rachel should have brought something – a casserole, even shop-bought biscuits.

'It will always be not very long,' Ella replied, her voice hollow.

Rachel reached into her rucksack and pulled out the letter that had come in the post. 'Do you recognise the writing on the front of the envelope?' she asked.

The way she paled told Rachel what she wanted to know.

'Why was he writing to you?' Ella narrowed her eyes. 'Were you and Eric having an affair after all? And you dare to come here!'

'We were not having an affair. I've told you. He adored you. You and the children were his world.'

Ella slumped back in her chair and closed her eyes. She sighed deeply, sat up and looked directly at Rachel. 'So why *was* he writing to you?'

'He wasn't.' Rachel tipped the key into her palm and held it out. 'He sent me this.' She waited until Ella took it from her before continuing. 'Do you recognise it?'

Ella rubbed the key with her fingertip as if it were made of gold. 'I don't think I've seen it before. Why did he send it to you?'

'That's what I was hoping you'd be able to tell me. Are you sure you can't think of a lock it fits? A desk drawer, perhaps? Or a filing cabinet? I know he was freelance. I assume he worked from home?'

'Sometimes. At other times he'd go to Starbucks or the pub. Work there. If the kids were home he'd find it too noisy. But to answer your question, he doesn't have an office as such.' Her lips twisted in a wry smile. 'A three-bedroom house, two children and a job where income can't always – ever – be depended on, doesn't allow such luxuries.' Her face crumpled as if it had just hit her all over again that her husband, whom she had clearly loved, wouldn't be working from home or anywhere else for that matter.

Rachel waited in silence for Ella's sobs to subside. She couldn't be thirty yet, far too young to be facing life on her own while raising two children.

When she was calm again Ella turned the key she still held, over in her palm. 'He had a small bothy in Glencoe. I told the police about it when he first went missing. He used to go there to work sometimes when he was on a deadline. I only went once, before we got married and once after our first was born. It's tiny. Just large enough for a bed, a table and a couple of kitchen cabinets really. Maybe he had a cupboard there he locked, a safe even. It's pretty remote. He bought it when he first joined Lochaber mountain rescue, so he could be close if he had an emergency callout. He used to leave it unlocked in case a climber or walker needed shelter. He stopped when the numbers of tourists increased, and he started finding empty cans and rubbish left behind. The key to the bothy is still here. Somewhere. The police had it, but returned it after they'd searched it.' She stood, her movements stiff and slow like that of an old woman. 'I'll get it for you.'

When she left the room, Rachel let her eyes linger on the photo of Ella crouching down with her arms around two boys. One on either side. In time the two children would learn that their father *really* was the hero they undoubtedly saw him as now. He would remain a shadow, his heroic status gaining with every year his grieving wife and mother remembered him until he was more myth than reality. Was that what Eric would have wanted?

Ella came back into the room brandishing a set of keys – a Yale and a mortice. 'Found them.'

'Where is the bothy exactly?' Rachel asked, dropping the set of keys into the front pocket of her rucksack.

Ella crossed to a bookcase, hunkered down in front of a shelf of OS maps, and rifled through them until her fingers came to rest on one which she pulled out from the others. 'I assume you can read a map?'

When Rachel nodded, she unfolded the map and laid it on the coffee table. 'Google Maps will only get you so far in Glencoe. It's about three kilometres from the village, going north towards Ballachulish and around halfway up the path that leads to the hidden valley. Obviously you can only get there on foot. Maybe you should ask Mike or one of the others from the search and rescue team Eric worked with to take you. I know they had a session or two with him there after a particularly difficult rescue.'

'I'll keep that in mind,' Rachel said, although she didn't think it would be necessary. She knew how to use a compass. She stood as the sound of squabbling children came from outside the front door. Their kids coming home from school.

'I'm truly sorry about Eric,' Rachel said. 'He was a good man. And sometimes that seems to be a rare thing. We'll get them,' she continued, hoping that she was not making an empty promise. 'Whoever killed Eric. And make sure they can't hurt anyone else.'

FORTY-SEVEN

Rachel had always loved the drive along the A86, particularly the stretch from Ballachulish through Glencoe to the empty expanse of Rannoch Moor. The journey took her through one of the most desolate, yet stunningly beautiful parts of Scotland with the road snaking through a valley, majestic mountains and empty glens on either side. It always seemed to her that the ghosts of the MacDonalds murdered by the Campbells still haunted the glen.

When she reached Glencoe, she parked at the visitor centre and pulled on her boots. She'd located the bothy on the map before she'd set off and thought she could find it without too much trouble. It was a couple of miles, a difficult walk rather than a climb.

Bothies in Scotland had been used as shelters for shepherds in the past and were now primarily used by walkers. They were small, usually with enough space for a couple of sleeping bags, maybe a rickety chair or two, but almost always a place to lay a fire. There was a tradition that anyone could take shelter in one at any time, so they weren't usually locked, even if they'd been bought by a private owner. It was a shame Eric felt the need to keep his locked.

Eric's bothy was slightly larger than most. On one side it had a bunk bed complete with mattresses and blankets, two worn armchairs on either side of a fireplace and a couple of free-standing kitchen units, with sugar, tea and coffee in one and a wash basin and a camping stove and Tilley lamp in another. There was no running water. If required it could be collected from the nearby stream. There was an outside chemical toilet. Eric's needs were clearly simple when he stayed on the mountain.

On first inspection there was nothing in the bothy that needed a key. To make sure, Rachel checked under the mattresses, in the cupboards, even the outside toilet, with no luck. She walked around the property searching for places where Eric might have buried something, but again found nothing.

The key was a puzzle Eric intended her to solve. Could the solution have something to do with climbing? It was the only thing they had in common.

Rachel retraced her steps to the car and drove to the hut where the search and rescue team had a base.

When she arrived there was a van parked outside bearing the rescue team's logo so she assumed the large brick hut was open. It was, although there was no one inside. That suited her. She didn't really want any company when she was searching around for Eric's stuff. At the back of her mind was the lingering anxiety that other players could be here searching for the same thing.

At the rear of the hut was a communal staff area with a small kitchen and a couple of locked storerooms. Her pulse racing, she tried her key in both locks. They didn't fit. Not even close. She glanced around, her gaze falling on a row of steel lockers, some with their owners' names, some without. But which one was Eric's? Not seeing his name she put on a pair of gloves and started working her way through the anonymous lockers with her key. She was starting to despair when she got to the bottom row and suddenly, the key turned.

Heart in throat, Rachel opened the locker and peered inside. Hidden behind his official rescue clothing was a thick folder of notes. She lifted them out and flicked through them, conscious someone might come in at any moment. She was in no mood to explain herself. To her dismay not one page was legible – at least not to her. They were covered in what looked like squiggles. It was as if Eric was determined to make whatever information he wanted her to know as difficult as he could make it to decipher. Why couldn't he have just sent her an email?

Could the squiggles be shorthand? That would make sense. Presumably if Eric was taking notes when listening to someone and hadn't been allowed to record them, he'd have to write it down as quickly as he could. But it didn't look like shorthand. Maybe it was his own made-up code? In which case she was screwed.

Scrawled on a separate piece of paper was a string of numbers and letters. Adrenaline buzzed through her veins. It looked like a password. Maybe to files he kept on the cloud. That's what she would have done if she were in his shoes.

She shoved the pad into her rucksack.

'Can I help you?'

She swung around to find a large man with a bushy beard standing behind her. He was wearing a fluorescent jacket.

'Just picking up some stuff for a friend,' she replied, quickly closing the locker again and hurrying to the door. She didn't want to waste time answering questions. She needed to get these notes to Du Toit as soon as possible. One of his analysts was bound to know how to decipher them.

FORTY-EIGHT

Rachel had passed the turn-off to the north at Invergarry when she noticed that a dark Range Rover that had been behind her since Fort William was still following. She was annoyed. The driver had been driving too close for the windy narrow roads and, despite Rachel giving him plenty of opportunities to overtake, he hadn't taken advantage. Instead he'd slowed down whenever she had and sped up when she pressed on the accelerator.

It was probably a tourist using her as a pacer – someone to clear the road ahead. Having driven this road more times than she could count, she knew every bend and blind corner and drove accordingly.

She had just passed Fort Augustus, where the southern tip of Loch Ness started, when the car behind her decided she wasn't going fast enough for his liking. He pulled out into the lane on the opposite side of the road. But instead of passing he hung back on her rear bumper.

Why the heck didn't he hurry up and go past? A blind corner was approaching, and a car could be coming in the opposite direction.

Rachel slowed to encourage him to pass but the Range Rover slowed too. Had he changed his mind?

Crap. Now there was a car coming towards them. The idiot needed to make up his mind. If Rachel sped up and he did too, they could both crash.

He fell back again but he must have misjudged it as Rachel felt a crunch as his left wing clipped her rear fender. It wasn't a full-on impact, but the four-by-four was far heavier than Rachel's car and she felt it blow out one of her rear tyres. Her car careened over to the other side of the road and into the path of the car coming towards her.

There was nowhere for it to go to avoid her except the loch.

Rachel yanked the steering wheel to the left, only just managing to drag her car out of the path of the blaring vehicle on the other side. It passed her close enough to make Rachel's vibrate. Unfortunately, in her desperation to avoid a head-on smash, Rachel had over-corrected. Her car's passenger-side wheels left the tarmac. Hanging onto the steering wheel, Rachel braked as hard as she dared to without sending the car into a spin.

She almost got the car back on the road. But at the last minute its wheels hit the bank on the verge. The car tilted to the side and came to a sudden halt. Rachel cried out as her face connected with something hard.

She sat there for a minute, stunned. Apart from the blow to her face she was OK.

She was just in time to see the car that had hit her disappear around the corner. The idiot hadn't even stopped. She became aware of frantic knocking on the driver's side window. A woman with greying hair twisted into a bun was peering in at her. 'Are you all right?' she asked, in a local accent. 'Do you need an ambulance?'

Rachel stretched, testing her body, feeling for broken bones.

Apart from her smarting face, it appeared she'd escaped relatively unscathed.

'No. Please don't. There's no need. I'm fine,' she told the woman.

'For crying out loud, what was that driver thinking?' the woman said, looking unconvinced.

'I have no idea.'

'Should I call the police?'

The driver of the Range Rover had long since gone. It would only hold her up, and she'd wasted enough time already.

Rachel shook her head. 'No. I'm fine, really. I just need to change my tyre and get my car back on the road. Can you help?'

'Not personally, but as it happens I do have a tow rope and my son in the car.'

FORTY-NINE

On her return to the COPFS building, Rachel went straight to police headquarters, showed the officer on reception her ID and told him she had an appointment to see Du Toit. He let her through without argument.

As she walked past the workstations spread across the rest of the open-plan area, Audrey looked up from her desk and gave Rachel a surprised nod. Selena was nowhere to be seen.

'Rachel! I didn't expect to see you!' Du Toit said when she announced herself at the door. He peered at her. 'What happened to your face?'

She'd forgotten about her swollen cheek. 'I was driving back from Glencoe when some idiot ran me off the road.'

Du Toit's expression darkened. 'I'm assuming you called the police and reported it.'

'What? And wait there until they came? I know the patrol officers are stretched – as you keep telling me. I might have waited hours.'

'It's the law, Rachel. As you know. And it applies to you just as it applies to me.'

'Never mind that now! I was in a hurry to bring you this.

Anyway I have twenty-four hours to report it before falling foul of the DVLA so I'm reporting it to you.'

She dropped the sheaf of papers on his desk and explained about the key, her search of the bothy and the search and rescue office where Eric had a locker. 'I believe he sent me the key, guessing I would be able to work out where he kept his notebook. And that's what I found.' Du Toit stood and closed his window blinds. Now no one could see in.

'What does it say?' Du Toit asked.

'I don't know. It's in some sort of code. One of your analysts will need to decipher it. I think it contains details of the story Eric was working on and I'm going to guess it will lead us to his murderer.' She tapped her finger on the single sheet of paper with the line of letters and numbers. I think that's the password to his cloud account.'

Du Toit frowned. 'Did it not occur to you that someone might have run you off the road deliberately? Are you sure you weren't followed from Glencoe?'

The same thought had occurred to her although she couldn't be certain. 'I only noticed the car when I left Fort William. You know what the roads are like. It's not unusual to have the same car behind you for miles on end.'

'What kind of car was it?'

'A Range Rover, I think.'

'Colour?'

'Black. Oh shit!' Finally the obvious struck her. It should have done before but she'd been too focussed on getting the notes and password to Du Toit. 'Could it have been the same one the woman on Skye saw on her croft? Selena was going to try and find it on the ANPR.'

'I don't suppose you got a registration number?'

She shook her head. 'Sorry.'

Du Toit stood, placed his palms on his desk and leaned forward. 'Listen to me, Rachel. You've done your bit. Your life could be in danger. I want you to stop investigating these deaths. I want you to stop looking into OCGs. Even better, get out of Inverness, preferably out of the UK.'

No chance. 'I'm not going anywhere. But now will you get Ella some protection?'

FIFTY

The next morning Rachel eased herself out of bed and examined her face in the mirror. The graze on her cheek was crusting over and she had a whopper of a black eye. But although her elbow throbbed it could have been so much worse.

There was nothing wrong with her legs, yesterday's rain had vanished and the skies had cleared, so she was going to go for a run before she did anything else.

It was still early when she hit the canal path, deserted apart from one other jogger, or power walker, someone making some sort of shuffling movement at any rate – a man in his late fifties or sixties with a paunch.

For a startling moment she'd thought it was Mainwaring, dismissing the notion immediately. Never in her wildest dreams would Mainwaring – overweight and slothful – be out running at this time. But as she drew closer, she saw, to her horror, it was. He was wearing knee-high socks, shorts, thankfully not running shorts – and a T-shirt that had seen better days with The Smiths in white lettering on a black background. This morning she'd decided to run along the left side of the canal towards the cemetery, so there was no chance of avoiding him. She had no doubt he was as loath to encounter her as was she him.

On the other hand she had something she needed to ask him. She ran up to him and stopped.

'Douglas! How are you?'

'Bloody awful. Doctor says I have to exercise. The bastard.'

'I'm sure it's better for your health.'

'Did I ask for your opinion?' he snarled. 'What the hell happened to your face!'

'A small altercation with a ditch,' she said briefly. 'I'm OK.'

He searched her face for a while, clearly doubtful. 'Walk with me. Tell me what's been going on in the office. I gather you've been up to your usual tricks?'

Linda. The snitch. The office administrator who Rachel liked a great deal had been keeping the office updated as to Mainwaring's progress. Clearly communication had been a two-way process.

'I assume you know about Eric Hunter and the body found in the graveyard?'

'Of course I know. Why is it murder appears to follow you around?'

'It's nothing to do with me!' she protested even as she wondered if that was true. Murder did appear to have become her personal stalker.

'Is Alastair handling the cases?'

'No. I'm not a hundred per cent certain John McLean was murdered yet. We need more evidence first. As for Eric Hunter, his murder has been pushed up the line to the COPFS in Edinburgh. Eric was a pretty high-profile personality, and I suspect they think Alastair doesn't have enough experience yet to handle it.'

Mainwaring harrumphed. Rachel was relieved to see his colour was beginning to return to normal.

They reached the end of the canal, the point where it and the sea met. Douglas turned and searched her face.

'Come on. Spit it out. What's really going on? Don't think you can pull the wool over my eyes. I had a heart attack, not a lobotomy.'

'Do you remember a Monika Troka?'

He was silent for a moment as if searching a giant database in his head. 'No, should I? Who was she?'

'A young woman. A witness in a sex-trafficking case. Drowned a month after she testified. Apparently you signed off her police report as No Pro.' No further proceedings.

'I think that's unlikely. Scan the report and email it to me.'

'Bit of a problem. We can't find it. Linda thinks it might have been misfiled.'

'Tell her to call me.'

'I've been ordered to stay away from the office.'

'By whom?'

'Ginny. She found out about the knife.'

Mainwaring shook his head like a lion about to charge.

'And I am ordering you back.'

FIFTY-ONE

When Rachel arrived in the office the next morning she was astonished to find Douglas ensconced in his office along with Ginny Plover. Yesterday he'd given no indication that he planned to be there too. It sounded as if he and Ginny were arguing, although Rachel couldn't hear what they were saying. Only certain shouted words. MY STAFF. COMMON COURTESY. NOT ON.

Linda was hovering outside his office, an anxious smile on her face. Spotting Rachel she scurried over.

'He's back! Says the office has gone to hell in his absence. I don't know why he thinks that! I've been telling him we're getting on fine so he should stay home resting, but he won't listen to me. He kept swatting me away like I was a fly.'

Rachel hid a smile. The brush with death hadn't helped their boss's irritability.

'Goodness! What on earth happened to you?' Linda asked, her eyes raking over Rachel.

Instinctively Rachel's fingers went to her cheek. 'It's just a bruise.'

'Some bruise. Anyway, Douglas wants you, Alastair, and

Suruthi in his office as soon as they arrive. I should warn you, he's in high dudgeon. He's been talking to DI Du Toit, I gather.'

While she waited for the others, Rachel rang Selena.

'I was about to call you,' Selena said. 'But Du Toit had me checking out black Range Rovers registered with the DVLA with an Inverness-shire address. No joy as yet. But we'll find it. None of us intend to put up with one of our fiscals being threatened. Or run off the road.'

Rachel glanced up as Ginny Plover swept out of the room. Douglas leaned back in his chair with a satisfied smile.

'A bit of good news,' Selena continued. 'We found CCTV of John the day before his body was found.'

Rachel's pulse kicked. 'And?'

'It's from the CCTV of a homeowner, so not great quality. It shows John walking along the street. A car pulls up, some sort of sports car, and moves away a couple of minutes later. When it does, John has gone. He either got into it of his own volition or was forced into it. We can't say.'

'Can you make out a number plate?'

'Not so far. We're trying to get it enhanced.' Selena continued: 'There's more. Audrey and I went to Johnny's flat with a couple of local officers. There was nothing of note to see. But get this. We found a credit card statement. The same one used to buy the shoes. We checked it out. It appears it's a shared credit card account. With a certain Lord Christopher Hughes.'

'Jesus! As in the judge?'

'The very same.'

'Does Alastair know?'

'An email is winging its way as we speak.'

By the time Rachel disconnected, Suruthi and Alastair had arrived. Judging by the stricken looks on their faces, Linda was bringing them up to speed regarding Mainwaring.

Rachel joined them in Douglas's office.

Although, this thinner version of Douglas took up less physical space in the office, his presence was still overwhelming.

'Is someone with a modicum of sense going to tell me what has being on in my absence?'

He jabbed a finger in Rachel's direction. 'I've found out from DI Du Toit that the story you told me was a load of bollocks . How many times have I told you to stay in your lane – and not only when you're driving! Why do you find that so difficult to do?'

'I'm not sure what you mean.'

'You know exactly what I mean. I had a long chat with Du Toit yesterday. He was delighted to bring me up to speed. He told me you were up to your ears in pig shit, most likely the target of some serious criminals, and that he'd strongly advised you to take time off work. Leave the country even.'

'Ginny and I did suggest she keep her head down,' Alastair said, giving their boss an oily smile.

'As for you,' Douglas rounded on Alastair, 'you were supposed to be taking the lead on homicide. First case you get, and you let it slip out of your grasp! Furthermore, I expect loyalty from this team. You are supposed to watch each other's backs. You've not done too good a job so far.'

He brought his fist down on his desk, making everyone jump. They shared alarmed glances. No one wanted to be responsible for bringing on another heart attack.

He pinned them one by one with steely eyes. 'Remind me, why are we here? I mean, what is our role? Our purpose?'

Suruthi raised her arm as if she were a school child. 'To make sure crooks go to jail.'

His eyes swivelled to Alastair. In the face of Mainwaring's wrath he'd lost most of his bluster. 'To make sure we have sufficient and appropriate evidence to prosecute them in court,' he said stiffly.

Then it was Rachel's turn.

What answer did he expect? Want? Whatever she said, it was bound to be the wrong thing. Might as well tell it how she saw it then.

'Justice?' she said.

'Expand?' Douglas demanded.

'Justice for those people who can't speak up for themselves. And for those who need the protection of the law.'

Looking unimpressed, Douglas harrumphed.

'Then what are you all lolling about for? I want reports from each of you by the end of the day, detailing exactly what you have been doing in my absence. Leave nothing out. I want every single detail. Do I make myself clear?'

FIFTY-TWO

Rachel had been writing her carefully edited report for Mainwaring when Greg Berkeley phoned to tell her he had something for her.

He'd been happy to come to the Ministry of Justice again. This time, for privacy, they'd squeezed into one of the tiny rooms normally used by reporters.

'I'm sorry to tell you I haven't been able to do anything more with your John Doe's DNA. But you also sent me DNA from under the fingernail of your neighbour – the one who was attacked.' He smiled. 'This time I did get a hit.'

'But that's great! Who did you find? Do we have a name for our culprit?'

His expression fell. 'If only it were that simple. I didn't find a match on GEDmatch, unfortunately. Not a direct one, anyway. But I did find a cousin. Can I talk you through what I've discovered?'

'Yes, please,' Rachel said, aware the urgency in her voice contrasted with Greg's slow and deliberate manner.

'The DNA under the fingernail is a close match with someone who is likely to be an older cousin or second cousin.

Very helpfully, that individual has included his family tree on the website. His own son is a more distant match, so that takes out that branch of the family. We now have to look backwards. The DNA similarities indicate that the attacker and this cousin share a set of grandparents. I've used that family tree and excluded those descendants who are far too young or old. That leaves only three grandchildren of the common ancestors. One of them is female and the DNA you sent me is definitely male. That leaves two names.'

He slid a folded piece of paper across the table.

'The man who attacked your friend is one of them.'

FIFTY-THREE

Selena was with Du Toit and Audrey as they interviewed the man who paid John's credit card bills. Rachel was listening on the other side of the two-way mirror.

'I loved him,' Christopher said, his voice hitching.

It was a broken man they had in front of them. Christopher Hughes was a tall, heavy man, clean shaven, anguished brown eyes, fair hair receding at the front.

Shamefaced.

'How did you meet him?' Du Toit asked.

'In a brothel here in Inverness. I was defending a client in court at the time. I know how it looks, but no one knew I was gay, least of all my wife and family.'

Selena and Audrey shared a glance.

'Go on,' Du Toit encouraged.

'I fell for him straight away. He told me he was eighteen.'

'Did you believe him?'

'Not really.' He hung his head and flushed.

'How did he end up in the brothel?'

'He told me he was there voluntarily. Said he found it safer than being on the street. He'd been beaten up on a couple of occasions. He soon realised he was mistaken. Conditions were brutal and when he tried to leave he was caught. They snapped his arm with a sledgehammer.'

Selena winced.

'Why the hell didn't you bring this to the police?' Du Toit demanded.

'Come on. You must know why I didn't. But I got him out of the brothel. Set him up in a flat. I needed him to be safe.'

'And because you wanted him all to yourself?' Audrey asked. 'Were you jealous?'

'I didn't want to share him. But not because I was jealous. It was safer in term of STDs. I did love him, but that came later.'

'So you moved him into the flat in Stockbridge. Didn't your wife notice?'

'I bought the flat before we were married. When property was still affordable for a man on a starting salary for a new lawyer. I never told her about it.'

'How long did he live there?'

'For the last fifteen years.'

'What did you think when he disappeared? Weren't you alarmed?'

'He told me he was going to visit his grandmother in Skye. He said he'd be gone for a week, possibly longer.'

'Were you aware a body had been found in Inverness?'

'No, I wasn't. Even if I had been, it would never have crossed my mind it was John. I thought he was still with his grandmother in Skye.'

'Didn't you try to get in touch with him over that period?'

'He didn't want me to phone him. His grandmother didn't know he was gay and he didn't want to answer any questions about his private life. He also said that the part of Skye where she lives had very patchy phone connection.'

John hadn't stayed on Skye. He'd left after only a night. Why? Perhaps he was meeting someone else – a lover Christopher didn't know about – in Inverness. The visit to Skye could have been a ruse. Could Christopher have found out and killed him in a jealous rage? Was it Hughes that John had been hiding from in the empty building? Gentleman Tim had said he'd seemed frightened. That would mean he'd tracked him there.

'Did you and John use your phones to track each other?' Selena asked. Joe had suggested they use their iPhones to do that.

'No!' Christopher sounded genuinely horrified. 'I respected his need for privacy.'

'Did John have a job? How did he earn income? Pay for things?' Audrey asked.

'I paid for almost everything. He planned to support himself eventually. He was a songwriter and hoped to make it big one day.' He ran a hand over his scalp. 'He sent demo tapes – no bites. Sometimes he busked in the town centre.'

'What about friends? Drugs?'

'He didn't have many friends. We had each other. I never saw him take drugs. He put it down to his religious upbringing.'

'His grandmother said that he was expecting to come into money. Was he blackmailing you?'

He shook his head. 'Never. John loved me as much as I loved him.'

'Someone else then. Who knew about your relationship?' Du Toit asked. 'Maybe they threatened to kill him if you didn't pay up?'

Christopher buried his face in his hands and sobbed for a while. 'No. I'm about to retire. My wife and I recently agreed to part ways. Although she wasn't thrilled to learn I was gay, you are barking up the wrong tree. The reason John died was nothing to do with our relationship, I promise. But there is something. He phoned me from Skye to ask me to see what I could find out about an Eilidh Souter.'

Selena shared another glance with Audrey. 'Did he say why?' Selena asked.

'Only that he'd seen her in Skye, having a coffee with someone he recognised from the brothel he was kept in when he was in Inverness.'

'And what did you find out?' Audrey's voice was icy.

'That Souter had been a detective in the force at the time.'

'So you did speak to John?'

'Yes. But only that once. We always used burner phones when we wanted to speak to each other.' He gave Du Toit another shame-faced look.

'But you spoke to him again? To let him know what you'd discovered?'

Christopher shook his head. 'I texted him the information.' He blew his nose and looked Du Toit in the eye. 'Someone else is responsible for his death and you have to find them.'

FIFTY-FOUR

Selena slid down in her Fiat 500 trying to look inconspicuous. Then realised that was the worst thing she could do. Thighearna's a Dhia, this detective lark wasn't easy. No wonder they didn't let new detective constables out on their own. Eilidh Souter was arranging a time with her lawyer to come in to be questioned and Du Toit had sent a similar invite to Jason Bright. Progress was painfully slow but progress all the same. Right now she had a couple of hours free until she was due in on the back shift, so had taken herself off to Skinny Ian's.

She'd seen the same man leaving Skinny Ian's house again, but this time she'd been in the car she'd bought to replace the motorbike she'd been using until she had to return it to her brother.

When he climbed into his car, she made an instant decision to follow him. He'd driven straight to this house in the Crown area. She parked up and watched him go in, then made a note of his number plate. She'd look it up when she got in to the office. She'd watched the house on four occasions now. Warrior Rachel, as she continued to call Rachel in her head, went off on her own on a regular basis and, while it wasn't orthodox, it brought results.

It was more difficult to do a stakeout in the middle of summer, when in this part of the world it only got dark for a few hours. But the men's visits weren't confined to the hours between eleven p.m. and three. Selena had seen plenty of businessmen enter and depart. They might leave their jackets in their cars and roll up the sleeves of their shirts, but that's what they were.

The punters weren't confined to the better off, either. Selena had seen all sorts. A couple of men in their thirties had rolled out of a white van and approached the house as if they were joiners or electricians on a house call. Perhaps they were. Homes used for brothels had to be maintained too.

The street was lined nose to tail with cars. People parked up here because it was easier to get a space and then walk into town.

There was an Audi in front of her and a small BMW behind. Otherwise, the cars were mainly SUVs or large four-by-fours.

A woman who couldn't have been more than five foot was in the process of climbing into the driver's seat of one such monster. She practically had to take a running jump to get in. Just as well that she was wearing leggings. Selena got that farmers might need four-by-fours to access their fields and farms, or even folk who lived in the more rural parts of Inverness-shire, particularly in the winter. But in town?

Selena felt immediately guilty. Who was she to judge anyone? Only God had that right.

The house she had under surveillance didn't look out of place in the street of sandstone terraces. It was easy to imagine that it was a home belonging to a doctor or a teacher. Which made it even weirder that the neighbours didn't seem to realise that they had a brothel in their midst. Yet, Selena had learned, a middle-class suburb was one of the best places to hide one. The neighbours were too busy, too polite to ask questions. Furthermore, the brothels moved on, usually within a six-week period.

She wasn't going to do anything stupid. She wasn't going to go in and arrest anyone, for example. She just wanted enough evidence – wrapped up like a gift with a bow – to deliver to the team. The problem was that Selena didn't yet have an iota of evidence to bring Du Toit.

Sugar. It was getting on for nine thirty. She was due to start her night shift in less than thirty minutes. She glanced at the door. Then up to the upstairs windows. Was it her imagination or was there a figure silhouetted in the window looking straight at her. She couldn't make out if it was male or female from this distance. Had they clocked her?

If someone had spotted her and become suspicious, they might check out her number plate, or worse come out to challenge her. She forced herself to stay put. She'd only make them more suspicious if she drove away now. She stretched as if she'd been having a rest, pulled out her phone as if she were checking Google Maps – or something.

She was about to give up and go home when the man she'd followed here emerged from the house and got in his car. This time he was carrying a rucksack. Could he have been collecting money on behalf of his boss? If so, was that where he was going? Her pulse skipped a beat. She was going to find out. As his car pulled into the road, she checked her side and rear-view mirrors, and prepared to follow him.

FIFTY-FIVE

Mags hurried along Castle Street. It was empty apart from a man getting into a fancy car. She was out later than she had been since she'd given up the game. Being out at night had never worried her before but if she were honest, since Ashley and Jody had been murdered, she'd become more feart. Being bashed around the head hadn't helped either, even if she'd given as good as she'd got. When she was a young woman she would have inflicted more damage – maybe seen him off.

No point in regrets. People got older. Maybe she should join the gym down at the leisure centre. Work on her upper body strength. If she was going to be any use to Rachel she'd need to do better. Because that lassie was going to continue to get into trouble. Mags would bet her life on it. Oh, she liked to pretend she was tough, and in some ways she was, but Mags saw right through her. That woman was hurt. Hurt to her very bones. In that way she was no different to Jody and Ashley. Every time Mags thought about them it felt like someone had taken a cheese grater to her heart. She had tried to protect them and failed. She wasnae about to fail Rachel too.

She'd heard on the grapevine that there was a brothel in the

Crown and thought she'd check it out before she brought the intel to Rachel.

But wasn't that the car belonging to the detective Rachel was pals with? What was she doing here, her head barely visible above the dashboard? If she was spying on the brothel she wasnae making a very good job of it.

Mags opened the passenger door and slid into the seat next to Selena.

'What the hell...' Selena said. 'Put your seat belt on.' And before Mags could protest Selena pulled out after the fancy car.

FIFTY-SIX

Rachel came to a halt outside the Fergusons' house. She'd stayed late at the office to catch-up on work and then driven over, not ringing ahead in case Lorna refused to see her. Why hadn't she mentioned she had power of attorney the last time Rachel had been here?

The gate was open so Rachel drove straight in. There was only one other car in the driveway on this occasion.

Lorna answered the door. She looked surprised and annoyed to find Rachel on the doorstep. 'What are you doing here Rachel? And at this time of the evening?'

'I won't take up too much of your time. I just wanted to ask you a couple of questions.'

Lorna gave Rachel a long speculative look before standing aside. 'You'd better come in. But I'm about to head out. I'm going away for a few days, so you'll need to keep your questions short.'

In a change from previous visits, Rachel was invited into a large sitting room looking onto the side garden. Lorna excused herself to make some coffee, leaving Rachel alone, wondering what info Lorna could give her. An explanation for the credits to her father's accounts, perhaps?

A photograph on the mantelpiece caught her eye. She picked it up and examined it idly. It was of Georgie and another woman. One she realised with a jolt, she'd seen before. It was the same dark-haired woman who had been in the graduation photograph on DC Souter's mantelpiece.

Rachel was still working through the implications of that when her iPhone pinged. It was a text from Nora, the social worker her mother had once worked with. She read it with growing disbelief.

> Dear Rachel. Hope you are well. So sorry to have taken so long to get back to you. I finally managed to locate the name of the person who took the minutes of the meetings when social work still had the luxury of admin support. It was a Lorna Ferguson. I remember her now. She worked part-time. Quite a pleasant woman, if I remember, never had much to say for herself.

As the pieces fell into place, Rachel's mouth went dry. A little cough came from behind her. She swung around to find Lorna carrying a tray set with a silver coffee pot and mugs, standing in the doorway.

'You look like you've seen a ghost, my dear. What a pity you chose to involve yourself in all this.' She put the tray down on the coffee table. 'Now why don't you tell me everything you know.' She tutted. 'You could have had a peaceful, long life if only you'd left well alone. Instead, all you've done is brought trouble to everyone's door.'

'I have no idea what you're talking about,' Rachel said, although she had her suspicions.

'I think you do. Nora rang me to ask where she might find the minutes you were asking for. When she couldn't find them, she remembered I'd been the minute-taker. People don't look twice at office workers, particularly if they are self-effacing women who hate to be noticed. I knew it wouldn't take you long to work it out.'

Rachel's growing suspicions had solidified into a knot of dread.

'You were the minute-taker? It was you who tipped off the trafficking ring when a raid was planned?'

Lorna tipped her head to the side like an inquisitive bird and raised her eyebrow. 'As I said, people continually underesti-mate me. Including you. It's never crossed anyone's mind I could be a serious businesswoman.'

Rachel ran her tongue along her lips, taking a moment to absorb was Lorna was saying. 'You're part of the OCG?'

'A little more than that, I'm afraid. I guess you could call the whole enterprise my baby.'

'You're the boss?' Prim and proper Lorna Ferguson? Rachel was having difficulty assimilating the fact. 'You're admitting it?'

Lorna gave a self-satisfied smile. 'Not much point in denying it now, is there? I have a jet on standby, Georgie, Bill and I are going to join Andrew in Dubai. They don't have an extradition treaty with the UK.'

She gave Rachel a disapproving look. 'You were warned to keep your nose out of our business but you kept on digging, following in that journalist's footsteps. When you tracked down Eilidh Souter, it was a step too far.'

'DC Eilidh Souter?'

'The very one.'

'She worked for you? What about Jason Bright?'

'Bright? That fool. No, I'd never take the chance approaching someone I couldn't be sure would be receptive. And nothing he said or did suggested he would be. Eilidh on the other hand was a different kettle of fish. When I saw her at the meetings it gave me an idea. As you've clearly picked up, it's helpful to have someone on the inside. I got Georgie to recruit her. They'd met through a mutual friend, one who worked for the firm – the one in that photo you were looking at actually. Eilidh was happy to make a few pounds. Actually, enough cash to buy that cottage in Skye. She's been a good employee. Loyal, discreet. Happy to do whatever was asked of her.'

Lorna sat down in an armchair. 'Why don't you sit down while I pour you some coffee?'

Rachel remained standing. She wasn't about to concede the only advantage she had.

'Eilidh removed anything from the interview notes that might have pointed to me,' Lorna continued with a smug smile. 'She couldn't do anything about the prostitute's testimony about hearing a woman – too many people had heard that. Unfortunately, I didn't think of the minutes.'

More pieces of the puzzle slotted into place. Yet there was still so much that didn't make sense.

'Unfortunately, Eilidh didn't really have the nerve for what was required.' Lorna continued. 'She left the force and cleared off to Skye. We left her alone, knowing she couldn't dump us in it without incriminating herself. Inmates don't care much for a police officer. Retired or otherwise. She knew to tell us about Eric Hunter though. He requested the trial notes, worked out she might have something to with my operation and tracked her down. She strung him along. Pretended she was going to give up names in return for money. Instead, she set up the meeting and told us.'

'You killed Eric?' Rachel felt sick.

'Not me personally!' Lorna raised her eyebrows in pretended affront.

'You tortured him.' Fury welled up inside Rachel like lava in a volcano.

'We needed to know what he'd learned. He wouldn't tell Ben and Eilidh where his notes were, the fool. He told us where to find his camper van. Said his laptop was there and we'd find everything on it. He was lying. When he wouldn't tell them the password, they put him out of his misery.'

They didn't know Rachel had found it.

Outside, tyres crunched on the gravel driveway.

'What did you take from his locker in Glencoe?' Lorna continued. 'We know you found something. I heard you ran straight to Inspector Du Toit with it. Ben cocked up, running you off the road. That's when we knew had to leave in a hurry. But it would be helpful to know what you found out first.'

'And John McLean?' Rachel asked. 'The man whose body we found in the graveyard in Inverness. Did you kill him too?'

'He saw Eilidh when he was in Skye. He recognised Lisa, the woman with her, from the brothel. She'd only been there twice, but it was twice too often it seems. John found out Eilidh had been a police officer and asked her for money. When the journalist started snooping around too, I knew something had to be done.'

A heavyset man with his hair in a man bun came into the room. He gave Rachel a dismissive glance before bending to whisper something in Lorna's ear.

'Time really is running out. Are all the cases in the car, Ben? We need to leave shortly.'

When Ben turned around, Rachel was horrified to see he had a gun jammed in the waist of his jeans.

She had to play for time.

'And Monika?'

'Look. You work it out. That jet won't hang about. We need to be gone before anyone realises you're missing.'

'What is that supposed to mean?' Rachel demanded with more bravado than she felt.

'You were warned to stop looking and you wouldn't. So now I'm afraid you'll have to accept the consequences.'

While Lorna had been speaking, Rachel had been searching

for something she could use as a weapon. There was no handy poker or knife conveniently left on the coffee table. Her gaze fell on a table lamp. The base was made of glass. Not much use against a gun – but better than nothing.

'There is something I need to know,' she said to Lorna. 'Did my father know what you were up to?'

'Of course he did. He was our solicitor. He could have walked away when he first realised that Bill's company was just a front for his other activities, but instead he made a deal with us. He'd keep our little secrets and do everything in his power to protect us from the law. For a price.' She poured coffee into two mugs.

'He made a great deal of money from this arrangement. Of course, it went into his pocket and not that of his firm, and there was the matter of how to spend it without attracting attention. Not easy when you are basically a small-town solicitor.'

So, Rachel had been right about her father money laundering for an OCG. It explained the money deposited in his personal account as well as the suitcase of cash.

'Did you frame my father? Blackmail him into taking the rap for my mother's murder?'

Lorna sighed, leaned forward and looked Rachel directly in the eye. 'You poor deluded fool. We didn't frame your father. We weren't blackmailing him. He was blackmailing us.'

FIFTY-SEVEN

Selena, with a pleased as punch Mags beside her, followed the car all the way to Moy, where it pulled up in front of a large house surrounded by gilded gates that wouldn't have looked out of place at the entrance to a country estate. As she drove past, the driver leaned out and spoke into a speaker attached to the pillar and the gates swung open.

Selena considered the merits of pressing the buzzer too and seeing if she would be admitted, but that would be reckless without backup.

To her horror, just before the gates closed, she clocked a red second-hand MG. Rachel's car. Now with a bump in its rear fender. What the heck was she doing here?

She parked out of sight of the security gate.

She needed to speak to Audrey or Du Toit urgently.

FIFTY-EIGHT

Audrey entered the first name Rachel had given to Du Toit into the police database. Nothing. Hugh Slater had never been arrested, didn't even have points on his licence, or as much as a parking ticket.

No luck with Ben Ramsey either. She blew out her cheeks in frustration. If the attacker had been arrested previously there would have been a DNA hit straight away.

On impulse she googled Ben Ramsey Inverness and came up with a hit on Facebook.

Ben Ramsey loved to post, particularly photos of him living the high life. He always seemed to be on holiday or having a good time. His photos were set in exotic locations and usually included expensive cars, cocktails, parties, one of which was on a yacht.

Audrey stopped at that one. Ben was bare-chested and in Bermuda shorts. He was standing on deck with one arm around the waist of a glamorous red-haired woman, the other around the shoulders of a man. Her heart lurched. The man looked familiar. His hair was shorter when she'd last come across him and money had been spent straightening and whitening his previously discoloured and crooked teeth. In case there was any doubt, someone had helpfully tagged him. Josh Carlton.

She entered his name onto the police database. And came up trumps.

Josh Carlton was what was known in the trade as a career criminal. He'd first come to police attention twelve years ago when he was seventeen. The eldest son of a teacher and a doctor, he had everything going for him, every chance of forging a successful career in a legitimate line of work. He'd done well at school, exceptionally well, and according to his teachers and parents had been expected to go to the university of his choice. Instead, to his parents' and teacher's bewilderment, he'd chosen to deal drugs, although apparently he didn't use. He'd started off running a few kids in the local estate and had managed to do that for a couple of years before being caught.

He'd been given a two-year custodial sentence and since being released had managed to avoid being arrested again, although Police Scotland was certain he was engaging in criminal activity. The fact that he always drove expensive cars, lived in a duplex flat and wore designer clothes, despite not being employed, was a bit of a giveaway. And he was pals with Ben.

It wasn't proof Ben Ramsey was the man who had attacked Mags, but what were the odds?

She saved the photo to her phone and was on her way to Du Toit when her phone rang. It was Selena.

FIFTY-NINE

Audrey returned to her computer and typed in the car registration Selena had given her . When it came up with Ben Ramsey, she hurried across to Du Toit's desk.

He looked strained. He was going to look worse when he heard what she had to say.

'Audrey, I was about to call you to a meeting. A couple of officers with the National Crime Agency are on their way. Using the password Rachel found, they've managed to get into the file on Eric Hunter's cloud account. It made frightening reading. He'd discovered the OCG ring he was investigating are arranging to take delivery of several crates of ex-military weapons. And he thought he'd only scratched the surface.'

'Bloody hell!'

'He identifies several names, starting with his contact, ex detective constable Eilidh Souter. There are other names – Josh Carlton, Ben Ramsey and Andrew Ferguson among them.'

'Did you say Ben Ramsey?'

'Yes.' His gaze sharpened. 'Why?'

'Because we have a problem...'

SIXTY

'What the fuck is going on?' Mags asked Selena. 'Who is that man and why is Rachel here?'

'That's what I need to find out. I want you to stay here. If I'm not back in ten minutes, call DS Kennedy.' She wrote Audrey and Du Toit's numbers on a piece of paper. 'If Audrey doesn't answer, call Inspector Du Toit. OK?'

'What the hell am I supposed to say to them?'

'Tell them I asked you to phone. That I think Rachel might be in trouble and in need of assistance.'

'Fuck's sake,' Mags opened her car door, 'if she's in trouble, I'm no staying put.'

'Listen, Mags. I need you to act as lookout. You've got my number. Text me if anyone else comes to the house.'

Ignoring further protests from Mags, Selena slipped out of the car and, keeping an eye out for cameras, ran to the house. She needed to see inside. The wall was too high to climb but perhaps she could climb the oak tree whose branches overhung the fence. She was considering her options when she felt a hand on her shoulder. She looked around to find a familiar figure.

Thank God! The cavalry had arrived although, she frowned, why wasn't Joe in uniform?

Mags was about to do as she'd been asked and call the police when another car pulled up. This time it stopped by the gates. A man got out. One Mags recognised. PC Joe. What the hell was he doing here? And why wasn't he in uniform or in a patrol car? He and Selena appeared a few moments later, but instead of coming over, Joe pressed the buzzer and the heavy gates swung open.

SIXTY-ONE

Rachel couldn't help but laugh.

'Dad, blackmailing *you*? Good try.'

'I don't know why you find that difficult to believe. As I told you, he knew all our dirty secrets.' She gave Rachel a quizzical look. 'What did he tell you?'

'That he'd been framed for Mum's murder. Although not by whom or why. It was you, wasn't it? Why frame him? He couldn't have told anyone what he knew,' Rachel said, her heart banging against her ribs. 'Not without breaking client lawyer privilege.' She had to keep the conversation going.

'Go on,' Lorna said. 'You're getting there.'

'He said he'd taken the rap for Mum's murder to protect me. I knew it couldn't be true, but he was warned off, so was I...' She tailed off as the final piece of the puzzle fell into place.

'Mum was at those meetings. Did she suspect someone was tipping off the crime ring. Did she work out it was you?'

Lorna leaned back in her chair and eyed Rachel speculatively for a long moment before addressing her. 'I told you the last time we met that you were like your father. I know now you're more like your mother. Too clever by half. Certainly too clever for your own good, both of you.

'Not to be underestimated either, your Mum. Unfortunately, she started with the questions when she found the cash. At first she thought she was crazy even to think along the lines. But she knew of your father's connection – that he was a criminal solicitor – and was putting things together. She knew I was always at the meetings.' She shrugged. 'The prostitute had talked about hearing a woman . Your mother added two and two and came up with five. It never occurred to her that I might be the one in charge.'

'The woman Monika heard was you?'

'Me? Oh no. I don't go near those places. Pay attention. It was Lisa, Georgie and Eilidh's friend. There was a problem at the brothel when someone tried to leave.'

'You killed Mum when you realised she was on to you? And framed Dad for it.' Rachel whispered. 'They were your neighbours, your friends. You used his love for me to keep him quiet, to force him to take the blame.'

A sly smile crossed Lorna's face. 'Is that what he told you? My my, maybe you're not so clever after all.'

'What do you mean?' Rachel demanded.

'You have it all wrong. He killed Mary Ann all right. They had a blazing row. She told him she knew he was involved in organised crime and that she was going to go to the police and tell them everything she knew. He couldn't allow that to happen.'

It felt as if ice were flowing through Rachel's veins.

'She told him she'd been putting money away for years and that she was going to leave him and take you with her. She started packing.

'Maybe he didn't mean to kill her,' Lorna continued with a shrug, 'but I guess we will never know for sure. He came over

here afterwards in a right funk – said we had to help him. He
threatened to go to the police and tell them everything if we
didn't help him cover up the murder. It was an offer we couldn't
refuse. Getting rid of a thorn in our side, without having to kill
her ourselves, was a no-brainer.'

It took every ounce of restraint Rachel had not to grab
Lorna by the throat. She was talking about her mother's murder
is if it was nothing.

'My children weren't involved, I want you to know that. Bill
and I helped David get her body out of the house. It was easy to
do it without being seen, by using the path along the burn.' She
grinned again. 'It could have been made for the purpose.'

Still frozen in horror, Rachel listened transfixed as Lorna
continued.

'We helped him dispose of the body – well, not me personally, but Bill and one of the crew. Because of his work, your
father knew how to cover his tracks. Your mother had told me
that she was leaving him and David banked on your mother
telling someone else. He was right, as it happened. He gave us
her passport and credit and debit cards to get rid of. Understandably, he wasn't his usual calm and collected self.'

'But all of that was found in the house after Mum's body
was found.'

'So it was. Weren't we naughty putting it there? He should
never have given me a key. You see, we couldn't take the chance
your father might have a change of heart and go to the police.
He was distraught when you ran away. Got it into his skull that
you knew what he'd done. He got worse when Mary Ann's body
was found. He'd been slowly going out of his mind over the
years – we were scared he would truly lose it one day. We told
him that if he ever revealed what he knew about us, or our part
in helping him get rid of the body, we would kill you – chop you
into pieces and leave what was left of you in his garden. He

knew we meant it, so he didn't need much persuading. We were happy for him to plead not guilty, to do anything he could to get off, but he really didn't stand a chance, did he?'

So her father was guilty after all. Even though she had always known, Rachel felt her heart shatter all over again.

SIXTY-TWO

Rachel was still staring open-mouthed at Lorna when Selena burst through the door, accompanied by Joe who was holding her by the elbow, propelling her in front of him.

What the fuck were they doing here?

When Lorna turned her attention to them, Rachel picked up of the jug of black coffee. It was still hot. At the same time she edged closer to the table lamp.

'Ah Joe,' Lorna said. 'Where did you find your girl? More importantly, what were you thinking, bringing her here?'

'I found her snooping around outside.'

Selena's face was a mask of confusion. 'You know these people, Joe?'

Rachel was equally confused. Was it possible Joe was undercover?

'Where's the man I followed here? Do you know him? Are you working undercover?' Selena demanded, apparently as bewildered by his presence as Rachel was.

Joe pulled a face as Ben came back into the room, his gun in his hand. He pointed it at Selena.

'All right, Joe?' Ben asked.

'Sure.' Joe turned to Selena and gave her a regretful smile. 'Sorry, Sel. Nothing personal.'

Oh, Fuck.

'What's going on, Joe?' Selena asked, her eyes darting around the room before her gaze landed on him.

Lorna turned to the mirror and casually applied a slick of lipstick. At that moment, Rachel caught a glimpse of a face at the window. Mags! What was *she* doing here? It was only for a second, and luckily everyone's attention had been focused elsewhere.

Lorna turned back to the room and addressed the two men. 'Take them over to the McKenzie house. Use the path along the burn. Do what you have to and get yourselves to the airport. Bill is there already.' She glanced at her watch. 'Georgie should have been here by now. What the hell is keeping her? What a shitshow this is turning out to be.'

SIXTY-THREE

Before the gates closed behind Selena and Joe, Mags, keeping an eye on the rotating CCTV camera on the gate slipped through the gap. Huddling in the shadows, well out of the line of sight of the camera, Mags dialled the number Selena had given her.

'Is PC Joe Adamson working undercover?' she hissed, when the detective sergeant answered.

'No, he's not. Why do you ask?'

'Because he and Selena are in the hoose too.'

'Get away from there. We're on the way. We'll be there in under ten minutes.'

Instead of telling her to get stuffed, Mags disconnected. She crept around the house and peeked in every window, until she came to the sitting room. One glance was enough to freak her out.

Selena and Rachel were on the sofa and a man with his back towards Mags was pointing a gun at them. Joe was standing beside him. There was a woman Mags didn't know, applying lipstick at the mirror. Just before Mags hunkered down beneath the window ledge, she'd caught Rachel's eye.

The lass hadn't reacted at all but Mags knew she'd seen her. Fuck's sake, couldn't she stay out of trouble for a minute?

Keeping low, she'd hurried around to the front door.

She needed a weapon. Her gaze fell on a boot scraper. The one every fancy house had in the olden days so they didn't track the mud from their boots inside. This one was large and made of cast iron. Mags picked it up, pleased to feel the heft of it. Then she rang the doorbell.

As Mags hoped, the man with the gun answered the door. When he peered out, she didn't hesitate but slammed the boot scraper into his balls. He let out a scream of agony and grabbed at his crotch. Mags swung the boot scraper again, this time into his face. It landed with a satisfying crunch. He fell to the ground, the gun spinning from his grasp. Mags picked it up and, holding like she'd seen people do in the movies, she raised it as a woman appeared in the hall.

At the sound of the doorbell, Lorna had frowned. 'Ben, see if that's Georgie,' she'd said, picking up a set of car keys from the mantelpiece. She turned to Selena. 'It'd better not be more police. Joe, keep an eye on these two while I check.'

They heard a cry, followed by a thud.

Rachel knew this might be their only chance. 'Joe!' she screamed. When he swung to face her, Rachel threw the hot coffee at him. As he screamed and covered his eyes, Rachel lifted the table lamp and smashed it over his head. At the same time, Selena sprang up, swept his feet from under him, rolled him over and yanked his hands behind his back.

'Grab my cuffs from my back pocket,' she yelled to Rachel 'and help me get them on this piece of shit.'

SIXTY-FOUR

Rachel was with Du Toit and Selena in the interview room as they grilled Lorna. The cops had descended on the house a short while after they'd secured Joe, and Mags had appeared with Lorna in front of her, the barrel of a gun jabbed in her back.

Lorna sat with her arms folded and a mutinous expression on her face.

'You do know you are going to jail for a very long time,' Rachel said, 'for the murder of Eric Hunter and John McLean. You'll find that your fellow prisoners don't much care for women who traffic kids. Never mind all the rest.' They'd found John's car in the Eastgate Shopping Centre car park.

'I'm not going to jail,' Lorna said. 'Trust me, no one will testify against me.' But Rachel saw a glimpse of doubt. 'You won't be able to link the murders to me, or any of my family.'

'You think murder and sex trafficking is all we have on you?' Du Toit asked. 'We know everything about your group, we can tie you all together. We have access to the records of phones that you all used, who called who and when. We have seized the drugs from the house where you stashed them. Georgie talked – so did Bill– eventually. They realised we had too much on them not to. Your children and their accomplices are very careless when it comes to advertising on social media what they've been up to and with whom.'

Selena leaned forward. 'Thanks to Eric, your gang days are over. The kids you used to run your drugs have been identified. Most have their lives in ruins. As they are minors we won't be able to charge them – wouldn't want to anyway. We will try and get them and their families support. It'll be difficult, given that most of them are drug addicts, thanks to you, but if we save one, that will be something.'

'We know about the weapons too,' Du Toit continued. 'We've been liaising with forces across the UK and Europe. We know exactly when and where they are being delivered.'

Lorna's eyes turned black and she shifted in her seat. 'I've said enough. I want a lawyer.'

'Surprised it's taken you this long to ask for one,' Du Toit said. 'I don't think they'll be much help to you, now. The fiscals' – he nodded in Rachel's direction – 'are pretty sure they have enough to convict you easily. The question is, do you want to make it easier on yourself by helping us, or are you happy to take your chances in court?'

EPILOGUE

Apart from the crunch of rock underfoot, the occasional grunt or muttered swear word, the sound of their breathing as they raced up Ben Macdui, there was silence. Rachel was in the lead at the moment but that had changed time and time again throughout the duration of the climb.

They were neck and neck as they reached the summit, neither giving the other quarter. Rachel made it first. But only seconds in front of Angus.

Breathless and laughing they collapsed against a small cairn.

'I need to get fitter,' Angus gasped. 'I'm spending too much time behind the wheel of my car. If I'm not careful, you'll beat me next time too. And I can't have that.'

He'd been to stay with her twice since that night in Edinburgh and she'd been to his once. It was still early days in their romantic relationship and Rachel often thought about how she'd feel if he broke up with her. Every time the thought came into her head she pushed it away. She had enough demons to deal with.

In the weeks that followed Lorna and her gang's arrest,

Rachel had thought more about her father. He had tried to protect Rachel when he could have made a deal with the COPFS – might even have entered witness protection if he'd been prepared to turn on the Fergusons. On the other hand, even a short time in jail would have put his life in danger. She now knew that organised crime gangs had long arms as her father had suggested. Inmates and possibly even prison guards who could be persuaded to do anything if the money was right.

They'd given him a warning when they'd discovered Rachel was on their trail.

Joe had talked too. Lorna Ferguson had convinced Joe to join the force to be their man on the inside and he'd been happy to. His job, as far as the gang was concerned, was to keep his eyes and ears open for any inkling the police were on to them. They'd hoped that he would pass his exams and join the CID, but that hadn't happened.

He had targeted Selena as a way of keeping track of what Rachel was doing. Selena had been more than a little miffed to discover she'd been used by him but was getting over it. Along with the others, if the trial had the outcome they all expected, Joe was going away for a very long time.

Although Du Toit had been annoyed his new constable had gone Lone Ranger on him, he'd acknowledged her part in stopping the gang before they'd left the country.

Forensic accountants had traced the regular deposits Rachel had found in her father's accounts to an offshore account. That in turn was fed by an account set up and managed by Georgie.

It would be some time yet before Lorna was tried in court. Lorna's children, Andrew and Georgina, were still under investigation. Georgina for being the accountant for the OGC her mother headed up and Andrew as a senior member of the gang.

Angus reached for Rachel's hand and tangled his fingers in hers. She leaned against him. She didn't know if they were friends, friends with benefits, or lovers. She was still learning when it came to this relationship stuff.

She hadn't seen her father again. Had no intention of ever doing so. He was part of her past and had no place in her future.

Maybe, here, next to her, was the only person she needed.

Only time would tell.

A LETTER FROM THE AUTHOR

Huge thanks for reading *The Final Truth*, I hope you were hooked on Rachel's dramatic journey to uncover the truth about her mother's death. If you want to join other readers in hearing all about my new releases and bonus content, you can sign up for my newsletter.

www.stormpublishing.co/morag-pringle

If you enjoyed this book and could spare a few moments to leave a review, that would be hugely appreciated. Even a short review can make all the difference in encouraging a reader to discover my books for the first time. Thank you so much.

When I started the Rachel McKenzie series I had a clear idea of who she was and how her past had not only shaped her but would continue to inspire and torment her in equal measure.

I also knew Rachel would not let anything get in the way of her search for the truth behind her mother's murder.

I hope you enjoyed her roller-coaster ride.

Thanks again for being part of this amazing journey with me and I hope you'll stay in touch – I have so many more stories and ideas to entertain you with!

Morag

ACKNOWLEDGEMENTS

Thanks to everyone who helped me write this book, giving so generously of their time: Stewart Pringle, Karen Reynolds, Sigi Goolden, Lisa Clifford, Katy Hunter, Flora Van Kleef, to name only a few.

And as always huge thanks to my very patient editor Emily Gowers, as well as Anne O'Brien and all of the team at Storm.

Made in United States
Orlando, FL
16 December 2024

55629365R00203